SHADOW MONEY

Books by George Alec Effinger

What Entropy Means to Me
Relatives
Mixed Feelings
Irrational Numbers
Nightmare Blue (with Gardner Dozois)
Those Gentle Voices
Felicia
Death in Florence
Dirty Tricks
Heroics
The Wolves of Memory
Idle Pleasures
The Nick of Time
The Bird of Time
When Gravity Fails
Shadow Money

SHADOW MONEY

GEORGE ALEC EFFINGER

TOR

This is a work of fiction. All the characters and events portrayed in this book are fictional, and any resemblance to real people or incidents is purely coincidental.

SHADOW MONEY

Copyright © 1988 by George Alec Effinger

All rights reserved, including the right to reproduce this book or portions thereof in any form.

First printing: February 1988

A TOR Book

Published by Tom Doherty Associates, Inc.
49 West 24th Street
New York, NY 10010

ISBN: 0-312-93054-2

Library of Congress Catalog Card Number: 87-50886

Printed in the United States of America

0 9 8 7 6 5 4 3 2 1

Give me a dozen healthy infants, well formed, and my own specified world to bring them up in and I'll guarantee to take any one at random and train him to become any type of specialist I might select—doctor, lawyer, artist, merchant chief and, yes, even beggarman and thief, regardless of his talents, penchants, tendencies, abilities, vocations, and race of his ancestors.

—John B. Watson
Behaviorism

For Harlan Ellison, bonded messenger of the gods, who, Easter bunny-like, left an idea on my doorstep.

PROLOGUE

The Year-End Closeout

1.

Picture a young man, very well dressed, impeccably groomed, an ardent and indulgent smile on his handsome face. He is gazing fondly at the beautiful woman on his arm. It could be that he is Scott Fitzgerald, a few months after the publication of *This Side of Paradise;* now he is fortune's child. In that case, she would be the young Zelda, wide-eyed, desirous, making the young man prove he is worthy. In point of fact, they are not Scott and Zelda, but think of them so. How many of us have had just such a brief period of hope before the defeats of maturity begin, accumulating like snowflakes on a doorstep? It is right now, and for these two it will always be now, until—but they're not thinking about that.

The young woman bent slightly, a white fur stole curling sinuously through her arms and across the sleek and silk-clad narrow warmth of her back. "Oh, Jimmy!" she cried. "This is the one! This is it!"

The young man stepped back appraisingly. He smiled again at her excitement. "Take your time, sweetheart. Don't just grab the first thing you see. There are other stores in this city, you know."

"Oh, Jimmy, but this is just what I've always wanted!"

He shook his head in surrender. "All right, if you're sure."

She looked up at him, her eyes shiny. "I'm sure, I know I'm sure!"

"All right, Lisa, let's go inside and talk to the man." He held the door open for her, and then followed her into the jewelry store.

A tall, older man came toward them, a polite smile professionally in place. He had waves of silver hair and a neatly trimmed mustache. He wore an elegant suit that was even more expensive than it looked, and he had the suntan of a man who did nothing all day but clip bonds beside a swimming pool. "May I show you something?" he asked in a pleasant voice.

The young woman looked up at Jimmy. "The one in the window," she said.

"My friend is quite taken with the sapphire and diamond necklace in the window," said Jimmy.

"Ah," said the silver-haired gentleman. "That is an exquisite selection. Four lozenges of clustered diamonds, four carats and under, set in platinum. On each side there are links of fourteen-carat gold alternating with links of four large diamonds each, also set in platinum. The central sapphire is virtually flawless, one of the most perfect stones I have seen in my twenty-eight years as a trader in precious metals and gems. If you look here in this case, I have a matching bracelet. It has a smaller but no less stunning sapphire set off by the same pattern of diamond lozenges and gold links."

Lisa stared at the bracelet. "I've never seen anything so wonderful in my whole life," she murmured.

"I don't pretend that I know very much about fine jewelry," said Jimmy, "but I can recognize quality. What is the cost of the necklace and bracelet together?"

"Jimmy!"

The proprietor gave Jimmy a quick, knowing smile. "The two together are roughly fifty thousand dollars."

"Jimmy, look," said Lisa. "There's a ring that goes with them, too."

The young man laughed. "I'll consider the necklace and the bracelet, but not the ring, honey. I'm not ready yet to give a beautiful woman an expensive ring. It's much too symbolic, and I wouldn't want to be misunderstood."

"Oh, Jimmy, that's silly."

"We'd like to get the necklace and the bracelet, then," he said to the jeweler.

"Wonderful," said the older man. "They're very lovely, and they're certainly a sound investment as well. How will you be paying?"

"By check," said Jimmy.

"Well, in that case I'll give you a little discount, and we'll call it fifty-two thousand, five hundred dollars, with the tax."

"Thank you very much." He took out his checkbook and began filling in the amount. The jeweler went to his window showcase and removed the necklace.

"May I try it on?" asked Lisa.

"Certainly," said the jeweler. He clasped the necklace around her neck.

"How does it look?" she asked.

Jimmy looked up and gave an involuntary gasp. "You look like an empress," he said.

Her eyes went wider and one hand went to her throat. She hurried to Jimmy and kissed him on the cheek. "I don't know what to say," she said.

"It makes me feel good to give you something you really like," said Jimmy. "I just want to make you happy." He tore the check out and handed it to the older man. "Here you are," he said.

"Thank you, Mr. Valentine. Is this your correct address and telephone number?"

"Yes, it is."

"Good," said the jeweler. He turned away, toward his office, but a sudden thought made him turn back again. "Oh, I'm so sorry," he said in an apologetic voice, "I just realized that today is Friday and it's now past five o'clock. I'm afraid I can't actually release the necklace and the bracelet until I can contact your bank on Monday morning."

Lisa looked disappointed. "But your check is good, isn't it, Jimmy?"

"I'm sure it is," said the silver-haired man, "but you must understand, according to—"

"Listen," said Jimmy to the jeweler, "keep the check and call it in to the bank on Monday morning. I'm leaving town on business for a few days very early Monday, so when the check clears, I'd be grateful if you'd deliver the bracelet and necklace to Miss Parker's home."

"Well, I could be here first thing Monday to pick them up in person," she said.

"I'd be more than happy to hold them for her, or deliver them, as she wishes."

"Fine, then. Lisa, you'll have them in two days. You'll just have to be a brave girl and wait."

"It'll be murder, but I'll do it," she said.

"I know you can," said Jimmy. He shook hands with the jeweler. "Thank you for everything."

"Thank you, sir," said the older man. "I will see that everything is taken care of to your satisfaction. The young lady will pick up the jewelry, then?"

"Yes," she said, "but it's like waiting for Santa Claus to come."

The silver-haired gentleman laughed. "Have a pleasant evening," he said.

"Thank you," said Jimmy.

On the sidewalk, Lisa looked at the empty place in the window where the necklace had been. A tear slipped down her cheek. "I always dreamed of having something like that," she said. She raised herself up on her toes and kissed Jimmy. "You're wonderful" she said. Then he took her arm and steered her to the curb, where he flagged a cab. He gave the driver the name of an expensive restaurant.

The dinner consisted of one culinary masterpiece after another. Valentine chose a dusty bottle of Chateau L'Angelus to accompany their tournedos in marchand de vin sauce, and a Perrier-Jouet champagne to sparkle beside the simple but delicious dessert of lemon crêpes. The meal lasted almost two hours, each course introduced with hot loaves of French bread and a new basket of soufflé potatoes. They spoke little during the dinner, despite the relaxed pace—the food deserved all the attention they could give to it. When they finished, both Valentine and Lisa were comfortably sated. They walked slowly down the avenue, luxuriating in the evening and the weather, looking in the shop windows, enjoying each other's company.

"Would you care for a drink or two?" he asked.

She had to laugh. "I don't know what I'd do with a drink. My food and beverage compartments are crammed full. I may never have to eat again for the rest of my life."

"Would you like to go home, then?"

"Yes," she said. Valentine hailed another taxi.

They went to his apartment. He unlocked his front door and apologized for the clutter. Lisa did not even glance at the living room. She headed directly for the rear of the flat and Valentine's bedroom. Before he closed the front door behind him and caught up with her, she had turned down the covers on his bed and tossed her fur in a corner. She was waiting for him to help her with her gown's zipper.

They made love three times. The first time was quick and as consumingly passionate as the first few times Valentine had ever had sex. Afterward they talked and laughed together; they really didn't know each other very well. He had made her acquaintance through an advertisement in the Yellow Pages. Valentine told Lisa about his boredom with college and how he had written three wildly successful computer programs—one extremely useful for certain engineering applications, and two for the video-game market. He told her a little about what he did with the large, frequent royalty checks he received. It seemed that it was difficult to find enough uses to which to put his money. Despite his accountant's exasperated advice, Valentine preferred spending it to investing it. The investments just created *more* money, and that only aggravated the problem of what to do with it, making an ever-widening vicious circle leading only to a vast, unwieldy, unmanageable fortune. Lisa just nodded sympathetically. The second time they made love, it was slower yet no less intense. The third time was about three or four o'clock in the morning. Lisa woke from a bad dream and desperately needed comforting. Valentine thought that it was more like she were comforting him, but in the end she forgot her nightmare and came to a powerful, weeping, shuddering climax.

On Sunday they stayed in bed until well past noon, seeing how long they could maintain a gentle though fiercely erotic foreplay before one of them begged for completion. Again it was Lisa who needed more from Jimmy. When they emerged at last from the bedroom, they went for a walk through the city's large municipal park, where they listened to a free Mozart recital. Then they shared a second sumptuous dinner. Valentine reminded her afterward that he needed to pack for his business trip, and Lisa was disappointed, but she remembered that she had important business the following morning that would leave her just enough time to pick up her gifts at the jewelry store. They parted vowing that they would renew their sudden and consuming love as soon as Valentine returned to town. Lisa said she would break off with all her other gentleman friends in order to be with Jimmy as often as possible. She tried to thank him for everything, but she only stammered helplessly. He had thoroughly overcome her with his charm and generosity.

"You don't have to thank me, Lisa," he said between her kisses. "It really was my pleasure. I like to give presents to beautiful women. Then I can pretend that you really loved me a little."

"Pretend!" she cried. "Jimmy, I—"

He cut off her new spate of stammering. "Just promise that you won't forget me while I'm gone."

"I won't forget you. God, how could you ever think that?"

"Good. Go to the jeweler's early tomorrow morning. You shouldn't have any problems unless that shop is burglarized and your necklace and bracelet are sitting in a pawnshop in Biloxi."

"Hush, Jimmy, don't even joke about it!"

He laughed. "I'm sorry. I'll call you Wednesday."

"I'll be waiting. If you don't call, I'll just die."

He got her a cab and kissed her good-bye. "I had two perfect days with you," he said.

"There'll be more. As many as you want. We still have a lot of, you know, experimenting to do." She winked.

He closed the car door and the cab drove away. The stars were glittering in the night sky like chips of crushed diamonds. He walked slowly back toward his apartment, thinking about what he had to do before morning.

When he got home, the first thing he did was to kill Jimmy Valentine.

It wasn't difficult. He went down to the laundry room of his apartment building, where there were eight rusty metal lockers. Five of the lockers were open and contained odd electrical and plumbing parts, most of them useless, broken, or obsolete. There were also oily rags, clothes hangers twisted out of shape, mismatched remnants of bathroom floor tiles, torn sheets of sandpaper, and petrified paintbrushes. The other three lockers had combination locks on them. One of them belonged to Jimmy Valentine. He quickly opened his locker and sorted through a large stack of file folders. One of them was labeled with the Valentine name. He removed a biographical profile and character study of the identity, glanced through the pages briefly with some satisfaction, and tore the papers to pieces. He took his wallet from his hip pocket and removed all the Jimmy Valentine identification—driver's license; social security card; draft card; memberships to several clubs, professional organizations, and civic groups—and put the documents with the discarded personality sketches. From the file he withdrew an American passport in the name of James Valentine, and a legitimate, certified copy of a birth certificate from Lawrence County, Indiana. He destroyed these, too. Finally he added several credit cards and the checkbook to the pile, all that remained of Jimmy Valentine, except the memories in the mind of an enthusiastic but brassy paid female companion who called herself Lisa Parker. The credit cards were authentic, as well: Visa, MasterCard, American Express, oil companies and department stores, all in the name of James Valentine; he had paid for the meals and entertainment with them, and now it was time to abandon them before the bills came. He threw all these things into a fifty-five gallon drum that served the laundry room as a trash receptacle, poured paint thinner over it all, and struck a match. Just that easily, the final traces of Valentine became as ephemeral as soot and ashes. He felt no twinge of regret at all. This wasn't the first time he had destroyed one of his identities.

Now, though, it was necessary to choose another one, and to decide just what he was going to do next. He had career plans of his own, but his parents wanted him to finish college. The young man thought, not for the first time, that he might be able to accomplish both goals simultaneously. It was the middle of the summer. He had already been accepted as a transfer student at a small college in Michigan. He would let the course of events make his final decision for him. He had passed the test he'd set himself, that of improvising plausibly under pressure. Now he felt he could rely on his wits and his audacity in any situation he found himself in.

He carried the collection of unused identities upstairs to his apartment. Most of the things in his rooms had been bought with credit cards that now no longer existed. He would have no trouble leaving all of it behind—objects were easily replaced.

He spent two hours reading his files and selecting a new persona.

The next morning, just as he was about to leave the apartment for the last time, the telephone rang. He answered it. "Hello?" he said.

"Mr. Valentine? This is Robert Shattuck from Shattuck Brothers Jewelers. I'm calling concerning the sapphire necklace and bracelet. I phoned your bank just now, and they told me that your account does not have sufficient funds to cover the check you gave me."

"Yes, I'm afraid that's probably correct," said the young man.

"Is there some error? Did you give me a check on the wrong account?"

"No error, Mr. Shattuck. I just don't have that kind of money. I'm sorry for taking up your time, but I certainly *do* want to thank you for making possible one of the most memorable weekends of my life. Miss Parker was so grateful that she worked very hard endearing herself to me all day Saturday and Sunday. I can't tell you how grateful I am."

Shattuck was outraged. "Do you mean to tell me—"

"Thanks for everything, Mr. Shattuck. Good-bye." He hung up the telephone and smiled to himself. What harm had he done? After all, Lisa had just as good a time during the weekend. If he'd had some cash, he would have sent a dozen roses.

2.

David Caldwell's small car crawled in traffic toward downtown Detroit. Sometimes Caldwell hated driving. Sitting in a stalled line of automobiles, listening to music on the radio, he wished some of the bright-eyed predictions for mass transit made in his youth had come true: the monorail, the personal helicopter. That was a good one; whatever happened to his helicopter? Anything would be better than inching along in a very expensive vehicle, going nowhere, seeing nothing, internally combusting expensive gasoline in its engine. He hit the steering wheel in frustration, changed the radio station, and moved forward a car length.

He arrived half an hour late for his appointment. He left the car, locked but otherwise poorly defended, in a parking garage beside the medical building. He was late, but he knew that Dr. Loetz wouldn't be annoyed. Dr. Loetz liked him because Caldwell was an interesting problem.

Fixed up against the glowing white fluorescent screen were black and white X-ray pictures of the inside of David Caldwell's body, and Dr. Loetz plucked them down like dead leaves from a house plant. "I wanted to show you these first. From the year before last. That was, let me see, September. I saw you before that in February. I see you too often."

"That's what I was thinking," said Caldwell. "Why is that?"

"I can't say." Dr. Loetz studied Caldwell's medical history silently for a long moment. The folder was made up of many pages. "You've had these things grow in you a total of four times, right?"

"Yes," said Caldwell. "Once when I was a kid. Once three years ago. Once a year ago February, and once a year ago September. And maybe now."

Dr. Loetz closed the folder and put it on a formica-topped counter. He shuffled the X-ray pictures and put them in a manila packet next to the folder. "No maybes," he said.

"I've got one again." Caldwell tried to sound unconcerned, but it was a useless thing even to try to do.

"Not one, Mr. Caldwell," said Dr. Loetz. "Two. One up high, right side. One lower belly, partly hidden by the pelvic girdle. Look." He took five more X-ray pictures from another packet and put them up on the fluorescent screen. Caldwell tried, but he couldn't make them resemble anything he imagined he had on the inside. To him, they were just areas of black, areas of wispy white, bright, sharp lines, curves, and angles. They looked more like astronomical photographs than pictures of a living thing.

"Compare these to the ones from a couple of years ago," said Dr. Loetz. They meant nothing to Caldwell—nothing visually, at least. He couldn't even tell the body parts from the background. "When we had you in last time, we went through you pretty carefully. It wasn't just a matter of going in and cutting out the growth. It was your fourth occurrence. That just shouldn't happen. We wanted to find out why you get them, and we wanted to stop them. Well, you went over a year without a problem."

Caldwell was getting angry. He wasn't angry at himself or with the doctor, or even at the things growing inside him. He couldn't find an appropriate target for his feelings. "A year without a problem," he said. "So from now on, I'll never know if the situation is all over, or if I'm just in-between episodes."

"I've done a lot of work—the hospital's done a lot of work—tracking down other people around the world with this kind of history. You're the only person that I could find in the literature with a fourth occurrence. A fourth and a fifth, really." Dr. Loetz smiled briefly.

"How's that supposed to make me feel?"

Dr. Loetz pulled down the X rays and filed them away. He switched off the fluorescent screen, then turned and faced his patient. "I don't know how it's supposed to make you feel. Helpless, maybe. Concerned and worried, maybe, I guess. You're special, in a way, and I really can't offer you any good advice. I can't say, 'Don't worry about it,' because you will, anyway. But it can't do you any good to get overexcited this early."

"I'm in a life-threatening situation. Just tell me when it's all right to get excited about it."

Dr. Loetz frowned. He stood up and stretched, and rubbed his eyes. "You're playing with your imagination, now," he said. "You're fiddling with your emotions. If you leave these growths alone, they'll kill you. They have to come out. It's that simple. We take them out, and you're fine. Maybe someday we'll hit on the truth and we'll give you a bottle of little white pills that will stop the whole thing. In the meantime, I'll put you back on your medications again, and we'll see you in two weeks. Then we'll have a better idea of when you can expect to have the surgery. All right?"

"No," said Caldwell, "but what say do I have in the matter?"

"Okay, David, tell the nurse you want an appointment sometime around the first of the month. Go home. Get things organized. You have time to think things through. Call me if you can't handle it, and I'll give you something for the anxiety. I could also refer you to a psych—"

"Thanks, doctor," said Caldwell. Dr. Loetz wrote out three

prescriptions, then picked up the folder with Caldwell's medical history and the packets of X-ray pictures and went out of the examining room. Caldwell stared at the door for a moment, then finished getting dressed. He pulled on his shirt and hopped off the white paper-topped table. He put on his trousers and pulled the belt tight. He noticed how snugly his clothing fit around the waist. It wasn't fat, he knew. He combed his hair and put on his shoes, picked up his jacket from a plastic chair, then went out and made an appointment with Dr. Loetz's nurse. He left the office and the medical building.

Outside, it was a fine day for mid-January. The sky was a bright, cloudless blue. The infrequent birds that sang in Detroit were chirping in the few bare trees in the neighborhood. The sun felt warm on David Caldwell's shoulders as he walked toward the garage. He hated the day. He thought it should be bleak on the outside, as he was bleak in mind and spirit. He would not have been surprised—he wouldn't even have minded if the sun had fallen from the sky and hidden below the horizon until he had driven home. The sky might have covered itself with black thunderheads, out of respect. The birds should have kept their beaks grimly shut. There might have been a cold wind, and the other people nearby would all have been wrapped in their own thoughts, ignoring him, ignoring the world. But it wasn't like that at all. Caldwell tried to change the drift of his thoughts. He kicked, not angrily, at a stone on the sidewalk in front of him. It rolled forward, then curved across the tree lawn and into the street. A pigeon hopped across the curb, and Caldwell stopped to watch it. He wondered if the bird had secret things in its body sabotaging it.

No, goddamn it, thought Caldwell, none of this feeling sorry for myself. That's it, that's the last time. He walked on down the sidewalk. A couple of black schoolchildren were coming toward him. He had a vision of himself in a movie, played by an actor with a very tough and not altogether likable image. The actor playing Caldwell would be so obsessed with his own physical problems that he would thoughtlessly knock one of the little children down. The child—a girl, Caldwell supposed—would look up at him and cry. The actor-Caldwell would give her a rueful look and go on. That single act of unnecessary violence would mark the character: He had to die. By the end of the film the actor-Caldwell would be dead in a summer storm of bullets, or in the back of an ambulance while a weeping ingenue and a couple of paramedics watched. He would never have an epitaph, only final credits, fade to black, and house lights.

Caldwell didn't, in fact, knock down any of the black schoolchildren. He smiled at them. He figured that improved his chances for survival.

He wasn't filled with sorrow. He was happy to learn that. He *was* aware of a growing anger, the same anger he had felt in the medical building. The anger was more intense, yet it was still directionless, objectless. That was what made it so potent, so frustrating. He couldn't rely on his intelligence to solve this problem. There were just no options open to him. No effort of will in the world was going to change what was happening in his body.

He stared at the cars parked along the street. Each one of them was a masterpiece of modern industrial techniques. Many of them originated in or near Detroit. When anything went wrong with one of them, the owner took it to a garage, where a mechanic spent several hours making everything almost all right. These mechanics were the kind of guys Caldwell had known but slightly in high school, and now they held the nation's economy in their grease-slicked hands. It might take an hour or a whole weekend or even longer, but a good mechanic fixed your car. You had to pay a million dollars or so, but the car was fixed.

One of the bitter factors comprising Caldwell's anger, he realized suddenly, was that no matter how much time he spent in the hospital, the doctors couldn't do the same thing with his body. They couldn't just put in a new carburetor or change his points and plugs or something. They had spent the last few years putting him back together with safety pins and masking tape, and hoping the job would hold together. Instead of the hospital this time, Caldwell thought that maybe he ought to check into the Amoco station.

The parking garage was five stories tall, a high mound of concrete put down on a lot that had once been the site of an elegant hotel. The name of the hotel was still visible in blue and white tiles, set into the sidewalk directly in front of the entrance to the garage. Inside there were several color-coded levels, and a motorist cruised upward from one level to the next, searching for an empty slot in which to dump his car. There were arrows indicating the correct one-way direction, and if the driver ever made an error or decided that he wanted to get back to a lower level, he found that he was almost a prisoner. The simple business of finding a temporary home for a car while its owner ran his errands had been made complicated and frequently annoying.

Caldwell pulled a ticket from a hip pocket. It was stamped with the time when he had entered the garage. He went to one of the two elevators and pushed the up button. He waited. After a while he decided to walk up the stairs instead. He waited some more. He thought that because he had waited so long already, the elevator would *have* to arrive almost immediately. "Gambler's fallacy," he muttered. When the elevator door opened, Caldwell stepped inside. The automatic elevator didn't have buttons for numbered floors, just color-coded panels. Caldwell had forgotten at which color he had left his car. Goddamn it to hell, he thought. He pressed blue; it was halfway, and it sounded familiar to him. Blue. Sure, blue was a good color. Sometimes when he parked in the garage, he parked on the blue level. Sometimes he parked on the orange. Sometimes he parked on green, yellow, red. Caldwell knew that he was going to have to search for his car on foot, from level to level.

He got off at the blue level and made a quick circuit. His car wasn't there. He clenched his teeth and let his breath out slowly, feeling furious. If this had still been the Montpelier Hotel, he thought, there wouldn't be any problem at all finding his car. He could just ask at the front desk to have it brought around.

He walked up the stairs to the green level. He went around that level slowly, his hands making fists. He would be able to spot his Chevy Vega from a long way. It was odd, how familiar the old car was. If his Vega were parked among a dozen others just like it, he'd know his own from a hundred yards away. Just like he'd know Marianne, his wife. When he saw her walking from some distance, subtle characteristics of form and rhythm identified her. Caldwell's car was not on the green level. He was so frustrated that he kicked the fender of a long white Lincoln Continental. The car was so long that Caldwell imagined himself coming by in a pickup truck and tearing the Continental's tail end off. His kick had left a small but visible dent in the fender. Caldwell smiled. He rarely allowed himself emotional outbursts, but at the moment he felt like indulging himself.

He went up to the red level. His anger, which for so long that day had been free-floating and unaimed, was now directed viciously against automobiles. Millions of automobiles, he thought, had become things that people needed to stay alive, as much as they needed food and water. Were cars truly worth the inconvenience they caused people? Tear down buildings to make empty lots for cars to live in, reduce your own standard of living to feed your car, tend your car in the winter with more care than you give your own family—these things suddenly outweighed the benefits. Caldwell kicked at another car, a copper-colored Nissan, and this time he made a crease in the chrome trim on the passenger side. Caldwell grunted. He could do a lot of damage with the toe of a black K-Mart shoe. He walked along kicking cars and feeling his abdominal muscles tightening. He wished that he had something—a jack handle or something, maybe a brick—because he really wanted to smash a windshield. He really wanted to hear the satisfying sound of the impact, see the radiating cracks, hear the shattering of the glass. He felt a little better when he crumpled a Pennsylvania license plate with a kick right in the keystone, and when he cracked a taillight on a Dodge van.

He found his Vega around on the other side of the red level. For a moment he stood looking at it. About a month before, he had had to have six hundred and fifty dollars of repair work done. He frowned. He kicked the bumper hard, and it made a rattling sound. Caldwell was afraid for a moment that the whole thing was going to fall off. He almost opened the trunk to get something to break his own windshield, but he decided against it. The Vega would be dead soon, anyway. It was an old car, and it couldn't be expected to live much longer. The little pet turtles with painted shells that they used to sell at Woolworth's lasted longer than these powerful machines.

Caldwell drove the car slowly down from the red level. He stopped at the exit and paid the attendant. Then he drove home leisurely, in no particular hurry to face Marianne and tell her the bad news. She had been so brave the other times. His two children had been so brave. Caldwell kind of resented how brave everyone else had always been. They tried to comfort him and they tried to cheer him, and they worked very hard at pretending that everything was just fine and that everything was going along like normal. Caldwell hated that worse than he feared the pain and the danger. He stopped off briefly to fill the prescriptions Dr. Loetz had given him. The drugstore charged him more than eighty-nine dollars for the medications.

3.

Arthur Leyva was fifty-two years old, not very tall, not very fat, mostly bald, and discouraged. He was an associate professor of English Literature at Wray College in Detroit. The spring term was due to begin in little more than three weeks, and he was not prepared for it in the least. He would be teaching a Post-War Fiction course and a sophomore Survey of Poetry section. He was using the same texts he'd used the last two years, he knew how many papers he would require and how many exams, and he even had a general idea of what he would say at each lecture; after all, he had the notes he'd assembled the previous times he'd given each course. It wasn't the thin skeleton of facts that eluded him, it was an emotional involvement. For the first time in his career as an educator, he could not find the slightest interest in what he would be saying to the young people in his classroom.

Arthur Leyva had something more important on his mind.

Leyva had always been a good teacher; when he was younger, he'd had ambitions, he'd wanted to be made a full professor and, someday perhaps, chairman of the department. Those things had just not happened, but it was less painful to him than he would have imagined. He had found his niche and he was comfortable there. He was well liked and respected by his students and his colleagues in the English Department. It was nothing to do with the college that had him in such turmoil. It wasn't even anything he himself had done. It was all because of his sister's error in judgment. It was no good, he knew, to put all the blame on poor Abbie. She had been too trusting, of course; but pointing a finger would do nothing toward resolving their dilemma. What had Leyva so anxious was that he couldn't think of anything that *would* help.

He sat at the dining-room table, his texts, his lecture notes, and a blank calendar in front of him. He stared at the month of February, but the individual days blurred together before his eyes. He realized that it was impossible to keep his mind on what he had to do. He sighed and sat back in his chair, rubbing his forehead and feeling the first hollow pangs of panic.

"Arthur?" It was his sister, Abbie. She moved through the house like a ghost these days, touching photographs and framed mementos as if she were trying to reestablish contact with the living world.

"Abbie, where have you been?" asked Leyva.

"I've been in my room, thinking things over. I know that what I've done has you greatly troubled, and I don't want you to suffer on my account. I have always cost you a great deal of money, and I've never done anything to help pay the costs. Indeed, the opposite is true: Without me you would be in a more comfortable situation. So I've decided that—"

"I don't want to hear what you've decided," said Leyva. "Whatever it is, it's bound to be noble and tragic, and pointless. What are you suggesting, that you commit a self-sacrificing disappearance? Retire to an old-age home? Something like that, right?

Abbie looked embarrassed. "Something like that," she said.

"Just forget it. I don't understand how you could have so little faith or confidence in me. I told you that the best thing is a simple, direct approach. We'll work it out together. There won't be any need for either of us to make any dramatic gestures. That kind of thing only works in nineteenth-century novels, anyway, and they always require at least one person to die. I'm not going to volunteer, and I'm not going to let you volunteer."

"Well, then, whatever you think best, Arthur."

"Just forget about it all, let me handle everything. I have a better mind for financial matters in the first place."

"All right, Arthur. I'll be in my room watching television."

"Fine." Leyva watched his thin, gray-haired sister drift from the room and up the stairs. The whole house was beginning to feel like the setting of a Nathaniel Hawthorne story. Leyva shivered. He didn't have the slightest idea of what to do for her. He tried again to work up some interest in his class planning, but the idea of teaching was more tedious than ever, and less important. For the first time, his home life was interfering with his duties as an associate professor.

It really wasn't his sister's fault, after all. It wasn't fair to put the responsibility on her. For twenty years, since her husband's death, she had lived a lonely and inactive life, making meals for the two of them, embarking on one project after another, sewing or decorating or gardening, and never completing any of them. She had entirely lost her spirit, her taste for life. She had become a phantom so quickly, so mercilessly, knowing the effect it had on her brother but unable to exist in any other manner. Now she seldom dressed in anything but a long nightgown and a flannel robe, wandering upstairs and down, searching for something to occupy her mournful mind. She was as restless as if she were prematurely haunting the house. The sight of her made Leyva feel helpless. Her absence, when she was in her room watching television or reading, left him with a painful, furious anguish. He wanted so much to do something for her, and he had come to realize that was impossible.

Then, a year ago, she had met a man named Benjamin Jervis. He was some twelve years her junior, but that never seemed to concern either of them. Abbie had liked him from the beginning, and soon Jervis was escorting her to dinner, to concerts and films. Leyva was glad. It was the first time in two decades that Abbie had shown some excitement about anything or anyone. She was leaving the house, eager after her years of isolation to catch up on everything she had denied herself. Jervis was a polite, thoughtful man; after some initial suspicion, Leyva expressed his gratitude to him for the change he'd made in Abbie's self-pitying attitude. Leyva and Jervis had played golf together a number of times, and Jervis came to dinner at least one or two evenings a week.

Leyva closed his eyes and frowned as he remembered those days, and the illusion of happiness and promise he and Abbie had seized so desperately. Not long after Abbie's infatuation had deepened to the point where she could be truly hurt, Jervis had vanished, taking all of Abbie's savings with him. Much worse, he had persuaded her to cosign a bank note without consulting her brother; he told her he wanted to be securely set up in business before they married. Abbie had trusted him completely.

Now Jervis was nowhere to be found, and a stack of increasingly irate letters from the bank sat on Leyva's desk. He couldn't imagine what he could do about them. He prayed each day that something would happen to lift the burden from his shoulders. Every day, the burden only grew heavier.

Later that afternoon, Leyva had an appointment to meet with an officer of the Heritage Valley Bank. It would not be a pleasant meeting; the bank officer had been calling every morning at five minutes past nine, and Leyva had stopped answering the phone. He had nothing to tell the man. He didn't have the money, he wasn't going to have the money, there wasn't anything he could do about the money. What did they think, that they could get blood out of a stone? Yes, that's just what they thought, and what they intended. Leyva was the stone, and the house he shared with Abbie, the house they'd lived most of their lives in, that was the blood they would shed.

Leyva had an idea that might stall Heritage Valley. He went to his car and drove across town to a small branch of First City

Bank and Trust. He waited on a comfortable chair, watching a long line of customers depositing paychecks. It was Friday afternoon; Leyva wished he had a large sum of money to deposit, but it would be weeks before he was paid. He didn't even know how he was going to buy food for himself and Abbie, let alone give the Heritage Valley Bank anything. After a while, a smiling young woman asked if he needed to see an officer. "Yes," he said, and went to her desk.

"How can I help you?" she asked.

"I'd like to open a checking account," said Leyva.

"You know that we require an initial deposit of a hundred dollars to open an account."

"May I write a check from another account?"

"Of course." She took out a form and they filled in all the necessary information. She helped Leyva choose a check style and a checkbook cover, took his check from the Heritage Valley Bank, and disappeared for a few moments. When she returned, she brought him a packet of counter checks and told him his imprinted checks would be in the mail in a few days. Leyva thanked her and left. He got in his car and drove to the Heritage Valley Bank, in time for his meeting.

The vice president was waiting to see him. "Mr. Leyva?" he said. "I'm glad you could come in to talk. I'm sure you understand that your financial obligation is serious. We are more than willing to help you as much as we can, but we expect you to be cooperative, as well."

"I understand, Mr. Walsh. I hope we can work something out."

Walsh shuffled through the papers on his desk and selected one. "I see here that you missed the last two payments on the loan. If you were to miss the third payment, we would be forced to begin court proceedings to obtain our capital and interest."

"You mean some sort of foreclosure."

"I'm afraid that is the only means we have of recovering what we gave you. Unless you make the third payment and continue to make payments according to the schedule we agreed upon. Do you think you'll be able to make that payment? Before next Friday?"

Leyva chewed his lip and thought. "I'm really not sure, Mr. Walsh. Yes, I could give you the money today, but it would leave me with nothing, nothing at all for living expenses."

Walsh did not blink, did not show any sign that he would retreat from his position. "We're sorry," he said. "But we must have that payment as a token of good faith on your part."

Leyva cursed silently. He took out his new checkbook and started to fill in the First City counter check. "How much is that payment?" he asked.

"One hundred sixty-two dollars and seventy-three cents," said Walsh.

Leyva winced, and wrote in the figure. It was quite a bit more than he had deposited to open the account. He wondered how he was going to cover it. The check would bounce in a few days; he knew that if Walsh realized the check was bad, he wouldn't be inclined to give Leyva the least bit of sympathy in the future. Not that he had shown any remarkable compassion up to this point. Leyva signed the check, tore it loose, entered the amount in the register, and handed the check to Walsh. "Very good, Mr. Leyva. We'll expect the fourth payment on time in thirty days."

"Thank you, Mr. Walsh," Leyva said, standing up and walking out on shaky legs. He felt like a criminal. He was a criminal, he realized, knowingly passing a bad check. He got out of the bank branch as quickly as he could. He sat in his car for a few minutes until he got himself back under control.

That night he realized that he was going to have to make the check good somehow, and before it cleared at the First City Bank. He needed another sixty-two dollars and seventy-three cents. How was he going to get it? Pawn something? What? He didn't own anything valuable. A pawnshop wasn't likely to give him much on a matched edition of Thomas Hardy.

In the morning, without examining his feelings very closely,

Leyva went to a drive-in window of the nearest First City branch and deposited a check from the Heritage Valley account for sixty-five dollars. That would cover the check he had given Walsh. Then he went home and worked on his lecture plans for the rest of the afternoon, putting all thought of his debts out of his mind. He was able to lose himself in his work; by dinnertime, he had made an outline of the first semester's syllabus for both courses he would be teaching. He felt a little better when that chore was finished.

Over the weekend, Leyva relaxed. His problems seemed, for the first time, solvable as long as he kept a cool head. He couldn't let either fear or the bank vice president's intimidation provoke him to some desperate, foolish act. Of course, he realized that both he and Abbie would have to curtail their spending, but that was no hardship. Abbie assured him that she understood and that he'd have her full cooperation. After all, there was not very much that Abbie wanted to spend money on. Leyva, too, had never been a spendthrift. They would merely have to parcel out the available cash to cover the necessary day-to-day bills, and leave all luxuries until after their immediate crisis had passed.

On Monday morning, very early, Leyva got up and wrote out a check for sixty-eight dollars on his First City account, made out a deposit slip, and put both in an envelope. Then he drove to a nearby Heritage Valley branch and put the envelope in the overnight deposit slot. It would be collected and credited to his account as soon as the bank opened. That check would cover the sixty-five dollar check he had written Saturday morning. He saw already that in order to keep the whole succession of checks from being returned for insufficient funds, this process would have to continue every two or three days until he could cover the amounts with real money. Otherwise he would be ruined.

At lunchtime, Abbie came downstairs and made a casserole of macaroni and cheese. While they ate, Abbie asked if everything was under control. "Of course," said Leyva, "all I had to do was sit down with the bank officer and explain the situation. He was very considerate. He'd heard similar stories before. He was glad to help us repay the loan according to a refinancing scheme that wouldn't send us to debtor's prison. You don't have to worry about a thing."

"I'm so glad, Arthur," she said. "I haven't been sleeping well, ever since that man took our money."

He reached over and patted her hand. "The police have his name and description; they'll catch up with him sooner or later. I don't expect that we'll collect our money from him, but I'll be happy if they just send him to prison where he belongs. As for the loan, you don't have to concern yourself about it anymore. I'd just like to take over the management of your checking account, as well. It would simplify my figuring."

"Certainly, Arthur, whatever you think best. You know I trust you with everything we have."

"Thank you, Abbie. Now, just put all the worry out of your mind."

Leyva wished that he could feel as confident as he sounded. He wanted to ease his sister's anxiety, and he believed that he had; but he couldn't erase the nagging doubts that distressed him so much. He would sign Abbie's name to her checks now, and start depositing and writing checks on that account as well as his own two accounts. That way it wouldn't seem so suspicious that he was trading checks back and forth from two banks several times a week. He would have to draw up a formal plan, a rotation schedule with ever-increasing amounts to cover costs. Draw on Bank A, deposit in Bank B, draw on Bank C, deposit in Bank A, draw on Bank B, deposit in Bank C. Then he could reverse the direction of the flow for a while. One misstep, and the whole pyramid would collapse.

And the pyramid would grow quickly. Leyva was stunned to calculate that during the term of the loan, the bank balances would grow to over seventy-three thousand dollars.

He felt an ugly, cold feeling in his belly. How was he ever going to get seventy-three thousand dollars to cover it all? It was too late, because he had already begun the check kiting, it was already nearly beyond his ability to salvage. He needn't worry about the sixty-two dollars that had troubled him on Friday: Soon the amount would be hundreds, then very shortly thousands of dollars. Nobody but a loan shark would offer him money in that case, and Leyva had an educated reluctance about going to a loan shark. He didn't need sixty-two dollars, now. He needed a miracle.

4.

Judith Nominski was smiling and thinking of murder. She had never read Karl Marx, but she had an idea of what his philosophy was: liquidate all the bosses, seize control of the means of production, give all the deserving workers a raise, go to Cancún for a few weeks. It sounded all right to her, but the main problem was the same as it had always been—it was too damn difficult to put the program into effect. It was all well and good for Marx to advise the poor workers to seize the means of production, but how the hell was she supposed to do it? She gazed off into space and played a scene in her mind:

"Mr. Salicki, sir, I've decided to remove you from your position of authority."

"I understand, Miss Nominski."

"If you cooperate with our legitimate redistribution of power and wealth, nothing will happen to you. We admire your executive ability, and we have a place for you in our restructured corporate system."

"I'm very grateful. May I call you Judy?"

"Call me Andi. My middle name is Andrea. And I, in turn, will call you Dick."

"Call me Buzz, my mother does."

"Fine, Buzz. You will be working under a committee of

former wage-slaves and drudges who have been liberated and will govern the General Motors Corporation on a rational, humanistic, equal-work/equal-pay basis."

"I'm in favor of that, Andi, but doesn't it sound the least little bit like Communism?"

"Are you calling us Communists? I'm sorry, Buzz, but that just proves that your thinking is hopelessly out of date, locked into a counterrevolutionary, racist, sexist, bourgeois mode. There is no solution but elimination. It's too bad, but we gave you a chance to save yourself and you've shown that you are unable to conceptualize in a flexible and progressive manner. You will have to be purged for the good of your fellow workers."

"Of course I'm sorry that my life is coming to an end, but at least I have the consolation of knowing that my death will benefit the human race as a whole, and the General Motors Corporation in particular."

It made a nice fantasy, but that was all. Nominski couldn't even get the other clerks in her department to listen to her, let alone all the employees of General Motors. But it was fun to think about what might happen, *if* they—

"All right, Judy, you wanted to see me?"

"Yes, Mr. Salicki," she said. "You know the last time I asked you about a promotion, you said that it was too soon, and that I should wait. I thought it might be time now."

Her boss was a tall, thin man who wore a tie bar, tie clasp, cuff links, American flag pin in his lapel, and a plastic penholder in his shirt pocket. He was in his early forties and had his hair styled the way television gameshow hosts had worn theirs ten years ago. He was extremely nervous and sucked Mylanta tablets constantly so that when he spoke his words seemed to bubble forth from some dark, milky cavern. "Judy," he said sourly, "the last time you asked me about a promotion, it was only four months after your last one, and that was only one month ago. Using just very elementary arithmetic, we arrive at the conclusion that you have still another month before the subject can even be ripe for discussion. And if you insist on harping on it like this, you'll find out that your supervisor, *me*, is getting less and less sympathetic all the time. Now, isn't it about eight-thirty? Shouldn't you be getting to your desk?"

Karl Marx never had to deal with bosses like that. Marx wrote his goddamn book in the British Museum. If he had tried talking to somebody the way Salicki talked to her, the librarians would have shushed him.

She went back to her desk.

All morning long, until lunchtime, Judith Nominski thought about revenge. She processed the papers that crossed her desk and made an occasional call to the data entry clerks to see why everything took twice as long as it should. She'd never had any problems when she'd worked in that department, but then she'd had an intimate familiarity with the alphabet and the layout of a keyboard. These kids wouldn't even be able to type out their own names if you hid their operating manuals. When she wasn't doing her job and everyone else's, Nominski was seething about Salicki's cruddy behavior. Who did he think he was? Gen. Motors himself? Nominski wanted to teach him a lesson. She wanted to teach a lot of people a lesson, but Salicki was first or second on her list.

At lunch, she sat with another woman from the payroll office and complained about the company's attitudes. "They're just plain antiminority, all the way around," said Nominski.

"Who ain't?" said Arlene Williams, a short, heavy black woman a little older than Nominski.

"It doesn't bother you?"

Williams shrugged. "I been two minorities longer'n you been *one*, honey. You just learn what the rules are, see, then you learn what you can get away with. You got to get away with as much as you can get away with. Your trouble is you tryin' to get away with stuff by the rules. You can't mix gettin' away with stuff *and* rules. You does one or the other."

31

"Arlene," said Nominski in a bored voice, "you never make any sense."

"Judy," said Williams, "I'll tell you what your trouble is."

"I wish we could get through one lunch without you telling me what my trouble is. Every time you tell me, my trouble is something different."

"Cause you in a whole lot of trouble, and they all your fault. How long you been divorced?"

Nominski frowned; she didn't like talking about her marriage. "Seven months, eight months. I'm not keeping real close track."

"Yeah, and when was the last time you gone out with somebody?"

"What the hell business is that of yours?"

"Just answer me, honey. When was the last time?"

"Before I got divorced."

"You ain't met no boys?"

Nominski spat. "I ain't trying to meet no boys. I ain't in the market for no boys. I'm just fine by myself."

Williams shook a finger at her. "See? That's just what I been saying. Instead of getting mad at some boy, see, you got to find something else to get mad at. When you was married, you took it out on your old man all the time, didn't you? And now you ain't got nobody, you think you be mad at the company and Mr. Salicki. Hell, Mr. Salicki ain't nobody."

"You can say that again."

"And he ain't nobody to get mad at. Won't help you feel no better. It's like getting mad at the moon. No satisfaction, honey."

"So unless I go out with somebody, I'm going to be a frustrated, crabby old bitch, is that right?"

"Uh huh, now you got it."

"And if I go out with some guy, I can take it all out on him, and my life will be fine, and I won't hate my job so much."

"You right."

Nominski spat again. "It's not worth it, Arlene. I'd rather be like I am."

"Well, you ask me, honey, you talk like you been on the rag for a month."

"You don't have to sit with me, you know."

Williams smiled. "I like your spunk," she said.

"You go to hell," said Nominski.

During the afternoon, however, Nominski thought about what Williams had said. She still didn't think the woman knew what she was talking about, but Nominski had to admit that she was getting very tired of spending all her time at home. It was just that she had no desire at all to go out. The whole game of meeting men and pretending to be interested in their dinky little lives was too tedious. And what for? Just to get some obnoxious guy to buy her dinner, take her to a movie, and then fight him off at the front door? She'd had plenty of that in high school. She definitely didn't want to go through all that again.

On the other hand, though, maybe Williams had a point. Nominski *could* meet some jerk and go out with him, and she could be sure the relationship ran according to *her* rules this time. She could boost her sagging self-image by seeing how much she could get out of the fool. She might even enjoy taking charge for a change. It would show her ex-husband a few things, it would show that damn Mr. Salicki. It would show her, herself, that she had nerve and purpose and as strong a will as anybody else. That was the kind of person she wanted to be from now on.

So after work she went home, ate a light supper, changed clothes, and headed for a bar nearby. She sat on a stool and sipped at a daiquiri and looked around. It was still early, but already there were eight other people there, all talking and laughing. It wasn't like a singles' bar, and she was grateful for that; it was bright and pleasant and she didn't have to listen to awful music or a row of goddamn video games. She had nothing further planned. She was just going to enjoy her peach daiquiri, order a second one, and if nothing happened by the time she finished it, she would go on to another place. She expected that wouldn't be necessary.

She was right. After a few minutes, a kid sat beside her. "Do you mind if I sit here?" he asked. He looked like a high-school senior or a young college boy.

"Not at all. It's a free country," she said.

"My name is Adrian," said the kid. "I go to Wray."

"What's a Wray?" asked Nominski.

"A top-secret private college for kids with rich parents."

"Oh. You've got rich parents." Her tone of voice was calculated to let him know that she couldn't care less.

"My dad's rich," he said. "My mom just knows about it."

"Uh huh. Your mom ought to leave him. Then she'd be rich, too."

"Well, they like each other. What's your name?"

"Andi."

"Oh. What do you do?"

Nominski enjoyed making the conversation as difficult for him as she could. "What do I do? When?"

He frowned. "Monday through Friday. Nine to five."

"I work for General Motors."

"Big company." This kid was *bright*. "On the line or what?"

"On the line? What do I look like? I handle computers."

It was the wrong thing to say; Nominski saw his face light up. "Ah! Maybe you could tell me—"

"You bet," she said. "Another time." She got up, grabbed her purse, and started for the door.

"Wait a minute." The damn kid was following her out the door. "Listen, I'd like to talk to you—"

"What did you say your name was?"

"Adrian. Adrian van Eyck."

"Right. Buy me dinner."

"Okay."

Nominski's eyes opened wider. Why hadn't she tried this

years ago? "Dinner and drinks and that's all, Adrian," she warned him.

"Okay. I just want to ask you what it's like. Working for General Motors and all."

"It's your dime, sweetheart." They crossed the parking lot to her car. She wanted to be able to dump him when she felt like it, and she didn't want to be stranded anywhere. She was going to have to thank Arlene Williams for the advice. The world was already beginning to see a new Andi Nominski; the world would have to learn to adjust, and pretty goddamn fast.

Part One

The Drawing Board

1.

Detroit. The City Beautiful.

That was what Detroit was called a century ago. Since then, heavy industry has changed the face of the city and made it difficult to love in the old way. Few people except the most loyal of native citizens think of Detroit as other than the nation's machine shop. The Detroit River, once one of America's most beautiful, has gone the way of the beautiful blue Danube—as a shortcut to market for ore boats, tankers, and other merchant vessels. The industries have given Detroit jobs, growth, and the subsidiary benefits of commercial success, but they have forced Detroit to abandon some of the gentler virtues it enjoyed when it was "The City Where Life Is Worth Living." Detroit has never been "The City That Care Forgot"; that's New Orleans. Or "The Best Location In The Nation." That's Cleveland.

There used to be a cruise boat on the Great Lakes that traveled between Detroit and Cleveland in the 1950s. To someone from the south of California, that might seem like an odd and vaguely perverse way to spend a holiday. In those days some people might not have been able to tell which port was which upon arrival. "Is this Cleveland, or is this Detroit?" they would ask. In those years before the anxiety of the mid-sixties, only a born-and-bred local could tell the difference. Today, with the building of Detroit's downtown Renaissance Center and other more basic alterations in the metropolitan mood, that confusion is ending. But from certain vantage points, such as along various urban freeways or from the hazy layer a thousand feet above the ground, the two cities are still indistinguishable in many respects.

David Caldwell sat in his car, the engine running, listening to the radio. He was parked in his mother's driveway in Hamtramck, and he was trying to work up the nerve to go inside. The music on the radio made him feel old. Sometimes he went into record shops and the walls were lined with racks of albums completely unfamiliar; the records he wanted, if they were stocked at all, were in the $1.49 junk bins. A song ended, the deejay played a tape of some women singing the deejay's name and the station call letters. Then a voice came on and screamed, *"Sunday!"* There was an echo: *"(Sunday!)"*. That made Caldwell feel much better. He smiled and turned the volume up. *"Sunday!"* shouted the man again. It was a spot advertisement for a local auto raceway. *"Hanson Drag Raceway! Stocks, Rails, and Funny Cars! Special ten o'clock matinee Ladies' Demolition Derby! Sunday! (Sunday!) Hanson Drag Raceway, the Great Lakes' Racing Capital of the World! Route 24, five miles south of Pontiac! Sunday! (Sunday!) BE THERE!"* That ad and the bombeda-bombeda music that went with it and the super-hard, super-fast sell had been part of Caldwell's youth. Since the 1950s, every boy and girl in the United States had grown up with *Sunday! (Sunday!)*.

There was a commercial for an airline and one for a fast-food corporation. Then the deejay put on another song by a group Caldwell had never heard of. He switched off the radio, took a deep breath, and got out of the car. He walked up to his mother's side door. "Ma?" he called.

"Davey?"

"No, Ma, it's a robber disguised as the gas-meter man. Did Marianne call?"

Caldwell's mother came into the kitchen. She was very small, as thin and fragile as a bundle of sticks, and she limped as she walked. She wore a black dress with white dots. Caldwell had known that dress for years. He used to think that the white dots looked like the circles of paper he got all over his desk whenever he punched holes in typing paper. The old woman wore heavy black shoes. Her gray hair was pinned tightly to her head. Caldwell hugged his mother and kissed her. "Kids all right?" he asked.

"They're taking a nap. Marianne said she'd be late. The store's getting ready for inventory."

"I remembered. Let me just get the kids. You need anything while I'm here?"

Mrs. Caldwell glanced around the kitchen, as though searching for an empty space from which something important had disappeared. "No, Davey, I can't think of anything."

"Want to come have supper with us?"

She smiled wearily. "Thanks, but I've got supper started already. Remember that you have to take me to the doctor tomorrow."

"Right, Ma. I'll go pack up the kids' toys. They bother you any?"

She followed him out of the kitchen. Caldwell's children had strewn their toys all over the living room, under the furniture and hidden in the plants and among the old woman's odd knickknacks. "No, Davey, they were perfect angels." She watched her son collect the toys and put them in a brown corrugated box. "I have to go to the doctor tomorrow," she said.

"I know, Ma. I'll come get you. Two o'clock, right?"

"Yes, Davey. What did your doctor say to you today?"

He looked up. His mother's face was a spider's web of lines, creases drawn across her features by years of worry and loneliness. Caldwell knew that he had been responsible for a great portion of her sadness. "Doctor didn't say anything much," he said, going back to picking up the toys. "You know doctors. I just have to go back and see him again. Nothing definite, really."

"What about the tests? You had those tests last week. What did he say?"

"He said I may have to go back into the hospital."

There was a strained silence for a while. "Oh, Davey," she whispered, "oh, my God, I hope you don't have to go through all that over again."

"It's all right, Ma, I promise. Forget it. I feel fine. I'll get the kids."

Mrs. Caldwell waved one hand at him. "No, no, let me. I'll wake them." She left the room, a room where he had spent the first seventeen years of his life. The furniture was the same as always. He had hidden his own toy soldiers and cowboys in the same places, under the couch with the maroon-corded fringe. He could barely remember his father, who always sat in the same yellow wing chair facing the television. Caldwell realized that the television set was the only thing that ever changed in the room. He even recalled each stain in the carpet. He saw claw marks of the only cat he had ever owned, where the animal had ripped the corner of the couch until his mother had made him get rid of the cat. The couch itself—

"Hi, Daddy."

Caldwell looked up. Little Davey was rubbing his eyes. The boy was four years old. Behind him, Caldwell's mother carried Risa, his eighteen-month-old daughter. "Davey," said Caldwell, "you carry the box with your toys and I'll carry Risa. Can you handle the box okay?"

"I carry it," said the boy.

"Kiss Grandma good-bye." Little Davey kissed her, and Caldwell kissed her. "Thanks, Ma. I'll call tomorrow before I come over."

"Give my love to Marianne. And take this. Nut bread. And

some poppyseed roll." She gave him two long packages wrapped in aluminum foil.

Caldwell opened the side door and waited for his son to carry the box of toys out. They got in the car and he drove home.

He parked the car in the driveway. Marianne's car was already in the garage. They lived in a small house on Berwyn Drive in Redford Township. As a wedding present several years before, Marianne's parents had given them the down payment on the house, and they paid less a month on the mortgage than they had for their apartment rent before they were married. Caldwell got out of the car, locked his door, and walked around to the other side. He let Little Davey climb out with the box of toys. Caldwell carried Risa, still asleep, into the house. The house was a little isolated from the mainstream of life in urban Detroit—but that itself was a blessing, Caldwell felt. The place was a cozy cottage for two young newlyweds. Little Davey and Risa had turned it into a kind of prison at times, but it was far better than nothing. Caldwell was growing to appreciate the things in life that were better than nothing.

Marianne was in the dining-room–kitchen area, making supper. She was trimming cubes of meat. "Hi, dear," she called when she heard the door open. Caldwell had hung a string of bells on the door as a kind of burglar alarm, and no one could get in or out without everyone else in the house knowing it.

"How's it going?" said Caldwell as he walked through the kitchen. He went into the room Risa and Little Davey shared and put his daughter down in the crib. He came back out to talk with Marianne. He kissed her first. "I heard you've started inventory. Ma said so."

"I told you, day before yesterday. Don't you remember?"

Caldwell shrugged. "Sure. I was only saying that Ma said you said— Never mind. You tired?"

"I'm tired."

"Want me to make supper?"

Marianne snorted skeptically. "You're going to make a stew, I suppose. Just like I'm going to fly to work in the morning."

"I can make a stew."

"I mean a decent stew, the kind people eat. What did the doctor say?"

Caldwell took an unpeeled carrot and sat at the dinette table, biting off chunks and chewing loudly. It gave him a little time to think about his answer. "Dr. Loetz looked at the X rays. He showed them to me. He showed me the old ones, too. They're different."

"Different how?" asked Marianne without turning around. She was shaking the beef cubes in a plastic bag filled with flour and seasonings.

"All right, all right. Where there didn't used to be anything, now I've got something."

Marianne turned around quickly. Her expression was shocked. Her face had become suddenly pale. "David," she said, "do you mean another growth?"

"Yeah," he said. He took a large bite of the carrot.

"And another operation?"

"Yes."

Marianne just stared at him, holding a knife in one hand and a stalk of celery in the other.

"It's not so bad," said Caldwell. "It'll have to come out, right? But it's not an emergency this time. I have, oh, I don't know how long before I have to go in. He wants to operate as soon as possible, but I can stall him for a couple of weeks. So we'll put money aside this time, and it won't be so bad. We've got insurance that will pay some of it, remember? So it's just a matter of having me around the house nagging and moaning at you for six weeks or so. That's all. What you call an open and shut case. Forget about it."

"David," said Marianne, her voice low and cold, "I can't

forget about it. I have to worry. You could die. You could die, all alone, and I wouldn't even be with you. The last thing you'd see in this world would be the damn stupid ceiling of the operating room. Then where would I be?"

He smiled and shrugged to relieve the ominous tone their conversation had taken. "Here in this house. And then in that case Little Davey would be the man of the family. He could quit school before he starts. It would make it simpler for him. And you could lay Risa on a tattered shawl in the snow with a tin cup full of pencils. You'd get by. I'm not that important." He stopped talking when he saw that Marianne was crying. She dropped the knife to the kitchen floor. Caldwell got up and went to her. He held her. He could feel her tears, strangely warm, on her cheek. He said nothing; he always felt foolish going, "There, there," in situations like this. He just held her for a while, kissed her a few times, and waited for her to get over the bad news.

"We'll be all right," she said at last.

"See?" he said. "You're being brave already." Damn it, he thought.

2.

Several days after he'd met Andi Nominski, Adrian van Eyck paid a visit to her where she worked. He just walked into the payroll-department offices as if he had every right in the world to be there. That was one of the cornerstones of Van Eyck's technique: raw nerve. That, combined with painstaking preparation and unshakeable credentials—his "Adrian van Eyck" identity was as phony and as solid as "Jimmy Valentine" had been—allowed him to go almost anywhere and get people to do almost anything. It wasn't foolproof, of course, and he hated to admit that he enjoyed the small risks he took. That wouldn't have been professional.

"Hi, Andi," he said, standing beside her desk. It wasn't half past eight yet, but she was already paging through the first batch of personnel reports she would have to process.

Nominski looked up at him, squinted, and tried to remember who he was. "Adrian!" she said. "What the hell are you doing here?"

He smiled. "Keep your voice down, Andi. I thought I'd just come in and see this wonderful modern operation you were bragging about. Admiring complex money-handling systems is a hobby of mine."

"How did you get in the building? You couldn't even have

parked in the lot without ID. The guard downstairs wouldn't have let you—"

Van Eyck just shrugged. "I got in all right. No problem. Now, I don't want to interfere with your work or anything, Andi, but I was just wondering if you could arrange a little something for me."

Nominski frowned. "What do you want?" she asked suspiciously.

"Nothing much. I'd like to take a little tour, that's all."

"Then why are you bothering me? They give tours all day long. You go by the main gate and follow the—"

Van Eyck interrupted her. "I took that tour yesterday. It was very informative. They showed us the production line and all these men and women keeping American industry strong, and they talked about the Free Enterprise system and all that stuff we learned about in high school. I tried to ask a few specific questions about how the payroll is handled, and you'd think I'd made some kind of indecent suggestion. The girl leading the tour either couldn't or wouldn't bring us up here. What is this, some top-secret military installation disguised as a Cadillac plant or something?"

Nominski gave him a wry look. "What did you expect? You thought they'd just let you roam around here unsupervised with a quarter of a million blank checks? Payroll and accounting information is as secret as the designs for next year's new cars."

"I suppose I can't blame them," said van Eyck. "Anyway, after I struck out playing Mr. Average GM Buyer, I decided I might try a different tack. It was just a matter of luck that I met you the other night."

"You mean, you met me and your thoughts immediately strayed to the General Motors payroll."

"Something like that. It doesn't make any difference, really. All that matters is that both you and I are in the right place, and anytime could be the right time."

"Yeah, sure. Right time for what?"

He grinned. "Right time for I don't know what, yet. That's why I'm here. I want you to arrange a tour for me, a little more detailed than the official version. And concentrating on this building, here."

"We don't do that."

"What if I was some bigshot software salesman who thinks he can save GM millions of dollars a year by streamlining your payroll system?"

Nominski shook her head. "In that case, you wouldn't be dealing with me. You'd call Mr. Salicki and go through channels. Even in that case, you probably would get just a polite brush-off. We have our own in-house computer geeks, you know. We don't have to buy software from itinerant disk peddlers."

Van Eyck nodded. "Okay, but I don't really want to sell anything, in the first place. I just want to look around. Why don't you arrange for me to have that talk with your Mr. Salicki. I'll let him show me around and then he can politely throw me out on my ear. I won't use up much of his time, and I'll see what I'd like to see."

"Adrian, how do you expect to fool Mr. Salicki?"

He grinned again. "Didn't you honestly believe the other night that I'd spent the last two years helping my dad salvage sunken silver off the Florida coast?"

Nominski sighed. "You had me going there, I'll give you that. But fooling an expert in his own field—"

"Is even easier. I just let him do most of the talking."

"But—"

"Andi, don't worry about me. Let *me* worry about me. I just need you to get me into Salicki's office. Will you do that for me?"

Nominski thought it over. "What's it worth to you?"

"How about a nice dinner, anyplace you like?"

She snorted. "I can't get over how men think a movie and a meal can buy anything. I meant it, Van Eyck, what's it worth to you?"

He looked unhappy. "You mean you want money?"

"Hell, yes."

His shoulders sagged. "I don't have a lot of money now, but maybe if you do this for me, I'll think of a way to get some."

"Oh, you're going to tap General Motors for an unauthorized loan. It'll be worth it to me to see the cops throw a smug little bastard like you into prison. Give me a call later this afternoon. I'll put you on Mr. Salicki's appointment calendar. The rest is up to you."

Van Eyck smiled again. "Andi, if this goes well, it might mean real money. I'm beginning to get an idea."

"You'll need one."

"I mean it, sweetheart. If everything goes well here, can you—"

"We'll see, later. And don't call me 'sweetheart,' or I'll set you up on fraud charges faster than you can hightail it out of here."

"Thanks. I'll call you later."

"You do that." She looked back at her work, and in a few minutes she'd forgotten all about Adrian van Eyck.

3.

Of course, Detroit is more than merely the nation's machine shop. It has a fine orchestra and fine museums, expensive shops, and all the cultural attributes of any of the larger cities in America. It is also a seat of learning, for if you take in the city of Detroit itself, and then the not-too-distant cities of Lansing and Ann Arbor, some of the most prestigious and well-respected universities and colleges in the country are within a short drive on your favorite interstate highway. One of these, in Warren, just north of central Detroit, is Wray College, small in comparison to Michigan State, not so well rounded as the University of Michigan or the University of Detroit; still, the school fills a need for many of the college-bound young people of the Detroit area.

Caldwell's office was really just a small rectangular space in Krummer Hall, separated from other rectangular spaces by thin plasterboard walls. The walls were only nose-high, and they were all painted a pale green. Some of the offices had doors; Caldwell's did not. On one side of him was the office of Cathy Schumacher, an attractive young woman whose main occupation in life was pretending that her husband wasn't nailing every still-warm female body in the Greater Detroit area. It was a harmless hobby for her. On the other side of Caldwell's office was Walter Chance, whom Caldwell thought of as an idiot. Caldwell had to admit that Chance's obtuseness was so well managed, so efficient in its own dullness that he was something of a genius at it. Caldwell's opinion was apparently not shared by the hierarchy of the English Department, because Chance's office had been furnished with a door of its own with a frosted-glass panel.

Caldwell's office hours were from ten o'clock until noon. He was very tired; he hadn't gotten much sleep the night before, even though Dr. Loetz had given him a prescription for a strong sleeping medication. Caldwell hadn't taken it; he hadn't wanted to admit to himself that the crisis had already started.

He grabbed the pile of mail in his box and dropped it on his desk. He went to the window behind his swivel chair and looked out. Detroit in January had never given him much inspiration. The campus was genuinely ugly. In the brochures that were printed for applicants, the photographers had found attractive and lovely places to pose attractive and lovely students. Caldwell, in his malignant mood of the morning, doubted that either the locations or the models had any connection whatever with Wray College or Warren, Michigan.

He stared out across the campus. Let him be healthy, he prayed. Let it be late spring, a clear day with warm breezes. Let it be Florida or Southern California out there instead of gray and grimy Detroit. Let him be a successful author or even merely independently wealthy. And let him and Marianne and their children be happy and well, too. Was that asking for so much? He answered himself: Of course. It had always been too much; it still was.

Caldwell closed the venetian blinds and turned away from the window. He looked at the unorganized clutter that covered his desktop. He sat thinking for a few moments. With a mental effort he stopped his morbid thoughts. Caldwell cleared a space on the desk and opened his notebook. He saw that he had an appointment at eleven o'clock, and until then he had time to look through the mail. There was nothing of interest—there rarely was. He put aside three envelopes from publishers wanting to sell him new textbooks. These he would throw away unopened. There was a circular from the head of the English Department reminding him that final grades had to be made up and recorded by the end of the week coming up. There was a handbill from a fraternity asking him to give blood. There was another notice from another group asking him to donate old clothing and furniture to a rummage sale; that fraternity was going to use the profits to bring over an exchange student from Botswana. The last thing in the bundle of mail was a coupon good for a free chocolate-covered yogurt on a stick. It, along with everything else, went into the wastebasket.

Caldwell could decide not to be depressed about his health, but it was more difficult to decide not to be depressed at all. He stared at the various missives now in the wastebasket, all evidently vitally important to whoever sent them. Some people thought them urgent enough to spend postage to get them to their prospective audience. Yet they all ended up, rather quickly, in the trash. Just as the more rigorous aspects of college life would, sooner or later, also end up in the trash. Caldwell had no illusions about the importance of his lessons and lectures to his students. He remembered that he, himself, as an undergraduate, had celebrated the end of each term by burning the notes he had taken in the weeks before. Just as he cleared his desk of the notices and pleas, so too would the students clear their notebooks and minds of anything he told them. Possibly a thought would stick here with one student, an idea or concept there with another. For the majority, however, at the end of the term it was into the trash with Mr. Caldwell.

Just then, before Caldwell could well work out of this second, equally foolish depression, before he could settle back and put his feet up on the desk, a young man knocked on the wall at the open entry. "Come in, Mr. van Eyck," said Caldwell.

"Thank you," said the student, a junior in one of Caldwell's classes. He was dressed in blue jeans and a green rugby shirt with white stripes. He carried a small spiral-bound notebook but no books. Caldwell had asked to see the young man during office hours because Van Eyck had gotten himself into serious academic trouble. Van Eyck didn't seem to be the least bit anxious. The situation apparently didn't concern the student as much as it did the teacher.

"Sit down," said Caldwell, indicating the wooden chair. Van Eyck sat down and waited quietly. Caldwell leaned back in his swivel chair, swung his legs up onto his desk, and took a deep breath. He hated these meetings. "I guess you know it's next to impossible for me to give you a passing grade for the term."

Van Eyck tried to get comfortable in the chair, but Caldwell knew it would be impossible. The chair had not been designed for comfort. It had been designed only to be manufactured in vast numbers and sold for profit. "I know," said the student. "I didn't expect any kind of special considerations."

"I don't have any special considerations to offer," said Caldwell. "You know that I don't take attendance in class. That never has any bearing on my grading system. Even so, I doubt that you've been around often enough for anyone else in your section to know your name. You haven't appeared more than five times this entire semester."

"It's not that I don't enjoy the course—"

Caldwell held up a hand and interrupted Van Eyck. "You don't enjoy the course," he said. "No one enjoys the course. It's a tedious overview of Romantic poetry, and even I don't enjoy it. That's not the point. Would you like some coffee?"

"No, thank you."

"All right. Forget attendance. What I *do* require from everyone—and I mean everyone—are the assigned papers, the midterm exam, and the final exam. This semester, of the four papers I assigned, you wrote exactly one. It wasn't a bad paper, as I recall. But you still owe me three. You passed the midterm, but you didn't bother to show up for the final exam. You have maybe ten days in which you can turn in the other three papers. If you do that, I will permit you to take a special makeup examination. This is something the head of the department would disapprove of, but I believe in getting as many juniors as possible into the senior class."

"Thank you," said Van Eyck, who had listened attentively, but without any apparent enthusiasm. "The way things stand now, though, I don't think I can get the papers finished, and I'm not prepared at all for the final. That's why I didn't take it."

Caldwell took another deep breath and let it out in a sigh. He put his feet back on the floor and sat up straight. He shook his head. "You understand that I don't have anything further to offer you?"

"I understand, Mr. Caldwell," said Van Eyck quickly. "I don't think *you* understand, though. I don't expect to pass. Really, I don't have any desire to pass. At least, I don't care if I do or not. It doesn't matter to me anymore."

"You're right," said Caldwell, "I don't understand. How are you doing in your other courses?"

"I would say precisely the same."

"Then you're looking at academic probation, possibly expulsion, as the only likely actions open to the school. You or your parents paid a good sum of money for you to come here. You don't like it anymore? Is it our fault or yours?"

"No, it's not that."

"Personal problems?"

"No. It's just that I don't think college is the right thing for me. There are other things I'd rather be doing."

Caldwell nodded. This he could understand. He could think of a dozen things he'd rather be doing, too. "That happens to a lot of students. Usually freshmen, though. First time away from home, the sudden need for a self-discipline that was never developed before, a whole new social situation. But you have only a little more than a year before graduation."

"I know, I know." Van Eyck sounded tired of discussing it.

"Some people think it's best to drop out for a year or maybe two and kick around a little. Then you can come back when you know what you want to do."

Van Eyck smiled. "It's not that, either," he said. "I already know what I want to do."

Caldwell was losing patience. "And may I ask what that is?"

Van Eyck rocked the chair back and smiled again. "I'm going to go into crime," he said.

Caldwell didn't change expression, although his first thoughts were disdainful. He wasn't going to let this boy, this college junior who had never seen the real world, let alone dealt with it, affect him. "You have a surefire plan to get rich, I suppose. Or were you thinking of a long-term career?"

"No," said Van Eyck, "never mind. It's too early to discuss it with anyone else. I haven't got it completely thought out as yet."

"I see," said Caldwell. "I'm glad you can make that admission to yourself. In that case, I guess I'll have to swallow my disappointment; I was looking forward to your papers. I wish you luck, Mr. van Eyck, and perhaps I'll see you in a year or two."

"Thank you for your concern, Mr. Caldwell," said the young man. "You're one of the better instructors I've met in the college. You're the only one with the common courtesy to ask if I needed assistance. Maybe you will see me soon."

Caldwell stood up and walked the student to the entry. "I'm not going to go into a cautionary thing here about doing something foolish," he said. "Just don't do anything foolish."

"I won't. I know my talents, and they'll see me through."

"So," said Caldwell. He shook Van Eyck's hand and watched the young man walk down the narrow green hallway. Van Eyck seemed so young: Caldwell had been that age once, and he remembered that when he was that age his mental image of himself wasn't so immature—unfinished, like bread unbaked in the middle. "Crime," muttered Caldwell. He wondered what Van Eyck's plan was—stealing cars from the factory parking lots, hijacking things into and out of Canada, something that sounded foolproof to Van Eyck, but something that was going to get him into a lot of trouble. Caldwell worried for a moment about his own responsibility. What should he do? Tell Van Eyck's parents? Caldwell shrugged. No, the boy was old enough; he'd have to learn things the hard way. Just like everyone else.

The next day Caldwell went through his early classes almost without thought. The students, at the end of the term, were not desperate to hear what he had to say, and all he could think of doing was to go over an exam for the sake of form, and for the couple of students who invariably tried to chisel a few extra grade points. At noon he remembered that he had made a date with Arthur Leyva for lunch.

Leyva appeared at Caldwell's office on time, eating Jordan almonds from a large box. Leyva would never be a well-loved fixture on campus, he would never be a respected authority on anything, he would never be a full professor. It didn't bother him a bit. He had a few dark comb-over hairs disguising his bald head; his feelings about his departed hair, his departed youth, and his departed ambitions were about the same. They were calm, rational, and accepting. He waited for Caldwell and put another pastel-colored Jordan almond in his mouth. "Where do you feel like going?"

"The Doodle," said Caldwell, choosing a popular lunch counter that made some of the best hamburgers in the city.

"Fine." They took Leyva's car and drove in almost total silence. The news of Caldwell's serious illness had diffused thoughout the English Department, so that almost everyone had come in to say how sorry he was about it all. People who passed Caldwell in the halls week after week without a single word of greeting now pretended that they cared, and it was all part of the business indirectly related to being sick that he hated so much. Leyva knew enough to avoid the topic, but there was little else to talk about. If he started talking about, say, the department chairman, Caldwell would know immediately that Leyva was being careful, and that just underscored the situation. It was quiet in the car for several minutes.

At the lunch counter, Caldwell initiated the conversation. He was actually grateful for Leyva's loyalty, even though Caldwell knew that he himself had been acting self-centered and moody. "I'm scared," said Caldwell.

"You ought to be," said Leyva. "It's a frightening thing."

"I'm afraid of dying."

"Yes."

"I'm afraid of having to go through the surgery, and the whole period of recovery. It's so goddamn hard. Walking again. Hurting. Gaining all the weight back. Building up my body. If it were the first time, it might not be so bad; but I know exactly what I have to go through, and sometimes it seems like just too much effort. I just hate it. Thanking people for their lousy cards and plants. The whole thing."

"I know. No, I don't know, but I can imagine."

Caldwell ate his lunch. "It's not the danger. It's the hole this thing puts into my life. Months. And no money coming in. And Marianne doesn't know it yet, but the insurance doesn't cover nearly enough. This business about a preexisting condition. And the savings went the last time. And my mother, and the kids."

"All right, all right," said Leyva. "If there's anything I can do to help; but you need more than that."

"There's nowhere to turn. I've tried every possible source. For one reason or another I'm not eligible, or I've used up my benefits, or I'm the wrong color or religion or sex or something."

Leyva put down his grilled cheese sandwich with a disgusted expression. Caldwell couldn't tell if the grimace had been caused by the food or by Caldwell's self-pity. "Let me tell you a little secret," said Leyva. "It's helped me, Lord only knows how many times in my life. People say that you should save for a rainy day, am I right?"

"Yes, sure. But just try."

"Right. But if you don't, if you just spend your money on the things you want, and the rainy day comes, you'll survive somehow. You'll pull through. You have in the past, haven't you? Even without money in the bank?"

"Sure," said Caldwell, "but it was hard."

"All right, it was hard. But you're here. And you'll make it through this time, won't you?"

"That's the question, Arthur," said Caldwell. "No, I see your point. I will, but I'm not looking forward to it."

"I'm not telling you to have a party doing it. The thing is that if you forget about the rainy days, when they come you'll survive them anyway; and you have the benefit of all the things you've allowed yourself by not storing the money away. Think how much poorer your life would be if you socked away a good sum each payday. You wouldn't have all the things you've acquired, I don't know—"

"Things in the house," said Caldwell. "The way we live— eating out now and then, movies, books. Risa."

"Sure. Instead, you'd have a tidy balance which you could hand over directly to the hospital. That's never seemed to me to be all that wonderful. Working your best years for the sake of some institution. Which would you rather have?"

"You know what I want?" asked Caldwell. "I want more."

"We all want more. And I want another cup of coffee." He signaled to the waitress.

"There's got to be a way," said Caldwell, musing, almost isolated in thought. He had a sudden clear memory of the day before . . . Van Eyck . . . something criminal that might work. He could tell the judge that he had mitigating circumstances. He'd get out in fifteen years, maybe. Little Davey would be a full-grown man by then. . . .

"What are you going to do?" asked Leyva, intruding on Caldwell's reverie.

Caldwell finished his hamburger and drank the last of his Coke. "I'm not sure," he said, "but there has to be an easier way. Not necessarily a better way, but an easier way. I have to take the pressure off Marianne."

Leyva smiled, crumpling his napkin and tossing it on his plate. "Ah," he said, "I see, I see! Van Eyck's been talking to you, too!" Caldwell could find nothing to say; he just stared.

4.

The next evening, after Caldwell had gone home and eaten dinner with Marianne and the children, he realized that his anxiety was increasing. He went into the bathroom and looked for the vial of tranquilizers. He couldn't find it. Then he went into the kitchen, remembering that Marianne had hidden the drugs from Little Davey. He couldn't find the tranquilizers there, either. "All right," he called from the kitchen, "where are they?"

"In the hall closet," said Marianne. "On the high shelf. In the box of spare vacuum-cleaner bags."

Caldwell closed his eyes and grimaced. "Is this going to go on every day now?" he asked. "Why don't you just tell me if I'm getting hot or cold?"

Marianne came to him and gave him two of the pills. "Here," she said. "You don't want your son swallowing them like candy, do you?"

"Of course not. But why don't you find a decent place and leave them there? Then I could find them when I need them. And give me another couple."

"That bad?"

Caldwell looked at her for a moment. "Feel this," he said, taking her hand and putting it on his lower belly. "Okay? Now feel this." He moved her hand to the other side, up near his ribs. "They weren't there a couple of weeks ago."

"I know." Marianne's voice was quiet and thoughtful. "Still, maybe, you're taking the drugs too much."

Caldwell didn't want to be lectured. "I know how I feel," he said. "I know what I'm going through. I'll take them when I need them."

Marianne was about to answer, but she stopped herself.

"I'm going to go lie down for a while," he said. "Try to keep the kids from—"

He was interrupted by the telephone ringing. "I'll get it," he said. "Are you expecting anyone?"

"No," she said.

"Hello?" he said into the phone.

"Mr. Caldwell, I'm glad I caught you at home."

"Who is this?" asked Caldwell.

"Oh, I'm sorry. This is Adrian Van Eyck. I'd like to speak to you about something."

"Your papers? Your final exam? Just see me during regular office hours, all right? I'm very tired."

"No," said Van Eyck, "it's not that at all. It's really very important for both of us. I've heard about your illness."

Caldwell's weary mind caught up with the course of the conversation. "I see" he said, "it's your life of crime. You need someone to come down to bail you out. What was your scheme, anyway? Hub caps? That's what we used to steal. Times have probably changed, though."

Now it was Van Eyck who seemed to be getting annoyed. "Please, Mr. Caldwell, I need your advice. I'm at the Playmor Bowling Lanes. That's not far from your house. Could you meet me there in, oh, half an hour?"

"Why don't you just drop by here?"

There were a few seconds of silence, during which Caldwell could hear the sound of wooden pins felled by sixteen-pound bowling balls. "Please, Mr. Caldwell," said Van Eyck.

"I'm very tired," said Caldwell.

"This will only take fifteen minutes. And you could be changing my whole life."

Caldwell chewed his lip while he thought. Van Eyck had been dropping his ideas loosely enough, if Arthur Leyva had heard them. The boy did need some straightening out, but that wasn't Caldwell's job. So Van Eyck really might need someone to bail him out, one way or another.

"Playmor," said Caldwell. "All right, Mr. Van Eyck, I'll be there in a few minutes." He hung up the phone. He thought that heaving a heavy ball at a target of maple tenpins might help him work off some of the nervous energy that had been building again.

Why had Van Eyck chosen the bowling alley? It was convenient to Caldwell, of course, and it was a neutral territory. It was nonthreatening to both parties. That idea made Caldwell slow up and consider what kind of threats might be implicit in the situation. He couldn't think of a single one. Van Eyck wasn't going to strong-arm him right there. Maybe he planned to shanghai Caldwell aboard some mysterious ship.

"Who was it?" asked Marianne.

"A kid from one of my classes," said Caldwell. "He's in trouble."

"Oh." She watched as he went back to the closet and brought out his bowling bag. "What kind of trouble is he in?" she asked.

"I'm not sure," said Caldwell.

"But you thought you and he could solve it by bowling a few frames."

"Knock it off, Marianne," he said. He left the house by the front door, slamming it a little harder than necessary. He was immediately sorry that he had spoken to his wife so roughly. If he had waited a few minutes, the tranquilizers would have taken effect, and he could have been pleasant and almost charming.

Caldwell knew that it would take more than four Valium to make him charming, under any circumstances. But before he got into his car, he thought about running back into the house and apologizing. His embarrassment and his appointment with Van Eyck kept him from doing it.

When he got to the lanes he realized that there weren't any open for bowling; they were all occupied by regular league teams. He felt grossly annoyed. He sat down behind one of the teams and watched for a few minutes. He wasn't going to look like a fool, searching through the place for Van Eyck. It was the younger man's problem; let him find Caldwell.

He watched a team—their orange bowling shirts said that they were all from Schoolcraft Rd. Motor Parts—and knew after a few frames that they were being slaughtered by the other team, from Big Beaver Tap and Die. Caldwell didn't give a damn. He got up and went to the snack counter. He got a bottle of Black Label beer and a bag of corn chips. He sat down by his bowling bag again. The league's game ended, and another began. He wondered where Van Eyck was.

His imagination wandered as he stared, virtually hypnotized, at the men bowling. The rhythmic approaches, the graceful swings, the rumbling of the ball on its way to meet the pins, the quick explosion of wood, the mild congratulations of the other men, all grew tedious in a short while. It was more pleasant to imagine Van Eyck's crime. He pictured the student busing in crowds of illegal Canadian aliens to work as field hands beneath the cool Michigan sun. Going the other way, across the Ambassador Bridge or through the Windsor Tunnel, Van Eyck supplied Canadian freedom fighters with arms or drugs or bootlegged video cassettes.

Was this profitable, Caldwell asked himself, this sitting and staring and imagining? No. He continued.

Adrian van Eyck, criminal mastermind, had probably been arrested in Pontiac, scalping tickets to a Detroit Pistons game at the Silverdome.

After half an hour of this, Caldwell gave up. He carried his bowling ball into the lounge and ordered a scotch and water. He stared at the rows of liquor bottles behind the bar. He was almost unaware of the other people in the lounge. He didn't even notice when a woman sat on the stool next to his and very slowly, very deliberately moved his ashtray closer to her, although she already had her own ashtray.

"Do you mind?" she asked. "Waiting to bowl?"

"No," he said. He turned to look at her. She was tall, not particularly attractive, her features sharp, her hair cut short and spiky; he understood immediately that she was not busy for the evening. Or, he thought, for a certain part of the evening.

"Then why did you bring your bowling ball?" she asked.

"I was supposed to meet someone here and I thought I might get some bowling in. I completely forgot that it was a league night. Just a simple mistake."

"And your friend didn't come?" she asked. She didn't bother to wait for a reply. She beckoned to the barmaid, ordered a drink, and paid for it.

"Uh huh," said Caldwell. He wanted to gulp down his drink and go home. He wondered briefly about the effect of one drink and a bottle of beer on top of four tranquilizers, the ones he had taken almost an hour before. He didn't want to be found dead in his car. He dismissed the thought.

"No sense hanging around, I guess," said the woman. "I really hate to see peoples' balls going to waste, though." She tapped his bowling bag with her foot. "My name's Andi Nominski."

"Andi," said Caldwell. He almost stood up and left with her name hanging in midair. "With an 'i,' right?"

"Yeah," she said, smiling. "My first name's Judith, and my middle name is Andrea. My folks always pronounced it 'Ondrea.' You know. So I've been calling myself Andi, since my divorce."

Caldwell smiled, but Andi misinterpreted his motive. It wasn't a friendly smile. The thing he wanted most in the world was to go home and take the nap he had planned before Van

Eyck's call. "I've got to go," he said. "It's been nice talking with you."

"Would you like to talk some more?" she asked. "We could go over to my place. You could see my collection."

"Your collection?" asked Caldwell. "Your collection of what?"

Andi blinked, frowning. "Well," she said, "of almost anything."

"Do you really want me that much?" he asked. "Am I that terrific looking? I could show you this guy who bowls for Schoolcraft Rd. Motor Parts who has arms like a Marine weight lifter."

Andi swallowed the last of her drink. "You *are* David Caldwell, aren't you?"

"Yes," he said.

"Then I don't care what your arms are like."

"Let me get out of here," he said.

"Let me make one more good try," said Nominski.

"Good night," he said, "and give my regards to Van Eyck. I have this idiotic notion that he was using you as some kind of substitute for a whole semester's schoolwork, and I thought he was brighter than that."

"You've got it wrong," she said. Her tone had become tougher. She stood up, and when she spoke she jabbed hard at his chest. "Adrian doesn't give a good goddamn about your class. And if you think I'd let myself be used just to get that little creep a passing grade, you're not the man he wants anyway."

"I didn't realize that I was wanted."

Nominski picked up her leather handbag and walked toward the exit. She stopped and looked over her shoulder at him. "Mr. Caldwell," she said, "you're *not* wanted." Her expression looked like she wished she could squash him with a cocktail napkin.

He stared after her. She left the bowling alley and went out into the parking lot. He shrugged and ordered another drink. The barmaid was sympathetic. "Lots of other birds in the bush," she said.

Caldwell only shrugged again. When he finished the drink he went back out to the bowling lanes. The leagues were just starting their third game. He picked up his bowling bag and went out to his car. He didn't like the way he was feeling, and he didn't like having to go through a remorseful scene with Marianne.

He was pleasantly surprised when he got home. Marianne had forgotten his peevishness, or she had decided to let it go. "Did you see your student?" she asked.

"No," said Caldwell, putting his bowling ball back in the closet. "He never showed up."

"They're just children, David, some of them."

"I know. But they don't realize how they could be screwing up their lives. Nothing seems important to them now. But, goddamn, I'm *still* sorry about things I did when I was in college."

"Try to forget about it," she said. She sat next to him on the couch and they watched the last half of a movie on television. When it ended, they got ready for bed. Marianne had showered and was waiting for him. The telephone rang.

"Van Eyck," muttered Caldwell. "He can go to hell. It's almost midnight."

"You'd better answer it," said Marianne. "This late, it might be an emergency. It might be your mother."

I'm the one with the emergencies, thought Caldwell, but he went to the telephone anyway. "Hello?" he said.

"Hi," said a woman. "This is Andi. Andi Nominski. Sorry about before."

"I am, too," said Caldwell. "Well, good night, Miss Nominski."

"Wait! Don't hang up! Adrian wants to have a meeting tomorrow afternoon. Arthur Leyva's going to be there, and I'll be there, too."

Caldwell almost said something vicious. He toned it down a bit. "Well," he said instead, "in that case, how can I stay away?"

"Great, David, we were counting on you. Do you know Hoffman's, on Woodward? Nice place. We have reservations for six-thirty."

"Does that include Marianne, my wife?"

There was a short pause. "My God, of course not." Nominski sounded exasperated. "What do you think this is? Anyway, she has to stay home with the children, right?"

"Not always," said Caldwell. "She isn't just a mother-machine. She has other functions."

"I'm probably keeping you from some of them right now," said Nominski. "Never mind, this is more important. We'll all be there and we'll get this show on the road."

"What show?" asked Caldwell.

"What else? Money. Lots of money. Adrian is working out this terrific idea, and the four of us are going to make lots of money."

"I see," said Caldwell. "Sure. How?"

"We're going to steal it."

Caldwell licked his lips. He stared at the dark ceiling. "I really should have been able to guess. Who are we going to steal this lots of money from?"

"You'll find out tomorrow."

"No, I won't," said Caldwell angrily. "You go back and tell Van Eyck that he can take a hike. This *Third Man* stuff of yours is making me sick. I'm not getting mixed up in some ring of tape-player thieves. I'm surprised that Arthur's in on it. Go on back to your Adrian. I'm going to bed."

"Mr. Caldwell, please," said Andi Nominski in her sweetest, most insincere voice, "it's not tape players. It's money. Cash. Lots of money, like I said. You can't imagine how much. And we all have a part in it."

"Who are we stealing from?" He realized with a shock that he had said *we* instead of *you*.

"Who else in Detroit? General Motors, Ford, and Chrysler. All together. All at the same time. A *hell* of a lot of money."

There was a click as the woman hung up. Caldwell stared at the receiver for a moment before he hung up. Then he went into the bathroom to take a shower.

Standing under the water, Caldwell thought about Adrian van Eyck and the mercurial Andi Nominski. He wondered if they went together. On the face of it, it seemed absurd. Van Eyck was a college junior, maybe twenty years old. She was older, divorced, cynical, and had called Van Eyck some uncomplimentary things. They would make a very strange, very uncomfortable pair, but these were strange times, and the situation was already definitely uncomfortable. Caldwell decided that it wasn't any of his business yet.

The remaining notion, which he hesitated to explore, was that it would become his business if he allowed himself to become involved in a scheme to extort money from the automobile industry. Then, and only then, would it be necessary to know and understand the personal vagaries of all the other people involved in the crime. For his own protection, he'd learn everything he could about them and their quirks. The water splashed around him. His own thoughts seemed ludicrous to him; he wasn't going to challenge the auto industry. That was for other hands and minds. He was going to take a shower, go to bed, teach school, and go into the hospital. The Van Eyck gang would have to get along without him. He smiled.

"Who was it this time?" called Marianne from the bedroom.

"Van Eyck again. Apologizing for not coming to the bowling alley. The kid has a real problem."

"He sure waited long enough to call to say he was sorry," said Marianne. "Can I come in?"

"He's using psychology on me," shouted Caldwell over the noise of the running water. "I'll be out in a little while." He dropped the bar of soap, and when he went to pick it up, he felt a sharp, sudden pain. He felt agony like a knife blade slashed in anger in his side. He had felt pain like that before, but experience was no good to him. He cried out, he screamed, and he crumpled, thrashing, to the bottom of the bathtub. The shower was pouring hot water on his face, but he didn't even realize it. He thought he was going to be dead. He thought it would end right there. The pain was so intense that he prayed and clutched. It felt like every organ in his body had been torn loose, that his life was hanging by the thinnest, most meaningless of threads. In a way, it was.

Marianne, in the bedroom waiting, hadn't heard. After a few minutes, Caldwell felt the pain start to go away. It wouldn't fade completely for half an hour or more, but he could stand again. He stayed under the shower, bowed over like an old man, weeping. He didn't have time to live.

Sometime later he came into the bedroom. "A nice long shower, David? Out in a couple of minutes, huh? I'm glad I didn't desperately have to get into the bathroom."

"Sorry," he said. His lips were pressed tightly together. His mouth was dry.

"Come to bed. I was about to go into the bathroom and positively *drag* you out."

"Mari," he whispered. She undid her nightgown, and he thought about the pain. She touched him, and he thought about Van Eyck, Arthur Leyva, and the mannish Andi Nominski. He thought about their crazy plan to steal a huge fortune from three of the world's largest corporations, all at the same time. He thought about three things: pain, money, and his family. Marianne slid closer, and he forgot his children and the money. He thought only of his pain, and the possibility of dying, and the genuine hardships it would cause Marianne, beautiful Marianne, no matter what happened.

"You know I love you, David," she whispered.

"I love you, too, Mari," he said, and in a little while he forgot everything but her.

5.

Hoffman's Swiss Chalet was a moderately expensive restaurant that had a pianist knuckling everyone's favorite showtunes. When David Caldwell arrived, the pianist was the first thing that attracted his attention. It seemed to Caldwell like a form of blackmail. Maybe with a good stiff bribe the pianist would disappear and there would be one more waiter in the place. Caldwell didn't know how long he was going to stay, so he declined to check his overcoat. He looked around the restaurant, which was not badly decorated, until he found a small table where Andi Nominski and Arthur Leyva were eating crackers and drinking. Andi was swallowing her beer straight from the bottle. Leyva was sipping a glass of white wine. Caldwell shook his head; he didn't belong here, with them. He wondered where Adrian van Eyck was.

Caldwell indicated to the hostess that he was with the party. "Hi, Arthur," he said. He nodded to Nominski.

A waiter came to the table. "Will you order now, everyone?" he asked.

"One more," said Nominski. "We're still waiting for one more."

"Bring me a Coke, please," said Caldwell.

The waiter left, and the three of them looked at each other.

None of them knew exactly what was going on. It occurred to Caldwell that he didn't even know if he was expected to pick up the check for his own meal. No one had anything to say.

Caldwell was resentful. First of all, he had had to lie to Marianne about why he was going to miss dinner. He had told her that he had end-of-semester work to do and wouldn't be home until late. He really hated lying to his wife. He didn't like being ordered to appear at a restaurant somewhat above his own style; he was uncomfortable with the dimly lighted room, with furnishings more luxurious than he was used to, with the damn musician serenading the early diners. He resented the implications that his appearance here set a stamp of approval on Van Eyck's wild scheme. In truth, he didn't know why he had come. He was certain that he wouldn't be there if Arthur Leyva hadn't been involved. Maybe he was just trying to keep Arthur out of trouble.

Fifteen minutes later, Adrian van Eyck came in. Nominski had finished two bottles of beer, Caldwell had drunk two Cokes, and Arthur Leyva had begun sipping a second glass of wine. "Sorry I'm late, gang," said Van Eyck, taking off his overcoat and handing it to the waiter. The waiter didn't seem thrilled about checking it for him. "Bring me a Seven and Seven," said Van Eyck. The waiter nodded and moved away.

"Adrian," said Arthur Leyva after looking at the menu, "this dinner is going to put a bad crimp in my budget. I truly hope it's worth it."

"It will be, Mr. Leyva," said Van Eyck. "And don't worry; I'm paying for this dinner, of course. I wouldn't invite you out and then expect you to pay for yourself. This meal is being enjoyed thanks to the profits of one of my smaller criminal ventures. So feel guilty, if you want to indulge yourselves."

"You're crazy," said Andi Nominski. "I don't give a damn where your money comes from. Pornographic postcards? Robbing students out selling band candy?"

"Birth certificates," said Van Eyck. He glanced up and said

nothing more for a while. Later, while they finished their dinners, he outlined the job that would net almost half a million dollars.

"I was expecting a little more than that," said Nominski. "You talked a good show, but that isn't so much money these days. I was dreaming of a cool million each."

"Even so," said Caldwell, "it's totally absurd. You're talking about a sum of five hundred thousand dollars."

"Four-fifty," said Van Eyck. "It doesn't matter how much the money is. You set up the right circumstances, and you'd be surprised how quickly these companies can come up with the cash. Especially Ford and General Motors and Chrysler."

Nominski ate the last of her manicotti and sopped up the meat sauce with a chunk of bread. "You have, it goes without saying, the right circumstances," she said.

"It goes without saying," said Van Eyck.

"Say it," said Leyva. "Say it anyway." He signaled the waiter to bring him another glass of wine.

Caldwell had another short movie-fantasy. He was sitting in a small, smoke-filled room with hoodlums. *Hoodlums,* a great word. He, in the fantasy, was a hoodlum himself. The rest of them were played by faces so familiar and so nameless that a gangster picture would flop unless these character actors were in the cast. The only one Caldwell could identify was the gang's boss, the actor who played Van Eyck: It was Douglas Dumbrille or Charles Middleton, except those men were twenty years too old. Gangs of hoodlums rarely had bosses as young as Van Eyck. The actor-Caldwell wasn't sure that he wanted to be included in the job, but he knew that he either had to agree with the plan or try to escape the smoke-filled room, dodging bullets all the way. Caldwell decided to play it cagey. He leaned forward. "What's the caper?" he asked.

Nominski looked at him and groaned. "'Caper,'" she mimicked, shaking her head.

Van Eyck tipped back on his chair, burped quietly, and smiled. He was in complete control, he was the very center of the universe. For a short while, he was the focus of attention. Van Eyck was not unnaturally vain, but he enjoyed his role. "First," he said, "I want you to listen to a few numbers. In Detroit—and I mean, what, Greater Detroit, right? In Detroit there are four and a half million people."

"Wow," said Nominski, without the least interest.

"That's half the people in the whole damn state of Michigan," said Van Eyck. "And nearly half of them are in the labor force, of which twelve and a half percent of them are connected in some way with the construction and sales of automobiles and trucks. That comes out to about two hundred eighty thousand people."

"Looking for the Big Three," said Levya.

"Now the latest figures I get say that at every pay period, the Big Three auto manufacturers produce a payroll totaling on the order of four hundred million dollars, not including bonuses, overtime, and so on. The actual total is closer to half a billion dollars."

Nominski took Caldwell's glass and drank some of the melted ice water. "He gets all this from the *World Book Encyclopedia* at the library," she said contemptuously. "We're going out there in front of real bullets, because this champ spent half an hour in the reference room."

"Nearly half a *billion* dollars," said Van Eyck, smiling again.

"Half a billion dollars," said Leyva, raising his empty wine glass in toast.

"And we're not going to touch a penny of it," said Van Eyck.

"What?" cried Caldwell. All he could think of was that this was the lunatic mind that was going to lead them to riches and independent luxury.

"You're crazy, Adrian," muttered Nominski.

Caldwell stood up, his expression disgusted. "Let me pay you for the two Cokes, at least. I have to get home to my family."

"Sit down, sit down," said Van Eyck. "Let's run through the business at least once, first."

Caldwell's internal movie changed. Now it was Dagwood and Blondie, and he had to make up a daffy excuse for Mr. Dithers. "Sorry, folks," he said, "but I promised Marianne I'd get home as soon as I could."

"Listen, listen, listen," said Van Eyck, for the first time a hard edge evident in his voice. He had a spectacular plan for making himself more money than he could ever earn honestly, and these other three didn't have the imagination to wait for his explanation. "Think of the business world as a man carrying a pole across his shoulders," he said. "On each end of the pole is a bucket, filled to the brim with money. Now, a clever man can slosh a little here and a little there, and it will never be missed. That's all I'm saying. A simple idea. An idea so easy and so uncomplicated that there's no way to stop it. There's no *time* to fight it. It's really only blackmail, and a kind of petty blackmail, after all. Look at this." He put a newspaper on the table amid the dishes.

UAW, MACHINISTS' UNIONS NEGOTIATING WITH FORD, GM

That was the headline. As Caldwell read on he learned that the major unions were starting to meet with management of these corporations to discuss their contracts, which were due to expire in several weeks.

"So what?" he asked.

"They won't agree," said Van Eyck. "They never do."

"So what?" asked Nominski.

"So we'll aggravate the issue," said Van Eyck.

"So what?" asked Leyva.

"So between it all, they'll pay us our blackmail to get rid of us and get back to the real troubles they have."

"I don't get it," said Leyva.

"Of course not," said Van Eyck. "I haven't explained it all

yet. Look. We're dealing with a payroll of several hundred million dollars."

"And we'll get it," said Caldwell.

"Nope," said Van Eyck.

Nominski snorted impatiently. "I had to sit here and stuff myself with manicotti and wop salad just to hear you say we're not going to lift their money?"

Van Eyck had her just where he wanted her. "Not that money," he said softly. "*Other* money."

"What other money?" asked Leyva.

"Here's how it works, now. This is terrific, if I say so myself," said Van Eyck. "We'll go over it again and again, but try to understand as much as possible now. Once every pay period all the timecards and data sheets from the foremen at the plants come into the payroll computer offices, see? Okay? They have master files of all their employees—for the Big Three, that's more than a quarter of a million people, all told, remember? They're all on computer disks, stored on racks and labeled. They keep these weekly disks for five, six, maybe seven days, updating them. Then they reuse them, re-record them. They feed in the information from the cards and sheets, and the computers take out the withholding tax, the F.I.C.A., and the United Way contributions, and the company insurance and whatall, and figure out their hours and hourly rates, and print it all on perforated checks."

"We steal the checks," said Caldwell.

"No, that would be stupid," said Van Eyck. "What good would a couple of hundred thousand unendorsed checks do us?"

"They'd have to reprint them," said Leyva.

"They could do that overnight," said Nominski.

"What do we do then, for Christ's sake?" said Caldwell.

"We keep our voices down," said Van Eyck. "We're criminals."

"I'm not a criminal," said Leyva.

"And I'm not, either," said Caldwell.

"I am," said Nominski, and she sounded rather proud.

"We all are," said Van Eyck, with just a little smugness. "Conspiracy."

"Hell," muttered Caldwell.

"We take the disks, people," said Van Eyck. "Without the disks, they're paralyzed."

"I might point out that the disks are nonnegotiable," said Leyva.

"Nonnegotiable at the First National Bank of Anytown," said Van Eyck. "But the corporations would damn well like to get them back. They don't have time to make up new ones, because they won't know the disks are missing until too late. We call them up, tell them we'll give back the disks, and it won't cost them much at all. Suddenly those disks are as negotiable as your seventeen-year-old virgin niece."

"A hundred fifty grand a company," said Nominski.

"Right," said Van Eyck.

"And why will they pay it?" asked Leyva.

Van Eyck tapped the newspaper. "Major strike coming up. They can't screw up anything here. The management thinks we're labor union goons who've stolen the disks. I don't know if you realize it, but some of the union members get paid overtime—maybe time-and-a-half or more—for as long as their paychecks are late. And the unions will think we're part of management's strong-arm tactics."

"We're taking potential money," said Caldwell.

"Wonderful, Mr. Caldwell, an insight!" Van Eyck smiled, and Caldwell glared at him.

"Two hundred thousand angry workers without paychecks come payday," mused Nominski. "I'd dearly love to see that. It's worth it to have my own lost in the shuffle."

"So would I," said Leyva. "The hell with the money. Let's just do it for fun."

"Let's not get carried away here, Arthur," said Van Eyck. He was happy, because he knew that he had each of them hooked.

76

"What happens in that case?" asked Caldwell. "Two hundred thousand auto workers with no money?"

"A major strike," said Leyva. "The kind that Congress and the President have to step into. Possibly a slowdown of the steel industry as well. Ripples would be felt all through the country. It would be a major, gigantic blow to the national economy."

They were in better spirits, and ordered more drinks. "All we're asking for is a paltry hundred fifty thousand dollars from each, right?" asked Caldwell. "To avoid that kind of trouble."

"Uh huh," said Van Eyck.

"I think I've spotted the fly," said Caldwell. "I mean, the bug. They must keep quarterly files."

Van Eyck's smile got broader. He nodded. "They do," he said. "On other disks, permanent ones. We'll lift the last quarterly record, too. That way they can't just make up checks for, say, a few hundred dollars per employee and distribute them, planning to adjust plus or minus during the next pay period. With the quarterly file gone, a large fraction of the new employees wouldn't get paid at all; and maybe a quarter of the employees from two quarterly disks ago are no longer working there and wouldn't give up the free money without a fight. No, they'll give us a hundred fifty thousand. Nuisance money. We're no big-time billion-dollar swindle. We're just a few chiggers down the collars of the Big Three. They have more important things to worry about. Just reconstructing the lost records, the overtime for the data-processing people, the headaches, would come to a hundred grand, maybe."

"It's petty cash to them," said Nominski. "Otherwise, the disks go wherever Jimmy Hoffa's gone and we leave the Big Three to stammer excuses to the news media."

Van Eyck looked at his three recruits; he could tell that each one was already imagining what he'd do with his share of the payoff.

6.

There are some cities for living in. There are some cities for playing in. There are some cities for visiting, and some cities for working in and growing old. David Caldwell sat in his Chevy Vega and wondered what in hell Detroit was for. He stared through the windshield, at the dense knot of motionless automobiles around him. Evidently, he thought, Detroit was for driving in. Or trying to, anyway.

The sky was gray, and the sun was a weak area in the clouds which let through little warmth and only a meager light. Caldwell was already late for a departmental meeting at school, which didn't concern him overly much. The meeting would have been even more boring than the traffic jam; he wouldn't have had a radio at the meeting. He hit his fists lightly against the steering wheel, took the car out of gear, and tried to relax. He sat back and thought about the people who designed and planned highways. Why should one flat tire affect the lives of thousands of people? That is what modern technology has done, one of the serendipitous gifts of the twentieth century. Today, thanks to the efficient news media, we read or hear about every tiny human tragedy around us. A hundred years ago, wars and political scandals and economic panics made up the routine reading in the news journals. Today, they are pushed aside by individual sadnesses—people without mattresses, families unable to send their children to camp, widows too poor to afford new kidneys. Everyone is made to listen, too, as though everyone doesn't have enough problems already.

And here on the highways: If one car got a flat tire or stalled out, traffic backed up for miles, sometimes. Caldwell wondered why he should be made to suffer along with that anonymous person far ahead. Caldwell tried to shield himself from the intrusions of other people's grief, yet he shared every overheated engine along the way. It was something else to thank the auto industry for. It was a reason to go along with Van Eyck's implausible scheme.

Caldwell realized for the first time in the several days since the meeting that he was, indeed, counting up reasons. That implied that he would join the scheme, should he find enough reasons. He hadn't conceded that to himself before. He wondered idly how many more reasons he needed.

He saw the cars up ahead begin to move restlessly. He shifted back into gear and rolled gently behind the blue Buick ahead of him. The car behind him moved up a bit as well. All together the endless line of automobiles crept slowly eastward, toward the late morning sun.

Forty-five minutes later David Caldwell parked his Vega on the campus. As he walked toward his office he wondered what had originally stood on the site of the parking lot, the daytime home for cars between the gymnasium and new science building. It was possible that the school hadn't demolished an old building to house the cars, but had merely asphalted over part of the cross-campus landscaping. Caldwell knew that he could find out by looking at photographs of the campus taken a couple of decades ago, an activity in which he had no interest and in which he'd never participate. He wasn't that curious.

When he got to his office, the departmental meeting was

already over. Caldwell glanced at his desk, but he had no desire to get any work done. He was glad when Arthur Leyva looked in.

"Hello, David," said Leyva. "Are you hungry?"

"No, but let's go to lunch. If I hang around here, somebody's going to come in looking for me."

"Someone already has. Adrian."

"Oh?"

"Uh huh," said Leyva as they walked toward his office. He went in and got his coat and hat. "There's another meeting tomorrow night. The first official planning session. Adrian wanted to know if you and I are still part of the gang."

"Still? You mean 'yet.' I never told him that I was going along with this thing. It sounded interesting, Arthur, but the trouble is that it will never fly. It's not that it's too crazy. I can see that Adrian probably knows what he's talking about; but nobody has any experience. The stakes are too high for people like us to be messing with a lot of years in prison. Not a single one of us knows what's involved with this. Nobody has the faintest idea what's going on."

"Except Adrian." They walked slowly out of Krummer Hall, toward the cafeteria.

"Except Adrian," said Caldwell. "Our master criminal. Arthur, he may be one hell of a fine shoplifter, but this is kind of a felonious extortion scheme, see? He's talking about almost half a million dollars. He's talking about taking on the second-largest corporation in the world, plus Ford and Chrysler, too. That's three-quarters of a corporation per person and, to tell you the truth, I lack confidence in myself. I mean, I don't really think I could hold off the Ford Motor Company, if Ford really felt like being uncooperative. You know?"

"With the right plan, it might be easy. Maybe Adrian has the right plan. Don't panic until you find out. If you hear the plan, and then decide it's too full of holes, then duck out. That's what I plan to do. In the meantime, don't get all excited. Here, have an almond."

"Okay, Arthur, okay. If Van Eyck understands that, fine. I mean, I'm sure not going to give him a definite answer until I've heard the whole plan."

Leyva held the door and Caldwell walked by him into the college's cafeteria. "I just thought of something," said Leyva. "How desperate do you think Adrian is?"

"I don't have the slightest idea. You seem more in touch with him than I am. When he came to see me in my office, he wasn't desperate at all. Of course, things may be changed since then."

Leyva picked up a tray and put a paper napkin and silverware on it. He stared at the menu board on the wall. "Because," he said, "if he lays out the whole plan to us, and we say we don't want to be part of it, he might do anything. You know. Think of the books and movies. Desperate criminals can't afford to have people like us knowing the details of their plans unless we're part of the gang."

"Van Eyck? Rubbing us out?" Caldwell laughed.

"I don't know," said Leyva thoughtfully, indicating to a cafeteria employee which of the brown and gray entrees he had most confidence in. "He doesn't seem like the type to hold up a major industry for almost half a million dollars either, does he?"

"Oh, hell," said Caldwell. He chose the same entree that Leyva took. "Well, don't worry about it. Van Eyck seems reasonable."

"After we're caught, explain that to your attorney. Does that mean you're going to Van Eyck's meeting?"

"I'll go," said Caldwell.

"That's good. Can you give me a ride? My car's being temperamental." They slid their trays along toward the cashier. Neither man spoke again for a long while. Caldwell was hoping that Van Eyck was not, in point of fact, very desperate at all.

After they had eaten dispiritedly for a few minutes, Leyva spoke up. "Terrible food, isn't it?" he asked.

"Awful," said Caldwell. They looked at each other for a moment, silent again.

"Are you thinking about Adrian?"

"Of course I am," said Caldwell. "I'm thinking about how nicely a hundred thousand dollars will solve my immediate problems."

"Mine, too," said Leyva.

"What problems do you have that need a hundred thousand dollars?" asked Caldwell. "Gambling debts? You have a secret mistress bleeding you or what?"

Leyva frowned. "I don't want to tell you, David," he said. "If I tell you, you'll go along with Adrian just to keep your eye on me, and I don't want that."

"You have a problem, Arthur."

"Yes. I'm well aware of it."

There was another silence.

Caldwell stared up at the ceiling. "Well, for the love of Mike, tell me about it."

Leyva squeezed his eyes closed. "You know, you don't have a patent on trouble," he said softly.

"Are you sick, Arthur?"

"No," said Leyva. "My sister. I don't remember if I told you about her. She was going to marry this fellow from California. He was an import-export agent, whatever that is. Abbie was really in love with him. She hadn't kept company with a man since her husband died, and that was twenty years ago. I was glad to see it. Anyway, two weeks before they were to be married, he got her to cosign a bank loan. He took the money and went far away. She's never heard from him since. Emotionally, she's completely destroyed. Not to mention that she wasn't able to pay back the loan money."

"And you—"

"If I ever catch that bastard, I'll see that he never tries that game again. I take care of Abbie. I have for twenty years. She owns the house and has a little insurance and a little money in her account, but that's all. When the loan came due, she came to me. She hadn't told me before, because she was humiliated and she was afraid of what I'd say. I went to the bank and explained. They wouldn't listen. They wouldn't give her any more time. They wanted their money. They were talking about foreclosing."

"Banks are like that," said Caldwell, with a sick feeling in his stomach. He had an idea that whatever was coming, it wasn't pleasant.

"So I paid them, just to get them off her back for a while."

"Good," said Caldwell, relieved, "Then you're just broke, from paying the bank."

"Well," said Leyva, looking away, "I didn't have the money, either. I gave the bank a bad check from another account.

"Arthur."

Leyva didn't reply for a moment. Caldwell shook his head and waited.

"It was just a stalling maneuver, and I thought we could come up with the cash somehow. I was called in by the bank. They weren't at all cordial."

Caldwell understood. "So you have to go along with Adrian to clear up that bank business."

Leyva stared into Caldwell's eyes. "I'm not finished, David."

Caldwell sighed. "I was praying to God you were, Arthur. Honestly."

"I took over Abbie's account, telling her that we had to manage our money better. Lord, she was always ten times better than I was at managing money. Anyway, I wrote a check on her account to my account, covering the bad check I gave the bank. I deposited it. Before it could get back to her account and be marked for insufficient funds, I wrote one on my second account to deposit in hers. That was good for a few days. Then I had to write another from my first account to my second to cover the last one. This has been going on every few days for three weeks now, David. And the amounts have to keep going up in order to cover service charges. It's escalating out of control. I think I'm going crazy sometimes. None of the checks bounce because there's always a new one to cover the old ones. But if I miss one deposit, the whole rickety pyramid will collapse. I swear, I've been thinking of putting a bullet through my skull." By the time he had finished his confession, Arthur Leyva had begun to weep. Caldwell was totally unnerved. He knew that he could feel only pity or contempt for the man, and he hated being forced to choose either.

"I think I'll be running along, Arthur," said Caldwell. "We'll work it out. I'll see you tomorrow."

"All right, David," said Leyva in a choked voice. "Don't worry about me." Caldwell winced.

After lunch Caldwell was free for the afternoon. His mother was babysitting the children, and Marianne wouldn't be home until five-thirty. The house was empty; it would be too quiet. Caldwell put off the idea of going home until later. He sat in his car for a while, listening to the radio and thinking. He tried to see himself actually involved in Van Eyck's scheme, actually carrying out whatever part he'd have to play. He couldn't imagine what Van Eyck had planned for him. Maybe Caldwell would just be a getaway driver. That didn't seem likely. Van Eyck or Andi Nominski could drive the car. They wouldn't hire Caldwell and pay him a hundred thousand just to ferry them around. Then what were Caldwell and Leyva supposed to do? Look tough? The scene played itself in Caldwell's mind: He opened a door and stood aside. Adrian van Eyck, dressed very well, very expensively, brushed by him and went into an office. A clucking secretary hurried in, too. "I'm sorry, Mr. Ford," she bleated, "but these gentlemen refused to—"

"Get her out of here," murmured Van Eyck. Leyva growled and shoved the secretary out of the room.

"What's this all about?" asked Mr. Ford, starting to rise from his leather chair.

"Sit down, buddy," said Caldwell threateningly. Leyva shut

the office door. Van Eyck walked boldly to Ford's desk and leaned forward, smiling. Caldwell and Leyva stood behind him, each with one hand inside his suit jacket.

Guns?

That brought Caldwell out of his fantasy. He had been thinking of the job as a kind of long-distance matter, an impersonal white-collar crime that needed only a bare minimum of physical contact. They could phone in the threat after Van Eyck took care of the disks or whatever. Then they could all go together to pick up the money. But at that instant Caldwell realized that Ford, GM, and Chrysler were not likely to give up four hundred fifty thousand dollars without some kind of resistance. Van Eyck claimed they'd be more than happy to agree, rather than run the risks presented by the extortion plot. Four hundred fifty grand could buy one hell of a lot of risks, and Van Eyck might well be planning to cut through them all with guns, squealing tires, and the rest of the whole television program scenario.

"Nice place you got here, Ford," said Van Eyck with a sneer.

"Are you mugs packing heat?" asked Mr. Ford.

"We're heeled, you better believe it," said Leyva in another growl, uncharacteristic of him.

"You'll never get away with it," said Mr. Ford.

"Oh, we think we will, pal," said Van Eyck. "And you'll help us, unless you're looking to get pumped full of lead vitamins. Get the picture?"

Caldwell didn't want to think about the business any longer. There was time enough for that during and after the meeting the next day. He thought that what he'd really like to do that evening was sit in the Pontiac Silverdome and watch the Pistons wobble around the floor with the New Jersey Nets. There was a very good chance that neither team would win the game. He hadn't been to a basketball game in two years, since his wife had been pregnant with Risa. He couldn't ask his mother to watch the kids, not after watching them all day already. Baby-sitters were out of the question, according to the Caldwells' budget. And he wouldn't go to the game without Mari. She liked basketball, and he couldn't stand watching a game by himself.

Of course, if he really *were* going to make a hundred thousand dollars in the next few weeks, he could afford a baby-sitter, after all. Maybe he could count on that money and spend what he had now. If he wasn't going to get the money, it would mean that he would be either dead or in prison, and so he could *still* afford to go to the game. . . .

Caldwell shook his head abruptly, as though to clear it of this line of thought. He really didn't want to ponder the job any longer, he really didn't.

Should he tell Mari about it, though? What if he did end up dead or in jail? She should know ahead of time, but she'd think he was crazy. She'd probably turn him in rather than let him go through with it. And then he'd have Van Eyck, Nominski, and Leyva gunning for him. He could see that, too, just like a movie—

It wasn't even four o'clock by the time he got home to Redford. He let the kids into the house, then wrestled their toys into the living room. He opened a can of ginger ale and sat in front of the television and watched *The Flintstones*.

The cartoon figures moved rapidly before his eyes. They meant nothing. He wondered what Wilma would say if Fred came home with an extra hundred thousand dollars one day. "Oh, that's nice, dear. Where did you get it?" What would the stupid husband say? "I found it." That was impossible. "Barney found a lot of money and shared it with me, aren't we lucky?" That was worse. What could a stupid husband say that wouldn't arouse a wife's suspicions and fear? Maybe Fred wouldn't even tell Wilma about it. He'd keep it a secret, stuffed in the mattress, taking a chunk of it out now and then to pay the bills. No expensive purchases, no alterations in lifestyle. Maybe that was the best way. Could Fred pull it off? Caldwell chewed his lip. If he could successfully steal the money in the first place, spending it shouldn't prove any more difficult. But Marianne was a good deal shrewder than Wilma Flintstone.

7.

The next evening Van Eyck's gang met in his apartment. Van Eyck lived off-campus, in a three-room flat in Warren, close enough to the college. The walls of the apartment were decorated with posters from motion pictures, old movies from the forties and fifties. That upset Caldwell a little, because he was aware of how often his own thoughts strayed to Hollywood versions of criminal activities. He hoped that Van Eyck, who was asking them to trust his judgment and planning, had more on the ball than merely a good knowledge of movie crimes. If they tangled with the police, the cops would be shooting more than movie bullets. If they faced a judge, they would be in prison for more than a reel or two. Caldwell prayed desperately that Van Eyck was taking the matter seriously, more seriously than any of the other three beginner crooks.

Van Eyck's shelves were remarkably clear of books. Caldwell noticed that quickly. He always looked over the bookshelves when he entered someone's home for the first time. He felt he could understand a person better by seeing what that person liked to read. Van Eyck, apparently, didn't like to read. There were fewer than three dozen books. There were several in German, one by Goethe. There was a Bible. There were a few suspense novels by bestselling authors. There was a dictionary. There was a travel guide to the United States. And, Caldwell was unhappy to see, there was a book on modern American firearms.

"I give them away when I'm done," said Van Eyck.

"What?" said Caldwell, looking up.

"When I'm finished with a book, I give it away. To the library or a hospital. I know I won't read it again. Why hang on to it? Just have to carry it around the country with me. I give it away."

"Then these—"

"These I'm not finished with. Have a seat, Mr. Caldwell. I'm sorry I can't offer you anything to drink." Van Eyck was evidently ready to begin his discussion of their mutual project, so Caldwell took the chair he offered. Arthur Leyva and Andi Nominski interrupted their conversation. They sat in the living room, which was lighted by a floor lamp and a table lamp, both with red bulbs. The red light made Caldwell uncomfortable. He couldn't begin to imagine what Van Eyck's intended effect was supposed to be. Caldwell, Nominski, and Leyva waited for Van Eyck to begin explaining.

"I'm not going to pass out any papers," said the young man. "I still don't know who is going to be with me, and who is going to want to drop out. After tonight, I'll know. I'll want you to give me your final decision before you leave. If you decide that you're not going to be in, I wouldn't want you to leave with a page of notes that might, well, fall into the wrong hands. Understand? So no photocopied timetables and maps, not just yet; and please refrain from jotting down any notes to yourself. It won't be necessary for a little while. This is just an elementary planning session, after all. Everything is still tentative, but after this evening it will stop being tentative."

"How are we going to split up the money?" asked Andi Nominski.

Van Eyck gave her a very sour look. "Andi," he said. He

shook his head. "Four of us. Four hundred fifty thousand dollars. A hundred thousand each, the extra fifty to me."

"That's generous of you," she said. "You mean you're not going to take half for being the boss?"

"No, I'm not," said Van Eyck. "A hundred and fifty grand will last me a few years. Two hundred wouldn't last me much longer."

"You know," said Arthur Leyva, "if we're going to do this, I wish we'd raise the ante a little. Half a million sounds so much better than four hundred fifty thousand."

"And an even million sounds better still," said Nominski.

"I'm not greedy," said Van Eyck. "Remember that as our demands get higher, they get more difficult to collect."

"Maybe you ought to be greedy," said Nominski. "Think of a quarter million for each of us."

"Let him talk," said Caldwell, who had been sitting and listening to his new partners with a little uneasiness. "I have a wife and two children at home thinking I'm at school making up a syllabus for next semester. I had to tap-dance around a reason why I didn't bring the work home with me. So let's get this over with and get out of here."

"Right," said Nominski.

Van Eyck looked a little disappointed. This was another big moment for him, and he wanted it to last. "All right," he said. "We're going to commit a crime. Never forget that. Never forget that the penalties for failure are very severe. There's not much hope of getting off easy if we blow this. It means prison. Wall time. A long while behind bars."

"It makes the whole thing more exciting," said Leyva.

"No, it doesn't," said Nominski.

Van Eyck regarded them both silently for a moment. "There is a right way to commit a crime, and a wrong way," said the young man. "The right way is slowly, calmly, confidently, with the proper amount of preparation. Almost everything in this apartment was stolen by me."

"Petty thefts," said Nominski. "Nothing that would train you for a major scam." Caldwell nodded agreement.

"Okay, sure," said Van Eyck. "But a few basic principles stay the same. I don't go into stores and steal things anymore. I sneer at the common shoplifter, the smash-and-grab thief. When I did take things, I studied a store to reduce the risk to myself. I needed to feel safe in order to act confidently. The air of self-assurance is a great protection in itself."

"Wonderful, Adrian," said Arthur Leyva, "but—"

"I know," said Van Eyck. He raised a hand. "Let me continue. I got the idea for the present job shortly after I met Andi. I realized that it could work, if I used my old philosophy and, to a large degree, the same techniques. The changes that needed to be made were not beyond my creative powers. We will approach the auto industry as if it were a large department store, large enough for all four of us to work together at the same time. We will enter the store, take what we want, leave the store, and return home safely. We will work slowly and confidently. It *will* work, because I have fitted all the necessary pieces together. Mr. Caldwell will understand; this is what I have been doing in lieu of schoolwork."

"It's a shame there isn't a bachelor's degree in Felonies at Wray, Adrian," said Leyva. "You could graduate early, if this works out."

"It will," said Van Eyck. "I have already taken enough tours, photographed the pertinent buildings, checked the security, studied libraries, and gotten what I feel to be most of the necessary information. I've pretended to be a visitor, an employee, or a delivery boy. I've devised three different systems of dealing with the three corporations and their various payroll plans."

"So all you need are unskilled laborers to haul away the money?" asked Leyva.

"I wouldn't have put it quite that way," said Van Eyck, "but basically that's the idea."

"Do we get to choose which company we want?" asked Caldwell.

"You do," said Van Eyck. "Andi will take GM, of course, because she works there already. The easiest of the three."

"*You* think so," said Nominski.

"Let's continue," said Van Eyck. "Now we'll look at each of the three, and I'll describe the different plans. We'll start with General Motors. GM has already been infiltrated. In a way, this whole operation couldn't work unless part of it was devised as an inside job. The security systems used by the automobile industry are some of the most sophisticated in the entire business world. The payrolls are huge, but the days of blasting open pete boxes or waylaying payroll messengers went out with the Dalton Gang. Today, in a computer society, the holdup man is usually too far away from the real money. There isn't any cash for him to steal—just machine-coded data negotiable only under the most particular conditions. This makes the corporation feel safe. In theory, no computer programmer can put his hands on the millions of dollars he disburses. The secure confidence of the corporation is helpful to us, because the theory is wrong. They haven't understood that they're guarding the wrong things. They have a real golden goose sitting on a shelf, all alone, unprotected, waiting for us to take it away."

"You couldn't have done this without Andi?" asked Leyva.

"No," she said. "I gave him the idea."

"I might have given myself the idea eventually, though," said Van Eyck. Caldwell thought he detected a small amount of irritation in the young man's voice, as though he hated to admit that Nominski was indispensable to his plan. "I think I could have pulled this operation off by myself, all three parts, but it would have taken forever and been a whole lot more difficult. I could have gotten into GM and accomplished what Andi will do, but that would have required more months of preparation."

Nominski laughed skeptically. "I'm telling you, Adrian

dear, that you never could have done it. They never would have accepted you in the department. You can sweet-talk a lot of people out of a lot of things, but you're not going to get General Motors to turn its computer payroll system over to you unless you give them a good reason."

"That's what I mean, Andi," said Van Eyck innocently. "It would have taken a couple of months to make them think they had a good reason."

Nominski lit a cigarette. "God," she murmured, "sometimes I really hate him."

The little scene showed Caldwell something important, something that he doubted Arthur Leyva or even Van Eyck was aware of at this point. The interlocking mechanism of the plan depended on many variables. Adrian van Eyck believed that he had control over all of these things. He had to believe that. He couldn't think for a moment that some minor flaw in the scheme would explode in his face, dooming them all. In order to proceed with the job, he had to accept as an axiom that certain things would remain constant. One of those things was the personality of each of his gang members.

If Van Eyck was as careful about choosing his allies as he evidently was about everything else, then there was nothing to worry about. But if personality clashes developed, if someone—Caldwell himself, old Arthur Leyva, Andi Nominski—proved unable to handle the pressure and the danger, then everyone would feel the ax. They were all in this together, and they had to work together. They had to be able to count on each other, if it was going to be successful. As Caldwell looked around the room, he didn't see one other person he was sure he could count on in the toughest circumstances, not even Van Eyck himself. And he was sure that they were looking at him the same way.

"In any event," said Van Eyck, "when a new employee is hired by GM, the payroll and accounting people punch out two cards for that person. These cards are used to begin a computer file of that employee's records. The first thing Andi will do is punch up two cards for Mr. Caldwell, under some made-up name. Bango, Mr. Caldwell, you're an employee of General Motors. Once the red-tape machine starts rolling, it takes very little to keep it going. You'll get all the other wonderful things that go along with a new employee's number. We can use all of them, and then we can apply for more sophisticated benefits. You'll see what I mean. At first, all we'll need is a verifiable ID for you. You will be put on the payroll as a middle-level executive in the data-processing department. You will also be issued a magnetic passkey, without which no one gets into or out of anywhere. Not even Andi. But those two little punched cards in the entrails of the GM computer system will give her and you and me access to almost anything we want."

Caldwell nodded. "I thought she was handling GM, though, Adrian."

"Right, of course," said Van Eyck. "If you have no objections, you'll be tackling Ford, Mr. Caldwell. Just hang on for a minute, and I'll explain. If the three companies get together—which they *will* do—and compare notes, and they discover that three people hit them at the same time, with the same story, they'll figure things out quickly enough. But if one or two of the people are disguised as insiders, as victims rather than crooks, we'll be better able to control the situation. It will make our position a little more powerful. So: Andi sets up our Mr. Caldwell here as a boss-type at General Motors. On the day of the job, Andi will use Mr. Caldwell's magnetic passkey to get into the data-processing library herself. She will locate the specific, important computer disks plus the quarterly summary disks. All she has to do then is remove their identification labels and replace them with phony ones. She puts the disks back on the racks somewhere, shuffles the other disks around to fill the gaps, and walks out. GM is taken care of."

"Edgar Allan Poe's 'The Purloined Letter,' " said Arthur Leyva.

"Whatever," said Andi Nominski. "You sure you don't have anything to drink?"

"Sorry," said Van Eyck. "We won't be much longer."

"I'm getting hungry," said Caldwell.

"Come on," said Van Eyck, annoyed again. "Let's get this finished. This is worse than talking to a bunch of high-school kids."

"You ever run a heist with a bunch of high-school kids?" asked Nominski, leering a little.

"Nothing this big," said Van Eyck.

"Of course not," said Leyva.

"Just pay attention," said Van Eyck. "Mr. Caldwell, with his phony GM identity, will have made an appointment to see someone at Ford with roughly the same job description. I will brief you enough to get you into the man's office without sounding like a fool; you'd be surprised how little you actually need to know. You can carry on a business meeting for an entire hour without getting into anything more technical than the lousy snow and the lousy local teams. You won't have to worry. About ten minutes after you show up at his office, you will be in their data-processing facility, trying to unravel whatever trumped-up problem you've taken to him. You will get a call from one of us; actually, the call will be for the Ford employee. Mr. Leyva or I will tell the Ford man that some GM disks are missing and that there's been a ransom demand. He will be upset and want to check on his own. He will be relieved that they are still safe. Mr. Caldwell, you will then act very worried, and you'll instruct the Ford payroll man to tell the caller to keep the lid on things until you get back. The Ford man will naturally be concerned and relay your instructions. During the confusion and anxiety, you will take your best opportunity and switch the disks at Ford exactly as Andi did at GM."

Caldwell was shocked. "How?" he cried. "I don't have any business in the Ford data library. I won't be left alone very long. I don't have a passkey—"

"You will have a passkey," said Van Eyck.

"You're sure?" said Caldwell. Van Eyck didn't bother to

reply. "Even so," said Caldwell, feeling panic rise in him as he realized what he was expected to accomplish, "how am I going to manage a switch like that?"

Nominski, not Van Eyck, answered. "The same way I do, of course. Calmly, as if you had every right in the world to be there. Shut the doors behind you. It will take another executive passkey to open them; you won't be interrupted. It won't take five minutes to mix up the disks. The Ford man will be so upset about the news from General Motors that he won't be paying any attention to you at all. You're just afraid, Caldwell. You're just wishing someone else would do your work for you."

Caldwell stared at her, his eyes wide. Right at that moment, he would have liked to hit her. "What's wrong with that? Of course I'm afraid. I used to be afraid to stay home from school when I wasn't sick. I've never done anything wrong in my life, not so much as keeping a library book overdue."

"It all comes with practice," said Van Eyck evenly, smiling.

"How much practice are we going to get?" asked Leyva.

"Well," said Van Eyck, shrugging, "I guess we don't really have time for any, but don't worry about it."

"What about Leyva's part?" asked Nominski.

"Yes," said Arthur Leyva, "what about me?"

Van Eyck stood and paced for a moment. "I'm sorry," he said softly. "I didn't forget you, Mr. Leyva."

"Yes, you did," said Nominski. "Adrian dear, I think you're not quite the cool criminal mastermind you think you are. You're telling us again and again that this job depends entirely on attention to details, right? And you're telling us how wonderful you are about handling stuff like that, right? But I'm telling you that my ass is on the line, and I'd just like to know that the heartwarming trust I have in you isn't going to get me put away in the slammer for the rest of my life. You know? Don't forget dear Mr. Leyva, Adrian. Don't forget *anything*. I'd be very upset if you did."

Van Eyck looked a little shaken. He didn't say anything for

a few seconds. He took a couple of deep breaths, sat down again, and twisted a gold ring around his finger. "Mr. Leyva is valuable to us because he doesn't look like a hood at all," he said. "He looks like a retired former employee. That's what he'll be, that's the part he'll play. He'll be treated rather well—I've already observed a similar occasion at Chrysler. There will be no need for the complicated subterfuge I've described for Mr. Caldwell. Chrysler will do that work for us."

Caldwell sighed. He didn't want to think about what he would have to do. Suddenly he felt a sharp stab in his side. He stretched out one leg, hoping the pain would go away. It didn't.

"I'm glad to hear that, Adrian," said Leyva. "I don't know if I would do very well at anything complicated."

Caldwell winced as the pain grew. It climbed through him. He gasped a little and stood up, then bent over.

"Nothing to worry about, Mr. Leyva," said Van Eyck. "I've chosen you all for—Mr. Caldwell, are you all right?"

Caldwell waved a hand, frowning. He sat down again and tried to be inconspicuous. The pain was becoming so intense that he was barely aware of what was happening in the room.

"So," said Van Eyck, "what's the verdict?"

"I'm in," said Nominski. "I've always been in, but I'm out as soon as things start to look sour. I'm running. I'm taking what I can grab and running."

"Nice to know we can count on you," said Van Eyck. "Mr. Leyva?"

Arthur Leyva shook his head. "Adrian, so far this plan hasn't completely won my confidence. I still don't see how we're going to pull it off."

"I've got it all worked out, Mr. Leyva. Believe me."

"I have to, don't I? Or else get out. You're asking a lot of me on faith, and the risk is tremendous. The holes in the plan are so huge I could march the Michigan State band through them. You want me to walk into the Chrysler Corporation and pretend I'm an old employee. You're sure that's going to make them willing to let me mess around with their incredibly important records as much as I want. This business of Mr. Caldwell and Ford sounds like nonsense, too. The idea that these corporations will sit idly by while we play pranks, and then docilely pay up when we make our demands—I can't buy that, either. Big-time crime isn't this easy. People just don't do this kind of thing, because people just *can't* do this kind of thing. Corporations protect their money too well."

Van Eyck smiled. "Yes, they do, Arthur. But they don't protect anything else."

"Another thing. Have you given any thought to what happens to each of us immediately after it's over?"

The young man nodded. "Of course. By this time next week I'll have the groundwork done for our escape. I'll leave the choice to each of you separately, whether you want to leave the area or stay in Detroit. I assure you, whichever you choose you will be perfectly safe. If we get away cleanly, there will be no chance at all that we'll be arrested later." Van Eyck didn't mention the fact that his promise was valid only if everyone concerned did nothing stupid, like talking to the wrong people.

"I'll be able to keep my teaching position?" asked Leyva.

"That's important to you?" asked Nominski.

"It is."

"Then you'll do that," said Van Eyck. "No problem."

"All right," said Leyva, holding up a hand, "let me think."

David Caldwell cried out in a small, anguished voice.

"Is he all right?" asked Nominski.

"Are you all right?" asked Van Eyck. He turned to explain to the others. "He has this medical problem."

"I know," said Leyva. "David?"

Caldwell looked up, tears shining on his cheeks. He opened his lips, but he said nothing audible. He nodded, indicating that he was all right, but his bloodless face indicated that he was lying.

"Arthur?" asked Van Eyck.

"Oh. Let me see. I've mentioned my objections over and

over: None of us knows what he's doing; the idea of three separate operations increases the difficulty geometrically; the amount of money involved; the balancing of management and union representatives in our negotiations. It's too much."

"That means you're not with us, Arthur? That I'll have to find someone to replace you?"

Caldwell groaned and tried to stand up. He couldn't.

"No, not at all," said Leyva, looking at Caldwell. He pointed. "In addition to my own troubles, there's the reason I'll go along with you. Him. That means that we're both in this, David and I. We both feel the same way, but we're both in. Now help me get him home."

Van Eyck stood again, smiling broadly. "Wonderful," he said, "absolutely wonderful. We're a team now. The preliminaries are over and we can start the real work."

Arthur Leyva looked at Van Eyck with an expression of displeasure. "Adrian, my boy," he said, "will you stop prancing around like Dillinger or Jesse James and help me get Mr. Caldwell to his car? Miss Nominski, would you be good enough to drive us home?"

"I have my own car—" she said.

"I'll take care of it," said Van Eyck. The young man suddenly felt left out of his own group, as though he had, in fact, overlooked a very vital element in their scheme. Whatever that element was, he knew, it explained why he had very few friends. He hoped that the nameless factor wouldn't interfere with their plans.

"Here are the keys, Adrian," said Nominski. "Why don't you just follow along behind me? After we drop off Arthur and Mr. Caldwell, I'll drive you back here."

"Are you staying with me tonight, Andi?" asked Van Eyck.

"No, Adrian, no," she said in a resigned tone of voice. "How many times do I have to tell you? That business between us is finished. It's over, Adrian, and I wish you'd leave it alone."

Arthur Leyva listened to them and chewed his lip thoughtfully. He wondered, as Caldwell had wondered earlier, what sort of relationship there was between Nominski and Van Eyck, and if that relationship would hinder their cooperation. There seemed to be just a little tension in the air, and that could make things unbearable for all four people.

They led Caldwell slowly down the stairs to the sidewalk, and Andi Nominski went to get the Vega. They put Caldwell in the front seat on the passenger side. He slouched down, making small murmurs of almost delirious incoherence. Leyva sat behind the driver's seat. Nominski started the car and followed Leyva's directions. The older man looked behind them, at Adrian van Eyck alone in Nominski's car, following. No one spoke; the only sounds were David Caldwell's moans and the rumble of the car through the dark streets. For Arthur Leyva, it was not an auspicious beginning to their undertaking.

8.

The morning was very cold. When Caldwell finished shaving and dressing, he drank two cups of coffee and ate a bowl of cereal. He had been awakened by a telephone call from Adrian Van Eyck. The young man had asked to see Caldwell at nine o'clock. Caldwell had some misgivings. Since the meeting the night before, he had let his doubts about the illegal venture grow. He had balked at the same weaknesses in Van Eyck's reasoning that had bothered Arthur Leyva. Van Eyck tried to project an image of rascally competence, but as far as Caldwell could see, Van Eyck couldn't fall downstairs without help. After all, the only thing that Caldwell had to go on, as far as Van Eyck's credibility was concerned, was the young man's string of failures at the college. He had never been given any proof, other than Andi Nominski's labored assurances, that Van Eyck was good for anything at all.

Still, David Caldwell was getting ready to drive back to Van Eyck's apartment. He didn't really know why.

"Where are you going this early, David?" asked Marianne. "The term hasn't started yet, and they wouldn't be having a meeting or anything this time of day."

"It doesn't have anything at all to do with school," he said.

"You're right, honey."

"You've been going places a lot lately." She didn't sound precisely suspicious, but there was a hint of the jealous spouse in her voice.

"It's a surprise. I promise you, when it's all over, it will be the biggest surprise of your whole life."

"Bigger than Little Davey?" she asked, smiling.

"You bet," he said. It took him an hour to get ready, to get the children ready, to drive them over to their grandmother's, and to head east in rush-hour traffic to Van Eyck's Warren apartment. The sky looked as if it had refused to lighten at dawn, a simple decision by the clouds to stay black despite all the urging from the sun. It was going to be dark, and that was that. The sky looked like the kind of heaven that might have glared down during a plague in the Book of Exodus, or just before the cyclone in *The Wizard of Oz*. A couple of inches of new snow had fallen, but it didn't have much effect on the flow of traffic. It would take more than that; people on Schoolcraft Road wouldn't be bothered by snow unless it drifted deep enough to hide their garages. The cars moved in their long, long lines just as routinely, just as sluggishly as they did every other day of the year. The day wasn't pretty, but it didn't matter; no one was looking.

Caldwell listened to the radio. It was playing a song recorded by the Somebody-or-Other Strings. Caldwell thought that it was too bad they were all strings; they could have used a few musicians. He changed stations, and two men and a woman were discussing something in polite, urgent voices. He turned the volume down so that he wouldn't find out what they were talking about. He drove on. About half past eight he arrived at Van Eyck's apartment building.

"Good morning," said Van Eyck. "Feeling better today?"

"Yes," said Caldwell. He had gone through that whole conversation with Van Eyck on the phone. It was a conversation he hated to have with anybody, and he was determined not to let it start up again.

"What did you want to see me about?"

"Last night," said Van Eyck. He was slipping on a jacket, a green and white thing much too thin for the weather. On the back was a screaming Indian face and the words *Westfield Warriors*. At least it was a signal to Caldwell not to take off his own coat. "I wanted to find out if you were still sure about being in on the job."

Caldwell knew that this was his very last chance. He could still reasonably back out altogether, as though Van Eyck had never approached him. That was something Caldwell had wished over the previous few days—that Van Eyck had not come to see him, had not invited him to be part of a possibly lucrative but probably futile venture, that Van Eyck had simply chosen another English Lit course or another section during registration and had never heard of Caldwell at all. Now Caldwell could make that all true, in a way; but he hesitated long enough to tease himself with the vision of money. "I'm in," he said finally. "Arthur and I, we're in, God help us."

"I'm sure He will," said Van Eyck, smiling with obvious relief. He indicated the door and they left the apartment.

"And how is it that you have God on our side?"

Van Eyck showed mock surprise. "Do you think any loving deity would side with Ford and General Motors against such nice little guys as us? After backing the Israelites and like that? God's got a soft spot for people like us."

"For losers, you mean?" Caldwell unlocked the passenger door of his car. Van Eyck slid in and slammed the door. Caldwell walked around and got in, then started the engine.

"Aw, forget it," said Van Eyck.

"Forget what?" asked Caldwell. They looked at each other for a moment. "Where are we going?"

Van Eyck nodded, businesslike again. "We need working capital to put together supplies and pay for the expenses of this scheme," he said.

"Right," said Caldwell.

"There's a main branch of the Peninsula Commerce Bank downtown, on Fort Street near Kennedy Square. You know where that is?"

"Sure." Caldwell was already driving south. The trip would be about fifteen or twenty minutes. Suddenly Caldwell wondered how they would fill up all that time with conversation. They didn't seem to have anything to talk about. Caldwell dreaded the ride.

"You can leave the car in a parking garage near Congress and Second."

"I hate parking garages," said Caldwell. He hated conversation, too, but he hated uncomfortable silences worse. "What do you think used to be on the spot where this parking garage of yours is? I mean, did they pull down a beautiful old theater or temple or something to put it up?"

"I don't know," said Van Eyck. "But you got to have parking, right?"

Caldwell shook his head. "Even if there were abandoned tenements there, they would have been better. Even if there had been nothing but a dangerous hole in the ground with boards over it, or a city block of marshland with snakes and mosquitoes. Then at least there'd be potential. Something could be done there, but parking lots and garages are permanent. You put up a parking lot, it stays there forever. Have you ever heard of someone tearing down a parking lot?"

Van Eyck hesitated. He was a little surprised by Caldwell's vehemence. "No," he said.

"See? They just spread. They multiply, because the cars multiply. People can't find decent apartments. There's this terrible housing shortage, but they tear down potential homes and pave over the ground and paint stripes on it, and it's fit only for cars from then on."

"Mr. Caldwell, when did you first start to feel this way?"

"When they knocked down the elementary school I went to and made it a parking lot for a laundromat, a delicatessen, and an unoccupied shop that became a shoe store that went out of business. I carved my name and initials in that school."

"I see." There was silence again in the car for a while. "Do you mind going with me to pick up the money this morning?"

"No, I guess not," said Caldwell. It was almost nine o'clock, and he was getting into central city traffic. It kept him a little distracted. "Why should I mind? I mean, it's not as if—"

"Yes, it is."

"Oh. It *is* as if. I see. We're *robbing* this bank."

Van Eyck nodded. Caldwell looked at him sideways. Van Eyck looked very much like a bad little kid who needed to be hit with his father's belt a couple of times. "I guess I should have told you first," said Van Eyck.

"Probably. Do you do this often?"

Van Eyck sniffed and rubbed his nose. "Coming down with a cold," he said. "No, I don't think we'll have to do this again. Just once, just to get an initial investment to work with. I mean, I don't think you should be expected to pick up all your parking fees and lunches and all while we're putting the job together."

"That's very kind of you," said Caldwell coldly. He thought about how wrong he had been, how the ride into town had not been so boring after all. "Look, Adrian, I want to tell you a story. Once, when I was about eight, I found a dollar bill lying in the gutter in front of my house. I didn't see money very often, and at that age a whole dollar bill was like a hundred dollars is to you now, in a way. The only thing I could imagine to do with it was blow it, fast. I took it down to the corner store and bought twenty packs of baseball cards. Twenty packs, Adrian, all at once. And I tore off the wrappers and stuffed the gum in my mouth, and when I had looked through all hundred and twenty cards, I had thirty checklists and twenty Gus Bells and about four thousand Walt Dropos. I knew right then that it was God punishing me for not turning that dollar bill in to the police. Ever since that day, I have been a good, clean person, Adrian. I don't steal and I don't lie much. My only value to your operation is that I have need, and I'm sure it wouldn't be too hard for you to replace me."

"You're intelligent and I like you," said Van Eyck. "That's more important. Do you want to be replaced? Turn in here."

Caldwell turned into the parking garage, stopped at the barrier and took a ticket, waited for the barrier to open, and drove up and parked on the orange level. "Got a pen?" he asked.

"Huh? Sure. Here."

Caldwell wrote "Orange" on the ticket, then jammed it in a hip pocket. He sat on the front seat of the car and waited. He felt like a child waiting to go to the dentist. He and Van Eyck were going to rob a bank! The idea was too absurd to consider. "Why don't *you* rob the bank," he murmured.

"What?" said Van Eyck.

"Nothing," said Caldwell. He thought that he might go shopping or something until Van Eyck was finished....

"You want to know how we're going to rob this bank?"

Caldwell began to feel hostile. "Van Eyck," he said, "if you want me to help you with this, don't you think it would be a positive gesture if you told me what we're going to do? Or do you want me to just sort of go in there and wing it?"

"All right, all right, you're nervous. I can understand that, this is your first bank; but, believe me, banks are really nothing. It's just that you're kind of losing your virginity in this. But banks are the easiest thing in the world."

"Then why don't we rob a bank instead of this whole auto industry song-and-dance?" demanded Caldwell.

Van Eyck looked hurt. "Because there's no money in it, that's why," he said. "Not much money, anyway. A few thousand at best."

"All right. Give me my machine gun and let's get going."

"Mr. Caldwell, I brought you with me for just one reason. I know the misgivings you have. I understand. I appreciate your position. I brought you to show you how easy things are, if you do them correctly. I wanted to build your confidence. You don't have to play an active part. Just watch me. See how simple it is for me. Then you'll understand why the rest of the plan will be just as simple. Stand behind me in the bank and pretend you don't know me, that's all."

"And after?"

Van Eyck smiled. "Tell the teller you want traveler's checks. She'll tell you that you're at the wrong window. You act annoyed, then walk away. Meet me here, and we'll go have lunch."

Caldwell wasn't shocked, because he was growing used to Van Eyck's style. Still, the robbery didn't match the ones he had in his imagination. "No blazing guns? No ski masks? No high-speed chase?"

"Lord, I hope not."

"What about when she takes your picture?"

Van Eyck shrugged. "Then they'll have a picture. I'm not going to be around this part of the world at all in a few weeks. I've never been arrested for anything. That picture won't do anyone very much good."

"Let's go, then," said Caldwell, desperately wanting to be back home, watching television.

Van Eyck carried with him a gray cloth bag that closed with a heavy zipper. There was a metal ring in the bag, and a padlock joined the zipper to the ring. It was the kind of bag businesses use to make night deposits at banks. The padlock was open now, and Van Eyck put it in a pocket. He opened the zipper and checked the inside of the bag. There was a white envelope in the bag. Van Eyck closed the zipper again.

It was only a few blocks from the parking garage to the bank. Neither man felt like speaking as they walked. Caldwell pushed both hands deep into his pockets and hunched his shoulders against the cold. Every step was another step further toward some unforeseeable end to his criminal career. He felt no excitement, no thrill. That meant that he suspected the end would not be pleasant. What were the broader implications?

What would it mean to himself, to Marianne and the children? If he was caught and sent to prison, how would it affect their lives? Caldwell knew what he could do to protect them: He could refuse to take any more steps. He could go back to the car and drive home. He could let somebody like Walter Chance hold up the automobile industry in his place.

Caldwell and Van Eyck entered the bank. It was a large building, and the customer-service area was in a huge, high-vaulted room. Balconies ran around the room above their heads, one on the floor above, another a story above that. Men walked leisurely around those balconies, looking down over the bronze railings. Perhaps they were paid to patrol the bank floor from above, on the lookout for likely-looking robbers. Van Eyck was not likely-looking, Caldwell thought, and he was glad of that.

There were twenty-six teller windows in a long row. At the far end of the room were a dozen desks where officers smiled and opened accounts or frowned and turned down loan applications. Van Eyck paid no attention to Caldwell once they entered the bank, but went straight to the first teller window. There was a line of three people in front of him. Caldwell got in line behind Van Eyck; he waited, feeling cold, even in the bright, warm bank building. His stomach felt upset, as if he had eaten a large quantity of something objectionable.

"Good morning," said the teller when Van Eyck's turn came.

"Hello," he said. He slid the night-deposit bag under her cage. "There's a note in the bag."

The teller raised an eyebrow, but said nothing. She opened the bag, took out the envelope, and glanced at Van Eyck again. She looked to Caldwell to be in her late twenties, rather overweight, not terribly attractive, still sleepy, and very bored. Something alerted her, though, that Van Eyck was out of the ordinary. She held the envelope. "What's this?" she asked.

"Read it, and then I'll answer any questions you may have," said Van Eyck.

"We have a lot of customers waiting, sir," said the teller. "Maybe you should see one of the officers. There's a gentleman behind you who—"

Van Eyck interrupted her with a raised hand. He turned to Caldwell. "This may take a few minutes or so," he said. "Maybe you ought to go to another window."

"That's all right," said Caldwell innocently. "I'm in no particular hurry."

"Fine," said Van Eyck. He turned back to the teller and shrugged. "Open the envelope."

The teller brushed a strand of hair out of her eyes and tore open the white envelope. She took out a small sheet of note paper and read it quickly. When she finished she looked up at Van Eyck. "A robbery," she said softly. "I thought something like that when I saw the note, but I didn't believe it, really. You're crazy. I don't understand this."

"I don't have a gun," said Van Eyck. "Don't be afraid."

"I'm not afraid! How do you think you're going to get out of here without a gun?"

"I got in here without a gun, didn't I?"

"What does that mean?"

"Never mind," said Van Eyck. "There's a teller who usually works at window twenty-four. Her name is Joanne something. Short, dark hair."

"Joanne Reisch."

"Okay. A friend of mine is watching her right now. She's in my living room, her hands and feet are tied up, and there's a rag stuffed in her mouth. You know. You've seen it on television."

"Uh huh." The teller's eyes opened wider. Her breathing was coming faster.

"Now, listen. The plan is that you fill the bag with money and let me walk away nice and calmly. If I'm not home in half an hour, safe and sound, my friend will begin to hurt Joanne Reisch. He won't kill her; we're not like that. He'll just cut her bad. Long, bloody, horrible slashes down her back, her arms, legs. He won't touch her face until I'm an hour late. Understand? Now, in a normal robbery, you're just guarding the bank's money. You turn in the alarm, and your participation is over. But now, honey, if you do anything like that, you'll have the responsibility for Joanne Reisch on your hands. You'll be the one who hurts her. If she dies, it will be your fault. The money doesn't mean a thing to you. Just think about Joanne Reisch, the teller from window twenty-four. What happens to her is up to you now."

The teller looked terrified. Her hand fluttered in front of her mouth as though she were stifling a scream, but she couldn't have screamed to save her life. She stared at Van Eyck; a robbery was one thing, but being made personally responsible for the safety of someone else—that was an inhuman thing for a bank robber to do to her. "How will you know if you get away all right?" she asked.

"I have another friend watching outside. He'll wait and see what happens after I come out. Don't give an alarm for ten or fifteen minutes. Everything will be okay. We don't want to hurt Miss Reisch. We're not evil, honey, we just need money."

The teller nodded slowly. She started putting bills into the night-deposit bag. "You won't hurt her, now?"

"Not if I get home all right with this."

"How much do you need?"

Van Eyck looked thoughtful. "Fifteen thousand?" he said.

"I don't have that much here," said the teller in a worried voice.

"Let's hurry it up," said Van Eyck, for the first time sounding just a little bit like a bank robber. "How much can you get me?"

"Seven or eight thousand?"

"Good enough," said Van Eyck. "And no dye bombs or fancy tricks like that." In less than a minute the teller pushed the bag back to him. "Thank you for your help," he said. "Joanne will be very grateful to you, and she should be. That is, of course, assuming you continue to act smart. No panic, now, right? Everything nice and calm. Let me get home, and then we'll get Joanne Reisch back to work as quick as we can. I don't like the idea of cleaning blood out of my carpet either, you know."

The teller couldn't say anything. She stared as Van Eyck took the bag, smiled, and walked quickly toward the exit. Caldwell pretended to be startled, as though he had been daydreaming. "I always get in the wrong line at a bank," he said, laughing. "Always in the one that takes longest. Look, I need to get some traveler's checks, and—"

"I've just been robbed!"

"What?" said Caldwell.

"I've just been robbed!" cried the teller. She had forgotten Van Eyck's warning already.

Caldwell thought that the best thing he could do would be to stall long enough for Van Eyck to get clear of the bank building. "Whoa, easy," he said, as if he were talking to an excitable animal. "Robbed? By that kid?"

"Yes," said the teller, "with some crazy story!"

"Calm down, calm down."

"Here's his note! Look!"

Caldwell read the note thoughtfully. Slowly. "You ought to tell the guards now. They better get after him."

The teller looked up, nodded blankly, and ran away from her window. Caldwell put the note in his pocket, and followed Van Eyck out of the bank. They met back at the car. "What's this Joanne What's-her-name stuff?" asked Caldwell.

"She's another teller at the bank," said Van Eyck. "Just a phony thing to cause tension and distract the teller. Joanne Reisch is right there at work, down at window twenty-four, but it was too far for my teller to check. I could go into that bank right now, go up to Joanne Reisch, and pull the same thing on her, using the name of the first teller. They get so upset that they just follow directions, mostly. That's what people do in situations like that. So I didn't have a gun, didn't commit armed robbery, didn't have a prisoner or hostage, didn't kidnap anybody, left no clues except the note, and now I have a bag full of cash."

"Bank robbery is enough of a felony by itself," said Caldwell. "I picked up your note for you."

Van Eyck was pleased. "Did you?" he asked. "Did you really? I was wondering if you'd think of that." He looked at Caldwell like a proud father. The expression made Caldwell uncomfortable. They drove slowly down the ramp to the parking garage's exit. Caldwell paid for the ticket with a twenty-dollar bill from the bank. He handed the receipt and the change to Van Eyck, but the young man wouldn't take it. "Keep it," he said. "Expenses. I want to count this up."

"I thought that tellers put marked or counterfeit bills in bags when they get robbed," said Caldwell.

"Joanne Reisch," said Van Eyck, smiling happily. "Picture the lovely Joanne, completely at our mercy, flayed alive, found days later by the police. There's only a blurred photograph in the evening newspaper; a tearful interview with the bank teller: 'It's all my fault!' she sobs. We should take fifty bucks and send both the teller and Joanne Reisch some flowers or something. I'm a romantic."

He's a romantic, thought Caldwell, as he drove back toward Warren. Beside him on the seat, Van Eyck was carefully dividing the money by denominations into piles on his lap. He looked like a child on Christmas morning.

The traffic wasn't nearly so difficult as it had been going the other way earlier that morning; they arrived after fifteen minutes. Caldwell sat in the car while Van Eyck gave him some final instructions. The next day was Saturday; Caldwell, Leyva, and Nominski would have the weekend off, but Van Eyck had a lot of preparations to make. Monday morning they'd all begin their parts of the operation. "I needed you with me this morning," said Van Eyck. "Do you feel better about my leadership, now?"

Caldwell rubbed the bridge of his nose and thought seriously about how he felt. "Yes, Adrian," he said at last, "yes, I do. You can be an amazing person. You really know how to use people. You know how they will react, and you know just the right way to make them do what you want. That's a very dangerous skill to have, and until I saw you demonstrate it, I didn't think this job had the chance of a rat in a rain barrel. Maybe it will work. Maybe we can do it."

"We *can* do it, Mr. Caldwell; now even I'm more confident. I like the way you picked up my note at the bank. That was really terrific; you have a lot of natural ability, too. Well, I'll call you Monday. Have a good weekend."

"You too, Adrian," said Caldwell. A lot of natural criminal ability, he thought. He smiled and shrugged.

Caldwell drove to the campus and parked his car, then walked through the dirty snow to Krummer Hall. It was the last day of the semester break, and it was too late for the students to do anything about shoring up sagging grades. He was glad. He was glad to see them all disappear—not into memory, because they certainly couldn't be retrieved there. The time for point-chiseling had passed, the time for pleading and bribery. The grades were in and recorded, and the old term was history. Caldwell took out the folders that represented his work of the fall semester and tossed it with a loud clump into the wastebasket. "Good-bye, good-bye," he murmured. He wished he could set fire to the papers. The school, like Adrian van Eyck, was giving him a short vacation. His first class meeting of the spring term would be on Thursday. By then, Caldwell would have had his first solo hours as a master criminal.

He sat back in his chair and closed his eyes. The odd thing was that his involvement with Van Eyck now seemed in no way unusual to him. He no longer marveled at the transition that made him part of a plot to fleece three gigantic corporations. It was being at school, sitting at his battered desk, looking at papers and books and messages and departmental memos, that seemed dreamlike, unreal. Where was his true identity now? How would his friends and associates and Marianne react when they found out the truth about him? He knew. He knew that his experience as a teacher would see him through. Ultimately, he'd remain loyal to his principles. He would become a campus hero to the students; but when his crimes became known, the school would reprimand him. They would probably fire him, although he was an extremely popular section man. They would be compelled by the alumni and the federal government to remove him from his job, because he might influence his young, impressionable pupils to follow him in antisocial acts.

And they would, too. They loved him. There would be huge demonstrations, demanding that Wray College rehire Caldwell when he got out of prison in forty years. His students would send him food and money, drugs and *The New Yorker*. He would be tough behind bars, a symbol of defiance and rugged individualism. Then, one night just before his execution—*execution*—the chairman of the English Department and Marianne would pay a last visit to his cell. "Hello, David," his wife would say.

"Mari," he'd answer, almost grunting. The men in the other cells on Death Row would be listening; he had to stay tough.

"Mr. Caldwell," the chairman would say, "take a look at these." He would hand a sheaf of newspaper clippings to Caldwell.

"Swell, aren't they?" Caldwell imagined the photographs: students rioting, carrying picket signs that said *Free Caldwell! Free Caldwell!* There was a montage of guns and bags of money and volumes of Emily Dickinson. There were editorials angrily blasting the college for allowing such a degenerate and evil person as Caldwell to shape the minds of tomorrow. "You keeping a scrapbook, baby? For the kids?"

Mari would sniff into her handkerchief. "No, David, I don't want the children ever to know about you. I've told them that you died in the war."

"What war?"

"They think you're a hero, David."

The chairman would frown. "That's the trouble, my boy,"

he'd say unhappily. "These students think you're a hero, too." He'd wave a photograph of the protesting students. "You're not, you know. You are a sick, depraved man."

"Aw, let 'em have their fun, chief. They're just kids."

The chairman would stare deep into Caldwell's eyes. "Look, buster, tomorrow you're going to fry. You know that? You made your peace with God, buddy? If it were just you, I'd say, 'Burn him and be done with it.' But it isn't just you. Your legend will live on with these young men and women. They think you're some kind of Robin Hood, instead of a filthy animal not fit to live in human society. Do you want them all to follow you? Follow you here, down that long, lonely corridor into the hotseat?"

He'd have a point, and a good one. Caldwell would be jolted out of his smug complacency. "You're right, chief; I never thought about that before. I'll see what I can do."

"You're damn right I'm right. That's how I keep my job. Now say good-bye to this fine woman, whose life you've ruined almost beyond repair."

"Good-bye, Mari. Forgive me." He'd kiss her.

"Good-bye, David." She'd try to say more, but her tears would prevent her. The chairman would lead her away, to be replaced in the cell by an old priest. Caldwell would hardly hear what the man had to say.

The next morning, as he was being led along the final mile, Caldwell would begin to scream. "Stop!" he'd cry. "I don't want to die!" He'd behave like a coward. He'd cry like a baby, and they'd drag him toward his last appointment on this earth. The spectacle would be so pitiful that when it was shown on the evening news, the students who had supported David Caldwell would resolve never to mention him again. They'd be disgusted by his behavior . . . .

When Caldwell awoke, his telephone was ringing. It was his mother, calling to find out why he was late; it was almost five o'clock in the afternoon. Caldwell told his mother that he'd be right there to pick up the children. He hung up, stood, stretched, yawned. He thought about his dream. No, he realized, that's not how it would end, not at all; the end would be a lot less dramatic. He would never get to play a Jimmy Cagney part. His role would be way down the list of anonymous credits, about a fathom below Elisha Cook, Jr. It would be very mundane, not glamorous; but it would be final, one way or the other. It would be an end. And maybe that would be a relief.

Part Two

The Production Line

1.

There was a filing cabinet in the basement of the apartment house where Adrian van Eyck lived. He had the only keys to the locked drawers. The filing cabinet was the most important thing in Van Eyck's life; in fact, the young man often thought that in a certain sense the contents of the cabinet *were* his life.

The keys were on a rusted metal ring, hanging on a nail in the wall behind his refrigerator. Van Eyck waited until three o'clock Sunday morning. He took the keys and went down into the basement. He opened the top drawer and took out an armload of manila file folders. He carried the folders back up to his room and dumped them down on the couch. He sighed. Going through the folders and getting ready to leave Detroit would take the rest of the night and all day Sunday. The job was worth it, of course. He was glad to be doing it. Still, he didn't look forward to the chore. Usually, he'd get someone else to take care of the worst tasks he had to perform. Not now, though. The contents of the folders were the only things in the world Van Eyck wouldn't trust to another person, however dear or faithful that other person might be.

Van Eyck paced around his living room for a few minutes, collecting his thoughts and working himself into the proper frame of mind. He turned on the radio softly, but he didn't listen to the music. He sat down on the couch with a pencil and a large notebook. He opened the first folder. *Gerard F. Urbano. Born: 4/6/65. Hair: Brown. Eyes: Brown.* There was a birth certificate, duly embossed by the Wayne County Department of Public Welfare. There was a Social Security card. There was a Louisiana driver's license; the license had Urbano's name and Van Eyck's photograph. There was even a United States passport, once again with Urbano's name and Van Eyck's picture. There was a list of credit cards in Urbano's name at stores in the Shreveport, Louisiana area. There was a passbook for a savings account at a Detroit bank. There were copies of Federal income tax forms filled out for Urbano for the previous three years. He nodded to himself and placed the folder on the floor to his left. He took up a second folder. *Barry M. Howes. Born: 8/21/64. Hair: Brown. Eyes: Brown.*

Barry M. Howes did not fare so well as Gerard F. Urbano. Howe's folder began a discard pile on the floor to the right. Urbano was joined a moment later by Sheila D. Moser, no photographs. Both piles grew, and in a few hours Van Eyck had sorted through all of his alternate identities. He went to a closet and took out a suitcase. He emptied the contents of the selected folders into the suitcase, then locked it and put it back in the closet. He took the empty folders and the discarded identities and carried them all to a large wire basket in the backyard. The basket was for burning trash and leaves, an activity which had been against local ordinances for some time. Van Eyck dumped the armload of material into the basket, squirted it all with charcoal-lighter fluid, and ignited it with a match. He watched the flames eat through the product of his labors, seeing the various fictitious people die fictitious deaths. He stirred the charred papers with a stick until everything was burnt to powdery black ash. Then he went back inside.

Van Eyck still had to sort through the contents of the bottom drawer of the filing cabinet, which contained dozens of rings of keys, but he put that off until Tuesday. Sunday evening he ordered a pizza delivered, watched a movie on television, checked off his timetables, and went to bed early.

At seven-thirty Monday morning, he telephoned David Caldwell. Caldwell was not happy. "It's early, Adrian," he complained.

"I wanted to catch you before you left."

"I wasn't going anywhere," said Caldwell.

"Yes, you are," said Van Eyck. "You're going with Andi to work this morning. You remember."

Caldwell sighed. "I was kind of hoping you'd forget about that, Adrian."

Van Eyck's voice turned hard. "No more joking, Mr. Caldwell. You're in for the duration now. From now on I'm running things, and you'd better show just a little cooperation if you expect to get out of this safe and sound."

"You're looking to get slugged, Adrian," said Caldwell.

"Forget it. Do you have to do anything else today?"

Caldwell thought for a moment. "I have to show up at my office this afternoon. No classes yet, though."

"Good," said Van Eyck. "Andi will be by to pick you up at about a quarter after eight. All you have to do is wear a coat and tie and stand around while she processes your ID at General Motors."

"I don't see why I have to go. I'm not ready, Adrian. I don't think I've been prepared enough for what I have to do."

"Listen," said Van Eyck, "today all you have to do is smile a lot and keep your mouth shut. Andi will take care of everything. Today you're just a prop, all right? It won't take more than half an hour, I promise. As for your own part, I'll lead you by the hand through every bit of it. I'll rehearse you. Don't worry."

"I'm going to sound like an amateur."

"I *want* you to sound like an amateur. I don't want you to be glib and slick. I don't want any of us to be memorable. I want you to sound *real*. I want you to sound just a little dumb, so the people you deal with will feel superior. That will hold off their suspicion."

"Okay, Adrian, I'll go along today. But listen: They're going to take my picture, right? They have to, for the company identification tag and my personnel file. Well, if they have my name and picture, I don't see how you can assure me that afterward I'll be able to keep on living here and teaching and everything."

"Andi isn't going to use your real name. How foolish do you think we are? Amateur, yes, but not stupid. For General Motors, you're Bill Jahncke. It's not a strange name, and it's not something like 'Joe Smith' that might ring a little false."

"But my picture! I'll wake up one morning to see that picture in the post office and on the front page of the newspaper."

"They won't connect 'Bill Jahncke' to the people who are pulling off this job. There's no reason to. When you make the approach for the ransom money, you won't be dealing with GM. You'll talk to different people. 'Bill Jahncke' will be dead by then."

"What do you mean, 'dead'?" asked Caldwell nervously.

"His file will be closed. Andi will pull and destroy his personnel records."

"Good," said Caldwell. They both lapsed into silence.

"All right, then," said Van Eyck after a moment. "Get yourself together. Andi will be there in a little while."

"Okay," said Caldwell. "Talk to you later." He hung up the phone and went into the bathroom to get ready for his appointment.

Half an hour later an automobile horn sounded outside. Caldwell looked at Marianne, who was still asleep. He glanced at himself in the mirror, took a deep breath, and went out. Andi Nominski was waiting in his driveway, behind the wheel of her car, smoking a cigarette. When she saw him, she rolled down the window and called to him. "Hey, Caldwell! Come on, get in! It's cold."

Caldwell opened the passenger door and looked in. "Listen,

Andi, I'd better just follow you in my car. My wife will be suspicious if I'm gone and my car is still here."

Nominski frowned. "That's not the way it's supposed to go," she said. "Adrian wanted me to ferry you around today, to make sure you don't chicken out."

"Hell," said Caldwell sourly. "You're just going to have to trust me."

"It's not me that has to trust you," said Nominski, shrugging. She stubbed out her cigarette and lit another. "Get in your car and try to keep up with me."

"Right," said Caldwell. He walked toward his car, his stomach feeling just a little upset. It had been doing that a lot, lately.

Caldwell followed Nominski's Toyota toward the Cadillac Division plant where she worked. He thought about her: He didn't know much about her, just as he didn't know very much about Adrian van Eyck. He was allowing himself to be dragged along in this absurd scheme because Arthur Leyva was as well. It occurred to Caldwell that Leyva might be using the very same reasoning to explain his own participation. If that were true, it was possible that both men were making grave errors. Caldwell drove with one hand, putting the other over his aching belly. This wasn't his disease troubling him; this was pure anxiety. He fought down the nausea and kept his eyes on Nominski's filthy car.

At the huge GM plant, Nominski pulled into a parking lot and Caldwell followed. They searched for parking places and found them a good distance apart. She waited by her car while Caldwell hurried through the cold air to join her.

"Good morning," she said, smiling.

"You seem awful friendly today," he said. He couldn't figure her out at all.

"It seems the right thing to do. We're going to make a whole lot of money together. We ought to be friends."

"Okay," said Caldwell. "Then let's be friends inside. I'm freezing my ass off."

"What a shame," said Nominski. "Come on."

"I'll be following you all day," he muttered. Then he shrugged. He would put up with it; he was brave.

Caldwell walked with her into the plant. "Stay with me," she said in a low voice. "Normally you wouldn't be allowed in here, and for sure you couldn't get into the data-processing department, but if you look like you're with me, we'll get through."

There was a bored black man in a guard's uniform at the inner door. He stood there protecting the timeclocks. He paid attention to no one. Nominski and Caldwell were discussing football in a rather strained conversational tone as they passed him. The guard never noticed. She went to a timeclock, found her card, and punched in seven minutes late. They went down a long brick corridor, through two glass doors, into a newer part of the building, and up an elevator. Then they followed a branching hallway—carpeted, unlike the lower floor—to another pair of doors. Metal letters spelled out *Paymaster*. Below that were the words *Hourly/Salaried Paychecks*.

"I'd have thought you worked in the personnel office," said Caldwell.

"No," said Nominski. "We start you up here and run your stuff through personnel later, sort of ass-end backward, if it's a special hiring through a supervisor in the department."

"Is that what I am?"

Nominski smiled. "You're a special rush job for the big boss. He's always liked your type."

"After this is all over, maybe I'll quit teaching and keep this job instead."

"The boss would get tired of you soon, baby. You'd never last until summer."

"Oh, well, forget it, then. I'm no boss's plaything."

"You don't think so?" said Nominski, with her cynical expression. Caldwell had begun to like her a little, but now she was reverting to her less likable personality.

To get into the offices, Nominski took a magnetic passkey

from her purse and pushed it into a slot beside the door. Then she opened the door and indicated that Caldwell was to go through. "You already have a card, then," said Caldwell. "What do you need my new one for?"

"I have this one," said Nominski, "but it won't work on the disk library door. Only the big bosses have them, or you have to sign for one with Mrs. Joiner. She's a pig."

"Oh, okay. And you're going to make me a big boss, so I get one?"

"Right. Here's my cubicle. Sit down. I'm going to enter you into my terminal and then I'll go punch the cards."

Caldwell was surprised. "Doesn't someone else do the card punching? I mean, I wouldn't think they'd make someone like you do all the little chores, too."

Nominski lit a cigarette at her desk and nodded. "I haven't punched cards in more than a year. In this case, though, I'm going to see to everything personally."

"Good idea."

Nominski looked at him scornfully. "Thanks. Thanks a heap," she said. "I'm glad I have your approval."

Caldwell just blinked at her. Stick it, he thought. He said nothing. He waited until she had filled out the sheet on the life of William Joseph Jahncke. "How old are you?" she asked.

"Thirty-four," said Caldwell.

"Hair and eyes?"

"Brown on brown. Five foot ten, one-sixty."

"That's enough," said Nominski. "Come on, we'll get your picture taken."

"Maybe I could wear a disguise," said Caldwell. He was still unsure about having his photo taken.

"Sure," she said. "How about a padded bra and an Afro wig?"

"Funny," said Caldwell.

Nominski carried the information sheet and the two of them took the elevator down a floor. They split up when they got to the keypunch room. Nominski explained to a young keypunch operator that she needed to use the machine for a few minutes. "Would you mind taking Mr. Jahncke over to personnel? He needs to get his picture taken for his ID badge. I'd appreciate it. This is a hurry-up job for Mr. Salicki."

"Sure, Judy," said the young man. Caldwell remembered that Nominski's first name was Judith, and that only recently had she begun calling herself Andi. The employee indicated that Caldwell should follow. Nominski settled down at the keyboard and began tapping out computer cards, the cards that represented the newly born identity of William Jahncke, computer expert and payroll troubleshooter.

After the photo session, Caldwell found his way back to Nominski's office. He leaned against the plasterboard wall. "Is that everything?" he asked.

Nominski looked up from her desk. "Sure is," she said. "It will take a couple of days for the ID to be issued and the passkey and whatall. Wednesday, I expect."

"Can I go home now?"

"Yeah, of course. Unless you'd like to have lunch with me in the cafeteria. Cadillac food."

Caldwell shook his head. "I guess I'll see you at Van Eyck's tomorrow, then."

Nominski had already turned her back and was riffling through some papers on a shelf behind her desk. "Maybe," she said coldly, "and maybe not."

Caldwell left the office and retraced his steps to the elevator and then out of the building. He searched the parking lot for a few minutes, trying to locate his car. He muttered, his breath making pale clouds that wreathed his face. He sat in his car with the motor running, waiting for the engine to warm up. Then he backed out of the parking place and headed toward the college. He marveled at how Andi Nominski always managed to put him in a foul mood.

When he arrived at the school he felt he was on firmer ground. The college had not, in fact, been changed into Yale overnight. Not even into Michigan State. And Krummer Hall had not become a pleasant Holiday Inn over the weekend, either. He would be more comfortable in a quonset hut on the campus grounds. Anything would be an improvement. He climbed the stairs to the English Department offices, grumbling. He took his mail from the box and went into his office. Neither Walter Chance nor Cathy Schumacher had hours now, so he was almost alone. It was very quiet. Caldwell enjoyed the silence. There would be little enough of it in the next few days.

After he sorted through his mail, Caldwell left his cubicle. He met Arthur Leyva in the hallway. They looked at each other wordlessly for several seconds. When they greeted each other, both men were horrified to hear how hollow and false-sounding their voices were.

"Hello, Arthur, how are you today?"

"Fine, David, my boy. Are you feeling better?"

"Yeah. Have a nice weekend?"

"Yes, I did. Relaxed and watched a little television. Read a little. How are Marianne and the kids?"

"They're fine. Everything's fine with me. And you?"

That's where they decided to leave it. It seemed to them that if anyone were listening to their nightmarish drivel, they'd both be convicted as they stood there. A third party would know instantly that something was up, and would be duty-bound to report them to the police, the FBI, the head of the English Department, and the newspapers.

"I'm done for the day, David," said Leyva.

"I'm not, Arthur. I'm supposed to be in the office until four."

"You're done for the day, too, David. Come along."

"Let me get my coat." Caldwell fetched his coat and turned off the lights. He and Arthur Leyva walked slowly down the staircase.

"Look at this," said Leyva softly before they reached the ground floor. He handed Caldwell a .32 caliber pistol.

"Oh, my God, Arthur, you're crazy. Get rid of it."

"I might need it, David. I got it from Andi Nominski. Apparently she has a few of them." He took back the pistol from Caldwell's shaking hand and put it in his overcoat pocket.

"That's crazy. *She's* crazy."

"That may well be true, David, but we might need protection."

"But Adrian promised—"

Leyva stopped on the stair. "David, what does Van Eyck know?"

Caldwell thought for a moment, then shrugged.

"I'll keep the gun," said Leyva. "I can't bully my way out of some unexpected situation, and I can't even run."

"But, Arthur, *what* situation? There won't be any need—"

"I pray to God that's true," said the older man, "but in any event, I'll keep it."

Caldwell was almost pleading. "Don't you see? Guns change everything."

"Come along, David."

"Arthur, don't talk to me like that. Don't treat me like that."

Leyva looked at Caldwell for a few seconds. "I apologize," he said at last. "You're right, you know. A pistol in your pocket bends your thinking right from the very start. You hear yourself talking differently and you watch yourself acting differently. I guess I ought to get rid of it."

"Will you?"

Leyva continued down the stairs. "No," he said.

Sometime later, when Caldwell was picking up his children from his mother's home in Hamtramck, he received another scare. It came from his mother. It was the first time she had actually frightened him since his high-school years. In those days he suspected that she had some uncanny way of knowing just what he was doing: what he was really doing in the garage with Nancy from next door, while he was supposed to be shoveling snow; or what he was really doing upstairs at two in the morning when he said he was reading. There had just been too many situations like that. He had come to the conclusion that his mother was no ordinary human. He had forgotten this notion, but now here it was again, years later, catching him in a vulnerable moment.

Caldwell's mother wore a dark blue dress with white lace at the neck and shoulders. She had on the same stern shoes. She sat down slowly on the living-room couch and watched as Caldwell helped his son search for all the toys. "I want to talk to you, David," she said in a soft voice.

"Okay, Ma," he said absently.

"Listen to me, Davey." Caldwell started. He remembered that tone; he recalled those words too well. He looked up at her. "Davey, are you involved with something you shouldn't be?"

Caldwell tried to answer but his throat wouldn't let him. He swallowed and tried again. "What do you mean, Ma?" he asked.

His mother regarded him with kindness and pity in her face. She looked like a whole Renaissance full of Virgin Marys. "I could always tell when you were in trouble, Davey. You can't hide anything from your mother."

Caldwell felt stricken. He was kneeling on the floor, a blue plastic cowboy in one hand, held awkwardly and forgotten on its way to the toy box. He said nothing.

"I can tell by the way you've been acting the last few days, Davey. You haven't been yourself. You snap at the children. You're short with me, too. I don't know if Marianne has noticed a change, but I know you better. It's not good for you, David."

"I know, Ma," he said. His mouth was dry and his head was buzzing in panic.

"Well, I think you have to be a man about it, dear. You have to realize that the people you love come first. What do you think?"

"You're right, Ma."

She smiled. "All right, Davey. I know you're worried about being sick again, but you can't let it harm everyone around you. Stand up and be strong."

A wave of relief washed over him. He realized that she thought he was just being overly worried about his illness. There was no clue that she knew anything about Van Eyck's gang of villains. "Ma, I'm sorry I've been a burden," he said. "I'll do my best."

"For Marianne, dear, and for your children. You have to be strong for them."

Caldwell resumed picking up his kids' toys. "I will, Ma, I promise you."

"You're a good boy, Davey," she said. "You always were."

Her words stung him when he wondered how she would react if she knew what he was preparing to do with Van Eyck. Would she accept his reasons? Would they excuse his crime? He knew the answer to that: Under no circumstances could he be excused. His crime might be forgiven, but it would never be excused. Caldwell glimpsed the enormity of his situation. His mother must never know, whether the crime was successful or not. His mother must be protected, even at the cost of his relationship with his wife. He hadn't counted on such a complication, but only now did he realize that it had always been inevitable.

An hour later, while he stood in his kitchen watching Marianne making meat loaf, he suddenly put his arms around her and kissed the back of her neck.

"That's annoying, David, stop it," she said.

Caldwell felt rejected. "What's annoying about it?" he wanted to know.

"It just gives me the creeps, that's all. You've been acting strangely lately, you know. Is there something going on I don't know about?"

Caldwell felt cold, as though the bottom of his soul had dropped out and he was floating free in space. "Nothing important," he said hoarsely.

"You've been staying at school and coming home late, and leaving early on days when you said you didn't have to be anywhere. It's enough to make any wife suspicious, you know."

"It's just that I'm so worried about going back in the hospital, honey. I get nervous and agitated and sometimes I just feel like bowling a couple of lines or shooting a few baskets or something."

She put down the salt and pepper shakers and washed off her hands. She wiped her hands on a towel and turned to face him. Her expression was very serious. "David, your bowling ball hasn't been out of the closet since that night you had to go see your student at the bowling alley. The same thing with your basketball. A minute ago I was just complaining and I didn't really mean anything by it. I know you're worried. But now you're lying to me, and I want to know why."

I blew it, thought Caldwell. "Nothing," he said.

"That's a great answer," she said, frowning.

"I'm just scared. Maybe I'm acting a little crazy."

"It's more than that, David. Where have you been going for the last week?"

"You mean, is it another woman or something?"

"It isn't another woman," said Marianne.

Caldwell smiled a little. "How can you be so sure?"

Marianne shook her head impatiently. "I know you better than that. What's the explanation?"

Caldwell had no reply. The silence was accusatory and condemning. He tried to devise a story, a lie to fill the quiet, but his mind wouldn't work. The silence went on. It seemed to him that it might last for minutes, for hours, and the longer it lasted the guiltier he would look.

"It's those drugs, isn't it, David?" said Marianne.

Caldwell shrugged. He looked puzzled.

"You're taking far too many pills. You've got to get yourself under control. From now on, you let me take charge of them. I won't let you abuse them. You have to be strong, David, like before. You have to think of our children."

"That's what Ma said to me," he mumbled.

"There," said Marianne. "I agree. Just let me take care of you. I don't want you going into the hospital a strung-out wreck."

"You're right, Mari," he said. He needed a few pills right then. He left her in the kitchen and took some tranquilizers from their hiding place and swallowed them with a drink of water in the bathroom. He brought the vials of pills and capsules into the kitchen. "Here," he said, "they're your responsibility now."

"All right. Put them on the counter until I'm done. Supper will be in an hour."

"Great," said Caldwell, feeling intense relief once more. "I'll go rest for a while."

"See what the kids are up to."

"Okay," he said. He took a quick look into the living room, where Little Davey and Risa were sitting in front of the evening news. The kids were fine. Caldwell went into the bedroom, kicked off his shoes, and laid down on the bedspread. He put an arm over his eyes and tried to take a nap. He dozed, and his mind created odd images. He saw himself walking down a narrow, deserted street. It was twilight. There were no cars parked on the street, and there were none of the usual noises coming from the apartment buildings. Caldwell realized that it looked like New York or maybe Chicago. He had never been in either city, but he had seen them in movies. He walked down the silent sidewalk, frightened a little by the strangeness. He was wearing a well-tailored if antique double-breasted suit. He had on a snap-brim hat. He walked with a peculiar confidence, a sort of threatening flirtation. No one noticed. Ahead of him was a sign that said DEAD END. Suddenly he knew exactly where he was: He was Humphrey Bogart in a 1937 movie. Somewhere in these apartment buildings were the Dead End Kids, Leo Gorcey, Huntz Hall, Bobby Jordan, Billy Halop and the others. They all looked up to Caldwell because he was a former neighborhood kid who had left the slums to make good in the rackets. He was a hood, a well-dressed gangster who commanded fear wherever he went. And now he was coming around to the old neighborhood again.

Ahead of him, from a doorway, a familiar figure beckoned. It was a woman. It was an alluring female from out of his past, his former girlfriend, whatever her name was. She was smiling, pleased to see him, pleased that he recognized her, pleased that the old erotic bond between them was evidently as strong as ever.

As Caldwell approached even closer he saw that the woman's face was ravaged by the excesses of her tawdry life. The attraction was artificial, painted on the diseased flesh, rouged and powdered thickly to cover the corruption. The woman (was it Marianne? It couldn't be. Was it Marianne, or maybe Andi Nominski?) looked old, too old. She had been prematurely aged by sin, sensual gratification, and the abuse of liquor and drugs. She had moved away from the church; she had even abandoned the loose moral code of the slums. Her pleasure came only from her knowledge of Caldwell's money and power, and the hope that he would share part of that with her. In that she was wrong; Caldwell was repelled. He was truly sickened. In her face (was it Marianne?) he saw a reflection of his own, briefly, and he turned away quickly. He left her on the sidewalk without a word of greeting. He crossed the street and walked faster toward his destination.

"I put your things away."

Caldwell opened his eyes. Marianne was standing in the doorway. "What?" he said.

"I said, I put your medicine away. When you need it, tell me. Then I'll give it to you. Sometimes you forget that you've already taken some, especially those blue capsules. You can take too many that way."

"You're right, honey," said Caldwell. "Those things are a bad idea. I should stop taking them."

"You take them when you really need them, and leave them alone the rest of the time," she said. "They're all right, unless you start playing with them. They're like matches. I just don't want you getting burned."

"Me, neither," said Caldwell, remembering the woman in his vision. "Thanks, Mari."

Marianne turned to go back into the kitchen, but he called out to her and she stopped. "Mari," he said, "were you ever involved with anything like that before we were married? Say, in school or anything?"

"No, Davey," she said, "I skipped all that. I was a nice little girl from Troy. I wasn't spoiled at all until I met you. The very first time I ever had a drink was with you."

"I didn't know that," he said. He regretted what she had said. It made him feel guilty.

"A lot of things I did for the first time I did with you," she said, with a playful laugh. Caldwell didn't notice. He didn't catch her meaning.

"After it's all over," said Caldwell in a low voice, "I only hope you can forgive me."

"Supper in half an hour, David," said Mari. She left him alone once more.

Where was he going? Where was he headed in his snap-brim hat and Bogart face? He was going to visit his mother, his gray-haired old mother, his impoverished, care-worn, dear old mother, whom he had virtually abandoned to her grief and shame. He was a bigshot now, and she would respect him. She would forget their past differences. She would have to acknowledge his status in the world. He was returning to touch her, to receive from her the renewal and peace of her blessing. He was searching for his past, to prove to himself that his fears and self-doubts were groundless, and that all of his justifications had some essential content of truth.

He felt a sharp twinge when he stood at the foot of the stoop. He looked up at the old building, the tenement where he had been born, which he had fled before entering his teenage years, where his mother still dwelt. He skipped up the steps with a remembered familiarity, and paused to read the names on the mailboxes, to read the history of who had remained and who had escaped or passed away. He almost ran up the flights of stairs to his mother's apartment. When he got there, he looked for a long moment at the tarnished numbers on her door. He leaned on her doorbell, grinning to himself in anticipation.

The door opened just a little. Caldwell touched the brim of his hat. "Ma?"

"David?" His mother was wearing the black dress with the white polka dots. She looked ethereal, like a Norman Rockwell rendering, like a photograph taken through a filtered, slightly unfocused lens. She represented tenderness and love, she represented life and peace and safety.

Caldwell's hand moved toward her face slowly, hesitantly. He was afraid this powerful moment might vanish, leaving only illusion and decay, as it had earlier with the girl on the street. Before his fingers could caress his mother's cheek, she looked up into his eyes. Her expression was demanding, almost fierce. "David," she said, and there was little tenderness in her voice, "what are you doing here?"

"Ma," cried Caldwell, "I came to see you, Ma."

"You made a mistake, David," she said. "You aren't wanted here. You aren't wanted in this neighborhood, not you or any of your kind."

"But Ma," said Caldwell, stunned. "I can take the others saying that. But you! You're my mother!"

The old woman was not moved. She shook her head. "You are no son of mine."

Caldwell staggered as though he had been physically assaulted. "Don't talk like that, Ma. All these years, I've scratched and climbed just to make it to the top. Just so you'd be proud of me, Ma. You, Ma! You're the only person I cared about."

"You've cheated and robbed, David. No child of mine could do such things. I've disowned you in my heart."

Caldwell was so afraid of the immense emptiness to which his mother was condemning him that he forgot himself. Unthinking violence, his response to any threat, roused itself in him. He raised one hand to strike the old woman; but before he could move, she slapped him across the face. The sound of the blow echoed in the crumbling stairwell. The shock of the slap was unbearable. The finality, the terrible pain of this rejection was too great for Caldwell. He stumbled to the stairs, then turned to stare at his mother. She still stood in the doorway, solemn and righteous and infinitely sad. "Go away, David," she said. Her voice was cold and steady. Caldwell turned and fled down the stairs. His crimes would have to be paid for, he had always known that. He had never doubted that he'd have to square his accounts eventually. But he had never imagined this. The price was too great. It was too much.

He napped uneasily. When his wife woke him for dinner, Caldwell was greatly agitated. He could barely swallow his food. When Marianne asked what was wrong, he answered, "Nothing."

2.

One of the truly remarkable things about computers is that people trust them so much. Oh, of course, every once in a while there are mixups in billing, or a bank may make an error on a monthly statement, but these are mistakes entered by careless computer operators. The computers' cogitations themselves are virtually unassailable. It is extremely rare that a machine will add two and two and arrive at anything other than four.

Because of this, individuals, corporations, and governments have delegated to computers a great amount of responsibility. In the memories of the machines is a large portion of what was once stored in written records. Consequently a person trained in the ways of the computer may have the opportunity to manipulate data that once were tamper-proof, because they existed in writing on paper. Information about credit, transfers of cash, purchases and sales of securities, and other such financial transactions may be altered at a computer terminal in a matter of seconds. It is not difficult to instruct a computer to ignore an overdraft of any size in a bank account, and only the bank's auditors stand between the computer criminal and a clean getaway. That audit may not take place for many hours or even days, however, and a well-planned computer crime can be untraceable, unsolvable, and almost free of risk. The financial rewards are many times greater than those of the masked gunman at the teller's cage.

What a computer says is often regarded with simple faith. Computers don't lie, but they can be made to report a kind of unreal truth. The greatest business crime in history, the Equity Funding disaster, was a two-billion-dollar scheme that used computers to store and manipulate information on thousands of insurance policy-holders who did not, in fact, exist. These policies were sold at discount to other corporations. The false population on the printout sheets grew and grew. When the bubble finally burst, there was a sudden and profound loss of confidence in both the formerly unimpeachable computerized auditing systems and the very basis of modern big business, which relies on a combination of trust and accountability.

Adrian van Eyck knew that one didn't have to be as large as the Equity Funding Corporation to delve into the electronically guarded mysteries of cash and credit. There are many ways for an individual with a little knowledge and some specialized equipment to circumvent and exploit the computers' own security systems. Van Eyck had considered and discarded several ideas which had been used in the past with varying degrees of success. He decided at last that what had been successful before would likely fail disastrously now. The best chance for success lay in a brand-new concept; that meant creative thought and a genuine stroke of inspiration. He never doubted that it would come. He was right.

It was Tuesday morning. He was in the Detroit Public Library, looking through microfilmed reels of old local newspapers. The first reel was dated 1925. He skipped through the frames until he got to March. He picked March for no other reason than it sounded right to him. He read through the obituary column day after day until he found what he was looking for: on March 11, 1925, a four-week-old male infant had died. He made a note of the infant's name and birthdate. He turned back and got all of the necessary information from the birth announcement. He found nine other male infants who had died in 1925. It took him about half an hour.

After 1925 was rolled up and put back into its box, Van Eyck followed the same procedure with 1955, finding ten female infants who had died within a month of birth. And then he listed ten male infants who had died in 1950. He had spent two hours in the library for the sake of his three gang members. The labor might well save their necks at some future time. They were too inexperienced to do the work themselves, and he felt an odd paternal responsibility for their safety. Besides, if they didn't get away cleanly, he couldn't be certain of his own security. It was, in the end, in his own best interests. Van Eyck had an instinct for protecting his interests.

He stood up from the microfilm viewer; his neck and shoulders ached, but he paid little attention. There was a meeting of the conspirators at his apartment at noon. He had to hurry or he would be late. Then they would all be sitting at his locked door, irritated and beginning to doubt his abilities. He couldn't afford to let that happen.

When he got to his apartment, only Arthur Leyva was there. "Hello, Arthur," he said.

"I guess I'm early," said Leyva. "I brought some wine. I thought you still might not have anything to drink."

Van Eyck smiled. "Thanks, Arthur. I'm a great planner, but a terrible host. Come on in. We'll open the wine and wait for Andi and Mr. Caldwell."

Leyva watched Van Eyck searching for his keys. "Adrian," he said, "why do you call me Arthur and him Mr. Caldwell?"

Van Eyck turned to look at the older man. "I don't know," he said thoughtfully. "I think it's because Mr. Caldwell might well be dead soon. That seems to put a little distance between us and him."

"Well," said Leyva, "I might be dead soon, too, you know."

Van Eyck laughed. "Not if you follow instructions, Arthur."

Leyva made a sour face. "Instructions have nothing to do with it. You really don't know *everything,* my boy."

Van Eyck looked astonished. "Are you afflicted with something, too, Arthur? You never gave a hint."

"No, I'm not. I'm not dying of anything but age, inch by inch."

"You're not old yet, not at all," said Van Eyck. "It's ten to twenty years too soon even to have those thoughts."

"I'm nearly ten years older than I was when I was fifty," said Leyva. "I've tried to resist every one of those years, yet I wake up every morning feeling their accumulation in my bones."

Van Eyck shut the door behind Leyva. "You and Caldwell are the two most morbid men I've ever met," said the young man.

"It comes of reading too many nineteenth-century novels," said Leyva. "If I taught art history, I'd be out dancing every night."

"We'll give you something to take the edge off all that," said Van Eyck. "After this week, you'll be able to dance your life away."

"That's not what I had in mind," said Leyva. He accepted a glass of wine and sat down to wait for Caldwell and Nominski.

In a short while they arrived. Nominski, smoking a cigarette, leaned against a wall and listened noncommittally. Caldwell was anxious to know what the purpose of the meeting was. "Nothing happens until tomorrow morning, right?" he said, his voice a little strained. "My wife and even my mother are beginning to sense that something unusual is going on. I had to make up another lie about where I was going today, and I'll just bet Marianne takes it into her head to check."

"She's a dear, isn't she?" said Nominski.

"I want you to come downtown with me," said Van Eyck. "I want to get your pictures taken."

"What, again?" cried Caldwell.

"I'm giving you a way out of trouble, if you want it," said

Van Eyck. He passed out the lists of names he had compiled at the library. "Look at these names. They are babies born at roughly the same time you were, who died a few days later. You can use any of these names as aliases. If we had another few weeks, you could apply for photostatic copies of the birth certificates. You throw away the ones of the wrong race, or the wrong hair and eye colors. Out of the ten, you ought to have a few usable identities. With a certified birth certificate, you can get a driver's license, credit cards, and then a passport."

Caldwell looked up from his list of names. "But we don't have another few weeks, do we?"

"No," said Van Eyck. "The UAW strike situation demands that we go this week, or our advantage is going to disappear. Today we're going to fit you out with false birth certificates and driver's licenses. There's no way I can get you passports on such short notice. After we're all done and you have leisure and money, you can do what I suggested. Get certified birth certificates and build a separate identity. I've been collecting identities for some time. I have close to fifty, now. Of course, I've constructed them all in much greater detail, but all you really need to disappear are the basic items of identification. The passport will get you safely in and out of the country, no matter what information the authorities may obtain about our true identities."

Caldwell looked sharply at Van Eyck. "What the hell do you mean by that?"

Van Eyck smiled wearily. "Oh, just in case one of us gets caught and talks under torture."

"I never thought about that," said Nominski. "I mean, one of us ratting on the others to the cops. I better check into these names quick."

"Don't worry about me," said Caldwell. "I wouldn't talk."

"That's what they all say," said Nominski.

"Adrian," said Leyva, "is Van Eyck your real name, then? Or is it one of your constructs?"

Van Eyck laughed. "Ah, Arthur, you should know better

than to ask me that!" he said. "Now, let's get going. This is for your own good, you know."

"Okay, Adrian," said Caldwell, "but this business isn't turning out to be as simple and automatic as you implied it would be."

"I didn't imply," said Van Eyck. "You inferred."

"Go to hell, Adrian," said Nominski. "Let's hurry up. I've got to get back."

They got into Caldwell's Vega and went downtown, into a shabby neighborhood near the riverfront. They left the car on a gloomy street lined with warehouses; Caldwell kept looking over his shoulder as he walked to make sure the car was still there. He expected it to be stripped and gutted as soon as they were out of sight.

There was a small shop wedged between two grimy office buildings. A sign in the window advertised passport photo service. "Here we are," said Van Eyck.

"The place is filthy," said Nominski. "Are you sure we won't catch something in here?"

"Just don't kiss anything," said Leyva.

They crowded into the narrow shop. There was no one behind the counter. Van Eyck went through a gate into the rear of the place. "Eddie?" he called.

"Who is it?"

"It's Adrian van Eyck. I have some important rush business."

"Wait a minute," said the voice from the rear. In a moment the man came out, wiping his hands on a faded blue towel. "What is it?"

"Eddie," said Van Eyck, "I need passport pictures for these three people. I need them right now. And I need three birth certificate blanks and three of your Louisiana driver's picture IDs."

"Now? Right now? You're out of your mind. I have more work than I can handle today as it is. Tomorrow. Come back tomorrow."

Van Eyck shook his head. "How much do you want? I need it all now."

The man thought. "Not tonight?"

"Now," said Van Eyck.

"Double, then. A hundred fifty bucks for the lot, and I'll throw in some extra prints of the photos."

"All right," said Van Eyck. "Fine."

"Okay," said Eddie, "who's first?"

"I am," said Andi Nominski. She moved toward the counter.

"Come with me, all three of you." The man led them past the counter, into the rear of the shop. They posed for their photographs, then went back to the front of the store while Eddie made up the counterfeit driver's licenses. It was all done in half an hour. Van Eyck typed in the appropriate information on the three birth certificates. Under casual inspection, Andi Nominski, Arthur Leyva, and David Caldwell could now pass for three people who had been born in Detroit and now resided in Louisiana.

"It's going to take me a while to get used to this new name," said Leyva.

"Work on it," said Van Eyck. "The driver's licenses are laminated plastic cards. Put them in your wallets. If you want to age the birth certificates a little, fold them up and put them in your hip pockets. Carry them around and sit on them for a couple of days, and they won't look so new."

They walked back to the car, each person thinking about the possibilities their new identities opened to them. The unifying theme running through these dreams was escape. The potential of a brand-new life existed, unblemished, unspoiled, mistake-free, where an hour before there had only been disappointment and weariness.

"Where to?" asked Caldwell as he started his car.

"Back to my place," said Van Eyck. "I have something else to give you."

"I want to show you something, too," said Nominski.

"What?" asked Caldwell.

"Wait," she said, "let it be a surprise."

They arrived at Van Eyck's building. Inside his apartment they resumed their regular places: Leyva on the couch, eating a box of Jordan almonds; Caldwell on a kitchen chair; Nominski leaning against a wall. Van Eyck pulled a plastic bag from under the couch. "Here," he said.

"Very clever hiding place, Adrian," said Nominski.

"Shut up, Andi." Van Eyck took out three keyrings, each with two keys. "These are the keys to an apartment I've rented on Woodward in Highland Park. Tomorrow, all activities will be controlled through this apartment. I want to see you, David and Arthur, at the apartment before you go off to Ford and Chrysler. You will leave your cars down the block. I've also rented three cars for us to use. The apartment and each of the cars is in a different name, so don't worry about the possibility of being traced. When you're finished tomorrow, I want you to check in with me at the apartment. I'll ask you a lot of questions to see how things went. Then I'll call the right people and present our demands. Do you all understand?"

"Sure," said Caldwell. He was gratified to hear how thorough Van Eyck had been. It quieted his gnawing fear for a while.

"This is a reassuring bit of business," said Leyva.

"I'll have to stay at work until five o'clock, of course," said Nominski. "I can't leave early, but I'll call you at the apartment. What's the phone number?"

"Oh, right," said Van Eyck, "let me give that to you, too." He took out his wallet and looked at a slip of paper. He passed it to Nominski. "The apartment address is on there, also. Jot it all down on the tag on your keyring."

"All right, then," said Caldwell, "everything looks promising. We do a little work tomorrow and Adrian does a lot. That seems fair. Is there anything else?"

"I've got something, Caldwell," said Nominski. She

opened her large handbag and took out three pistols, a .25 automatic, and .32 and .38 caliber revolvers.

"Oh, hell," said Van Eyck. "Put those away."

"I thought one or the both of you might want one. The little one isn't much good except for punching holes in paper, and I'm going to keep the .38 myself, but that leaves the .32."

"Forget it," said Caldwell. The pistols upset him.

"I won't need anything like that," said Van Eyck.

"Oh yeah, I forgot," said Nominski, putting the pistols back in her bag. "That's right, you're magic."

"We won't need guns," said Van Eyck.

There was silence in the room for a long moment. All four people realized that there was nothing more to be said. In the morning the plan would be put into action for real. "Well," said Nominski, "I'll see you all tomorrow. Don't screw up."

Caldwell turned to Leyva. "I like her attitude," he said. "One thing I've always said about her is that I like her attitude."

"She's a peach," said Leyva. They got up, said good-bye to Van Eyck, and followed Nominski out to their cars.

3.

Detroit was a good choice of targets for two reasons. First, there is a lot of crime in Detroit already. That would help to mask Van Eyck's operation for a while, although the extortion of nearly half a million dollars is the kind of crime that attracts police attention no matter what else is going on. And second, a large fraction of the area's total payroll is distributed by but three major employers. If he hadn't hit the auto industry, Van Eyck might have tried Pittsburgh and the steel industry, or anywhere else where a great many people were employed by a handful of companies in one geographic center.

The motto of the city of Detroit, adopted after the town was destroyed by fire in 1805, is *Speramus Meliora* (We Hope for Better Things). This sentiment might have described the feelings of Adrian van Eyck and his team as they lay in their beds Tuesday night, trying to catch a little sleep before the balloon went up the next morning. There would be no problem sleeping afterward: Either the balm of one hundred thousand dollars would ease the terrors of the night, or the reality of a long-term stay in prison would remove all distractions.

Of the four, the least concerned was Andi Nominski. Van Eyck had known her for several weeks, but he had yet to figure her motivations. She was a curious blend of hostility and vulnerability. She was perpetually angry; her cynicism was a defense mechanism that only aggravated her relations with other people. She was the most enthusiastic of Van Eyck's crew, but he knew that the money wasn't the principle reason. The trouble was, he didn't know what *was* making her go along. He only hoped that she wouldn't fall apart under pressure. He was confident, though, that he had chosen well; she wouldn't allow herself to show weakness in front of the three men.

On the way to the Cadillac plant that Wednesday morning, Nominski hummed along with her car radio. She gave the scheme and her role in it barely a thought. She trusted that Van Eyck had taken care of the details, and that if she, Caldwell, and Leyva did their parts, everything would come out exactly as planned. If they didn't, if things blew up in their faces anyway, she felt she could get herself out. And now she had the added benefit of Van Eyck's gift of a second identity. It wouldn't bother her at all to cut and run, to hurry home to pack a suitcase or two and race off anywhere to build a new life. She even liked the idea. She had toyed with the notion of doing just that anyway.

She found a parking place and killed the engine. When she locked her car, she looked up into the sky. It was bright blue. The day was very cold again, but sharp and clear. It made no difference to her what the weather was like. She didn't believe in luck or omens. She believed simply in only what she could do for herself. She walked confidently into the plant, past the guard, to the timeclock. She was humming to herself as the elevator took her up to the data-processing offices.

It was five minutes after nine o'clock. Nominski looked at her watch. She knew that Van Eyck and Caldwell would be waiting in the apartment on Woodward Avenue. Leyva would check in there, too, before he went off to pretend that he was an old employee at Chrysler. She looked in her purse and took out the keys to the apartment; she had written the phone number on the cardboard tag on the keyring. She put that on her desk near a mug filled with pencils. It was time for her to fire the starting gun for the day's adventure.

"Chris?" she called. There was no answer. She sat for a few seconds, waiting and smoking. Then she stood up, brushed some lint off her slacks, and went out to find the secretary. Chris hadn't arrived yet. Nominski fretted. She decided to wait another five minutes. She stood outside her cubicle and stared at her watch. The time passed; Chris didn't show up. "Damn her anyway," muttered Nominski. She walked quickly to the elevator and went back downstairs, neglecting to take her coat in her hurry. She went to the personnel department, which was in another building nearby. She waited until one of the office workers there noticed her.

"Yes?" said the woman, an elderly lady with rigid blonde hair.

"Hello," said Nominski, "I'm from the paymaster's office. I put through a sheet on a new employee, a William Jahncke, on Monday. Mr. Salicki is crabbing at me already this morning about getting the man's badge and things. I was wondering if it was all ready to go."

The personnel clerk didn't even look up at Nominski. "Did you submit the punchcards, too? Sometimes they forget."

Under normal circumstances, Nominski would have shouted back. She kept herself under control, however. "Yes, we did," she said.

"Then it ought to be ready. Let me check. What was the name again?"

"Jahncke," Nominski said slowly. "William." She bit her lip.

"Let me check." The elderly woman disappeared for a few moments. She returned with a large manila envelope. "Here you go," she said

"Thank you very much," said Nominski. "Mr. Salicki wants the man's personnel file, too."

The elderly woman looked into Nominski's eyes for the first

time. "Why in the world would he want that?" she asked. "There's nothing in his file yet except his picture and a printout of the information you entered."

"Look, lady, I don't know why and I don't ask questions. Mr. Salicki just wants it. You can take it up with him if you want to."

"All right, all right," said the woman, evidently hurt. "I don't know if I like being spoken to in that tone of voice."

Of course you don't, you old bitch, thought Nominski. Tough.

Nominski took the file and the envelope back to her office. She sat at her desk and opened the envelope. Inside were William Jahncke's plant identification badge, a sticker for his car that permitted him to use the reserved executive parking area, a magnetic passkey for the outer doors of the data-processing area, W-2 forms to fill out, a pamphlet on what General Motors expected of its middle-management people, a pamphlet on the kinds of benefits he would be receiving, and similar printed material. There was no magnetic passkey to the data library. Nominski felt herself go cold. She picked up the phone and called the personnel office. "Hello," she said, "I was just down there picking up the material on Mr. Jahncke. There doesn't seem to be any passkey to the data library. Mr. Salicki's getting on my back about it."

"Let me check," said the woman in personnel. There was a long period of silence. Nominski felt her stomach muscles tighten. The woman's voice returned. "Sorry, Mr. Jahncke apparently hasn't been okayed for the key yet. Mr. Salicki will have to send down a written requisition for it."

"Okay, thank you," said Nominski absently. She hung up. Then she lifted the receiver and dialed Van Eyck's number. "Hello, Adrian?"

"Hello, Andi. Everything okay?"

"No, Adrian. They wouldn't let us have a key to the library."

"Oh, no." There was nothing but static over the line for a while.

Nominski grew worried. "What do we do, Adrian? Postpone the whole thing? We could do it next week."

"No, we couldn't," said Van Eyck. "We might lose the advantage of the union situation. And besides, Leyva has left for Chrysler already. He's already going through with his part."

"Damn it, Adrian, that was just stupid!" cried Nominski. "You shouldn't have let him go until you talked with me."

"You're right, but he didn't come by here. He just called me up and I gave him the go-ahead. I wasn't thinking."

Nominski swore softly. "You didn't think. What the hell else are you supposed to be good for? And that means the old man's in his own car, too, right?"

"I guess so."

"Okay, Mr. Mastermind. In that case, you tell me how we're going to get into that library."

"Andi, just shut up." Van Eyck's voice was frightening, icy, unlike anything Nominski had ever heard from him. "You're going to find a way. You're going to do it yourself, you clever little broad, and then you're going to call me and tell me about it. Then I'm going to send Caldwell off to Ford and we'll all meet tonight like planned."

"How? How am I going to—"

"Do it, goddamn it, Andi, or I'll wring your neck." Van Eyck slammed the receiver down.

"He's getting nerves," muttered Nominski. She took a deep breath and thought for a moment. First she took William Jahncke's personnel file and tore it all into many pieces. She carried them across the large room and tossed them into someone else's wastebasket. Then she headed for Mr. Salicki's office. She paused outside and knocked on the open door.

"Yes?" called Salicki.

"A little problem with the personnel department," she said.

"All right," said Salicki. "Let me see."

Inside, Nominski went straight to the man's desk. Before he could look up or say anything, she took out her .38 caliber pistol and pointed it at him. "No noise, now," she said in a low voice. "Don't even breathe. Stand up and come with me. No, leave your overcoat. This will be in my purse the whole time, but I won't hesitate to take it out and use it, so please don't be brave with me. You'll get your brains spattered all over the nice IBM terminals."

Salicki did exactly as he was told. He walked ahead of Nominski, and together they left the data-processing department. No one noticed them. "Where are we going?" he asked.

"Downstairs."

"This is crazy, you know. You'll never—"

"Sure I will. Now, just be quiet."

They rode the elevator down, alone and in silence. She directed him out of the building and around the plant, until they walked down a shadowy alley between a large building and a power station. "All right, stop here," she said.

"What's going on?" said Salicki nervously.

"Shut up. Give me your passkey to the data library."

Salicki took it out of a pocket in his suit jacket. He handed it to Nominski wordlessly.

"Now your wallet. Thank you. Your watch and rings. Any loose cash? No? Okay."

"What is this, anyway?"

"Well," said Nominski, "I want it to look like a robbery."

Salicki's eyes grew wide. "It *isn't* a robbery?"

Nominski laughed. "No," she said, "it's a murder."

4.

"All by hand," said Arthur Leyva with a shy smile.

"It's hard to imagine," said the woman. Her name was Olive Taggert, and she was a public-relations executive for the Chrysler Corporation.

"There weren't so many employees then, of course," said Leyva. "When I worked here, it wasn't such a large plant. So much has changed. They tell me that they can do a whole month's worth of salary and wage computations and check-writing in a few hours, with computers. I used to sit at a desk in a room with dozens of other people, and we did it all with pen and ink and blotters. That was forty years ago, though. This is amazing."

"It's really hard to imagine," said Mrs. Taggert, smiling. She was not particularly happy or interested, but she was paid to smile. Old employees, waxing nostalgic in their later years, sometimes came back wanting to see how much had changed. Mrs. Taggert had to jolly them all along and listen to their old stories, tales which held very little interest even if one knew what the old people were talking about. Then Mrs. Taggert arranged for the retired folks to tour the new facilities. She issued them guest passes and vouchers for a free lunch at the cafeteria. Then Mrs. Taggert would shoo the visitors from her office and get back to work.

"Well, Mr. Edwards," said Mrs. Taggert, standing and holding out her hand to Leyva, cuing him that the interview had come to an end, "just wait outside for a few minutes and I'll arrange a tour for you. We're always happy to accommodate our visiting veterans." She smiled, shooing Leyva from her office.

"Thank you, ma'am, thank you very much for your—" Mrs. Taggert beamed and let him out. "—kindness," muttered Leyva, as her door shut behind him. He walked over to a pale green sofa and sat down. On a coffee table were some magazines. None of them interested Leyva at all; they were the kind of thing left for children in doctors' offices, or brochures describing Chrysler products, or six-month-old copies of *U.S. News and World Report*. Leyva waited.

He was enjoying himself more than he ever thought he could. Part of it, of course, was the thrill of doing something illicit, knowing that he was part of a larger scheme engaged in illegal and dangerous activities. It excited him. He, too, gave little thought to the money—although he was aware that the money would be very pleasant to have around later.

Van Eyck needed Arthur Leyva. The young man had recruited Leyva more vigorously than he had David Caldwell. Leyva projected an air of wholesome, law-abiding plainness. He was the most solid of solid citizens. No one could possibly think that he was a threat. He wouldn't likely be taken for an extortionist and a felon. He was protective coloration for the entire operation.

"Mr. Edwards?" said a young woman about twenty years old. "My name is Josie Frankel. I'm to show you around the plant."

"How do you do?" said Leyva, standing.

"So you're an old employee. I mean, former employee, not that you're old." She stopped, embarrassed. "Things have really changed, I'll bet."

"You're darn right," said Leyva. He smiled.

"What would you like to see first?" the girl asked.

Leyva pretended to think for a moment. "I'd like to see the computers that took over my job," he said. "They fascinate me."

5.

"Do it, goddamn it, Andi, or I'll wring your neck." Van Eyck slammed the receiver down.

"My God, Adrian," said Caldwell, "I've never heard you talk like that before."

"Hold it, let me think," said Van Eyck. He began pacing the narrow room of the unfurnished apartment in Highland Park. "This was a simple job, wasn't it? It was foolproof. It was all set up so that nobody, no matter how stupid, could screw it up."

Caldwell shivered. "What's happened?"

Van Eyck stopped pacing. "Andi didn't get the passkey."

"But I thought—"

"I don't give a good goddamn *what* you thought. It was supposed to be there in that package, that's all."

Caldwell looked out a window onto Woodward Avenue. "What if, Adrian? What if all your plans are nothing but pipe dreams? What if you were just plain wrong, Adrian? What if what you say about the value of the disks is true, but what if you're absolutely dead wrong about the chances of getting into these places and doing the job?"

"Shut up!" shouted Van Eyck. "I have to think. My God, first that moron goes off to Chrysler in his own car—"

"You talked to him this morning, Adrian. You didn't remember to tell him about that, either."

"—and then I have a panicky woman on my hands. Who knows what she'll do? Andi's crazy."

Caldwell sat down and waited. He had almost decided to abandon the whole thing. A long time passed in silence. He was caught in a misfiring explosion, instead of a smoothly running operation. The woman *was* crazy. Now he was beginning to see that Adrian van Eyck might be a little unsettled, himself.

How could he get out, though? If he quit the job, Van Eyck and Nominski would come looking for him. He was trapped between two very unattractive alternatives. There was nowhere to hide.

The telephone rang. "Yeah?" said Van Eyck. The young man's expression softened as he listened. "Terrific," he said, and hung up.

"Who was that?" asked Caldwell.

"Andi. She said that she's gotten hold of the key to the disk library after all. All she said was that she used her usual sweet-talk. I hope she didn't do anything unusual. She has to hold down her job there to maintain our cover. If she did something drastic at work, they'll remember it when this is over."

"How likely is she to do something drastic?" asked Caldwell.

"What do you think? When was the last time you knew somebody with a mixed assortment of guns in her purse?"

"Yeah," said Caldwell. He wasn't cheered by the image.

"Anyway, that ought to take care of General Motors. It will be a cinch for her now. And Leyva is taking care of Chrysler even while we're talking here."

"You hope he is," said Caldwell.

"Sure, I know they both are," said Van Eyck. "There's nothing that could complicate things now. Everything is going along just as I planned. I just got a little overexcited a minute ago. I'm sorry for the way I sounded before. I'm just nervous. Now, though, about you."

Caldwell held his breath.

"Are you ready?" asked Van Eyck.

No, thought Caldwell, of course not. "I guess so," he said.

"Sit tight," said Van Eyck. "I'll set it up." He opened a notebook and found the telephone number he needed. He dialed the phone and waited. "Hello," he said, "I'd like the Hourly Employee Record Division, please." There was another short silence. "Hello. I'm calling for Mr. William Jahncke, General Motors Corporation, Office of the Paymaster. Mr. Jahncke would like an appointment this afternoon to see Mr. Wozniak. Concerning the purchase of some software. I spoke with someone about this last week. Yes, I'll hold." Van Eyck grimaced at the telephone. "Hello. That's all right. This afternoon, if possible. Right after lunch? Fine, what time? One-thirty. That's great. Jahncke. Right. Fine. Thank you."

Caldwell sighed. His die was cast, into the same muddy pool as the others'.

"There you go," said Van Eyck.

"One more thing, Adrian," said Caldwell. "You promised me that I'd have the Ford passkey I'd need."

Van Eyck nodded. He picked up an object that looked very much like a credit card. "Here you go."

Caldwell examined it. "What do I do with it? Just slip it in the slot by the door?"

"That's all," said Van Eyck. "Make sure it's strip-side down."

Caldwell put it in his breast pocket. "How'd you get it?"

The younger man smiled. "I had a job for a day as a maintenance man at the Dearborn complex. The place is immense. I bluffed my way around until I found what I was looking for, and then I just stole it. It was very easy."

Caldwell was doubtful. "Don't you think that as soon as they learned one of their passkeys was missing, they'd cancel its number?"

Van Eyck shook his head. "I found a whole box of them that hadn't been issued yet. I took the last one, the one with the highest number. They won't even know it's gone."

"Okay, Adrian, I apologize. Things seemed a little ragged there for a moment and I was losing faith."

"That's all right, Mr. Caldwell. Just let me do the worrying. If you and Andi and Arthur tend to your small tasks, everything will come together just fine. Now you have to wait until Andi brings your GM credentials by at lunchtime. Then you become William Jahncke, and you take one of the rented cars and you go talk to Mr. Wozniak about buying some computer programs for the General Motors payroll department. Tell him you'd like to compare your systems. They do this sort of thing all the time."

"If you say so, Adrian," said Caldwell.

"That's the point, isn't it?" said Van Eyck. "I say so."

6.

It wasn't even ten o'clock in the morning, and already Andi Nominski had done something that lifted her out of the category of con men like Adrian van Eyck. In a perverse way, she enjoyed the distinction. David Caldwell or Arthur Leyva could never commit murder. Van Eyck himself flinched from stealing private property or hurting anyone. None of that meant anything to Nominski. The only important thing was clearing away the obstacles that barred her from her goal. She would accomplish that in whatever way was necessary.

She sat at her desk, her hands shaking just a little. She lit herself a cigarette and stared at Salicki's magnetic passkey. The little object had cost him his life. It wasn't worth that much. It was worth only a hundred thousand dollars to Nominski, a rather low estimate of the value of a man's life. Nominski had fantasized often about committing some audacious crime, displaying courage and ferocity. Now she had killed a man. She knew that he had not needed to die, that she had done it only to test the strength of her new self-image. She knew, also, that she could never again be the person she'd been before.

She looked at the passkey and stubbed out her cigarette. She hadn't done it for Van Eyck; she had done it for herself. She thought of her first meeting with Van Eyck. He had seemed like an obnoxious, immature college kid, which was the opinion she still had of him. During their first conversation he made claims about his talents that interested her. She thought he might be worth cultivating, that eventually he might come up with something worthwhile. She encouraged his boasts and finally challenged him to do something to back them up. He accepted the challenge, and a few days later called her to say that he had an idea that might net them a considerable amount of money. Could he count on her help? Negligently, she had said yes, without even inquiring what his idea was. She had already written him off, and she was surprised that he was taking her dare seriously.

Nominski was sorry now that she had gone along with him. When she heard his scheme, and saw how simple it was, she was certain that she could have done it all alone, without him. Every clever thing that he did, she could have done: and then she wouldn't have needed to split the money with anyone. Her dark red fingernails tapped the magnetic passkey. She wished that Van Eyck, Caldwell, and Leyva weren't hanging onto her skirts. After all, none of their activities would have been possible without her inspiration and her participation. Maybe she should ask for a larger share of the money, she thought.

With the money she could go to Atlanta, where her ex-husband was living. She could steal her two children back and take them away where no one would ever find them.

Nominski took the passkey and walked to the steel doors of the library vault. She looked carefully about her, and was satisfied that no one was paying any attention to her. She slipped the key in its slot, and the doors unlocked. She went into the vault, closing the doors behind her. She consulted a master list of the library's resources in the control room; it didn't take her long to find the serial numbers of the disks she was looking for.

In the library itself, the computer disks were stored on metal racks. The disks were identical, and there were few signs on the shelves themselves to tell her where the most recent disks were. She had to glance from one rack to another until she got an idea of the system. She found what she was looking for after about three minutes of searching. There were several disks that held all of the current information on the employees at the General Motors plant, with their pay scales and hours for the preceding pay period. These were the vital disks. Nominski removed the labels from them and put them back on the racks, moving other disks to make room for them in widely spaced places. She shuffled the disks around until they were irretrievably mixed up. Everything looked normal. Nothing would seem amiss even under close inspection. Then Nominski remembered that she had to take care of the quarterly summary disks as well. She shook her head ruefully: She was capable of mental lapses, too, it seemed. It was the work of a few minutes to find the summary disks, remove their labels, and hide them elsewhere in the library. Nominski's job was finished.

She left the library, again looking to see if anyone noticed her presence there. No one did. She was in the clear.

Except for Salicki's passkey, which would be damning evidence if it was found in Nominski's possession. As she walked back to her desk, she wondered about the best way to dispose of it. She thought she might just leave it with Van Eyck and let him worry about it, but she dismissed that idea. If anything happened to him, he might decide to drag her down with him. She would toss the key into the river or bury it instead. It wouldn't pose any serious problem.

7.

"This building here houses the Chrysler Corporation's Hamtramck Assembly Plant's computerized payroll and accounting systems," said Josie Frankel. She was freezing but cheerful.

"This I have to see," said Leyva. "I promised my wife that I'd bring her back something. Is there something I could get in there to take home to my wife? Edna would be just thrilled. Some computer thing or other."

"I don't know," said Frankel. "Let's go inside, though, all right?"

"Sure," said Leyva. He was still enjoying himself, getting a kick out of creating a character.

They passed a uniformed guard and went into the data center. There were no locked doors here. A receptionist evidently recognized Josie Frankel and let them through without hindrance. They marched up the center aisle of a large, bright room where busy men and women did the paperwork that kept the automobiles coming off the assembly lines. No one looked up as Leyva and his guide walked by. "It's the same basic idea as when I worked here," said Leyva. "The only difference is that everyone works on those things—"

"Computer terminals."

"—instead of on mechanical adding machines. But it looks like the headaches and the deadlines are still the same."

"See?" said Frankel, trying to be friendly. "Things haven't changed all that much."

"Oh, yes, they have. Where are the computers themselves?"

"They're in the room below this, I think. No, they're back there, where the cafeteria used to be. I don't come in here very often."

Leyva spotted what he was looking for. He saw a man with a computer disk in his hands leaving the room through a heavy wooden door. "What's that?" he asked, pointing at the door.

"I don't know," said Frankel. "Let's take a look."

The door had closed and locked. There were no signs on the door to indicate what was behind it. "Oh, well," said the young woman, "it's locked. Now, over in this direction you'll see—"

"I'd like to look in here, if I might," said Leyva.

"I'm sorry, Mr. Edwards, but I don't have keys."

Leyva was ready for her answer. He walked over to a woman at a desk. "Excuse me," he said, "what's behind that door?"

"That's the disk library," she said distractedly.

"Would you be so kind as to open it for us?" asked Leyva.

"No key," said the woman. She pointed to another woman a few desks away. Leyva followed her directions and asked the other woman to open the library.

"I'm on a tour," he explained. "I used to work here forty years ago. Maybe I even had your job, though it was a lot different then, of course, and you probably earn a lot more than I ever did, but of course you have to know a lot more—"

The woman looked up in irritation. "I'm sorry," she said. "I can't let you in there."

Leyva smiled. He went on talking as though he were only barely aware of what she had said. "So they told me I could look around and they even assigned this charming young lady to show me, I mean she wasn't even born when I worked here, I doubt if you were either, Miss, but she doesn't have the key to the door and perhaps, just for a moment—"

The woman signaled to Josie Frankel. The guide joined Leyva at the desk. "Here," said the woman, giving the key to Frankel, "please get him out of here. I'm busy. And don't forget to return that key when you're done."

"I'm very grateful," said Leyva. "It's nice to see that common courtesy hasn't—"

"Come along," said Frankel, tugging at Leyva's arm. She unlocked the library door and they entered. The door clicked shut behind them.

"These are the disks, then," said Leyva. He was awed at how many there were. He was suddenly afraid that he'd never be able to finish his assignment.

"Yes," said Frankel. "Now if you're ready, perhaps you'd like to go get that complimentary lunch—"

"Miss," said Leyva, "I'm suddenly feeling very ill. I have a kind of heart condition, you know, and bad circulation. I need a drink of water very much. I have to take my pills. Would you be so kind—"

"I'm sorry, sir," said Josie Frankel, her voice becoming a little annoyed. "I couldn't possibly leave you alone in here. You can sit down outside. I'll get you a cup of water then."

Leyva was baffled. He had a memory of something that had happened to him while he was in school, something he hadn't thought of in forty years. He had been in a school play, and he had had a scene with a young woman, a classmate. The girl had gotten rattled during the scene, and had begun repeating the same three speeches over and over again. No matter what Leyva said or did, he couldn't get the girl to go on to the next page of the script. She just kept cycling around. He had grown increasingly distraught as the audience became aware of what was happening. The girl was terrified and almost in tears. Leyva finally walked offstage to find out from the prompter in the wings what the actress's next lines were. He came back, spoke the lines himself, then framed his own lines into a reasonable reply. The young woman picked the scene up from there, and the play continued without further embarrassment.

That was how Leyva felt now. He was in the library, all right, but his young guide was not about to leave him alone. He wondered if he had to fake a heart attack on the floor to get her to leave him. He grabbed his left shoulder. "My God!" he gasped.

"What is it?" asked Frankel.

"Nothing," he whispered, his face contorted. "I think I just need to rest. Some water, please."

"Come with me. We'll sit you down outside and call for the company's doctor."

Leyva made a quick decision. He was under a great deal of pressure, and he hadn't expected this turn of events at all. He took out the pistol he had gotten from Nominski. When Josie Frankel saw it, she gave a little stifled scream. "Don't be afraid," said Leyva. "I came here to do something, and you just wouldn't let me work in peace. Now I'm going to have to do it despite you. I don't want to hurt you, but I'm sure you understand my position. Will you let me do what I have to do?"

She nodded. Looking down the barrel of a pistol was more frightening than she had ever imagined it could be.

"Do you know where the payroll system disks for the last pay period are?" he asked.

She shook her head. "I don't know anything at all about computers," she said.

"Great," muttered Leyva. "Now what did Adrian tell me? There should be dates on them, I think. What if there aren't? What do I do then?" Leyva began looking at the disks. There were thousands of them. "It may take me all day to find what I'm looking for. Somebody else will come in before long, and then they'll find us here, you over there shaking in your shoes and me with my gun drawn. That will be just wonderful." He began to perspire. He hurried from rack to rack, listening to the blood roar in his head. He wanted to be home, or at work, or anywhere else. He was beginning to panic, because the disks did not, after all, have dates on them. Then he found a section of racks labeled *Current Wage/Salary*. Near it were the other disks he needed to locate, the quarterly files. "Here we are!" he cried jubilantly. "Just a minute more, Miss Frankel, then we'll get out of here." He removed the identification labels from the disks, switched them with others on various racks, and adjusted the spacing so none appeared to have been moved. He examined his work and was satisfied. "Good," he said. "Now we can go."

Josie Frankel stared at him with huge, frightened eyes. "What about me?" she asked.

"What about you?" asked Leyva, pocketing his pistol.

"I saw what you did."

"Ah," said Leyva, suddenly realizing what she meant. He hadn't thought about it, but as soon as he pulled out his pistol, it had become necessary to dispose of the pretty young woman in some way. "My God," he murmured. He rubbed his forehead. He hoped that Nominski and Caldwell were having an easier time of it. He could see only one solution: He had to take the young woman with him. "You'll have to come with me," he said. "I'm really very sorry, but it's the only way out. I don't want to harm you, you see, so you'll just have to be a prisoner. It's much the more pleasant of the choices, I'm sure you'll agree. Now, don't do anything rash as we leave here. We'll just go down to my car and drive back to the apartment."

Leyva held the door for her. Josie Frankel was still afraid, but Leyva's calm, courteous manner took the edge off her terror. She didn't like the idea of being a hostage, but she preferred it to being dead. Leyva held her arm as they walked across the plant's parking lot. "Holy Mother of God," whispered Leyva, "is Van Eyck going to be unhappy about this."

8.

Caldwell and Van Eyck were sitting in the apartment waiting for Nominski. There was nothing to read, no television, just a radio. The two men were listening to a station that played easy-listening music. It was driving both of them crazy. Caldwell got up to find another station; before he got to the radio, Leyva came in with Josie Frankel. Caldwell's reaction was simple: He stared open-mouthed, paralyzed in midstep. He felt as though prison bars prevented him from moving.

Van Eyck's response was a bit more vocal. "Hello, Arthur," he said, in what might have been mistaken for a pleasant tone of voice.

"Uh, hello, Adrian. Now, Adrian, before you get angry—"

"Arthur, sit down. What do you mean, 'get angry'? Why don't you introduce us to your friend?"

Leyva was frightened. This wasn't the reaction he had expected. He didn't know what Van Eyck was leading up to. "Adrian, this is Josie Frankel. She was my guide at Chrysler."

"Hello, Miss Frankel," said Van Eyck. His eyes glowered at her. "I'm sorry we have so little to make you comfortable. Please sit down, though. Arthur, I'd like to speak to you."

"Certainly, Adrian. Adrian, look, I'm terribly sorry. I guess I just lost my head. I don't know what—"

"Let's go outside, Arthur." Van Eyck grabbed his jacket. "One thing first. Did you finish what you were supposed to do?"

Leyva rubbed the back of his neck. "Yes," he said in a low voice, "at least I got that part right."

"At least," said Van Eyck. "Come along." They headed for the door, but before they got there it opened and Andi Nominski came in.

"Hello, guys," she said. "I got the—" She caught sight of Frankel. "All right, who's she?"

"A friend of Arthur's," said Van Eyck serenely. "He decided to bring her along when he left Chrysler."

Nominski turned on Leyva. Her voice was high-pitched, a mad shriek. "You goddamn *fool*!" she cried. "We were looking at ten years in prison. Now, thanks to you, you bastard, it's ninety-nine years. It's kidnapping now, baby, and first-degree murder when you have to get rid of her. You *are* going to get rid of her, aren't you?" She turned to look at Van Eyck. "Or are they engaged?"

"Arthur didn't say," said Van Eyck. "I think they're just good friends. I was just going to speak to him in private. Man to man. You understand."

"Good," said Nominski.

Caldwell interrupted. "Adrian," he said, "here's something you might want to know about. The radio just said that police are investigating a homicide that took place this morning at the General Motors Cadillac plant. There were only headlines. The full story will be on in a half hour."

Van Eyck took a deep breath. "Andi," he said calmly, "when I'm done with Arthur, I think I'd like to talk to you as well. In any event, we really ought to stick to our schedule. Mr. Caldwell, if you'd be so kind as to take your material from Andi and be on your way. Mr. Wozniak will be expecting you. And please, try not to outdo your two friends here."

"I won't, if I can help it," said Caldwell. He glanced at both Leyva and Nominski. He suppressed a shudder. He looked at Josie Frankel, cowering in a corner. He looked at the ferocious expression on Van Eyck's face. He put his hand on the doorknob.

"You would have done the same," said Leyva. "It was the only sensible thing."

Caldwell spun to face his old friend. "You're all lunatics," he said.

"Don't," pleaded Leyva. "Don't judge me. I did what I had to do. I didn't want to hurt the girl. I just showed a little compassion."

Caldwell was incensed. "Compassion? What about my mother and Marianne? Did you think about them?"

"David, please, I don't understand what—"

Caldwell ignored the older man. He opened the door and left the apartment. It was colder outside, but it was peaceful, clean, and quiet.

9.

Caldwell drove to the Ford plant in River Rouge, his thoughts seething. He was no longer the slightest bit afraid, or even apprehensive. He had gotten past those feelings suddenly. He was filled now with anger, directed at the madness of Andi Nominski and the folly of Arthur Leyva. Van Eyck was still an unknown factor. A lot depended on what the young man made of the situation Nominski and Leyva had created.

When Caldwell arrived at the River Rouge assembly plant, he left the rented car in a visitor's parking lot. Then he telephoned the apartment to let Van Eyck know he had arrived. In twenty minutes Van Eyck would make the call to Mr. Wozniak, rescuing Caldwell from his charade and setting up the Ford Motor Company. Caldwell had a feeling that it was going to be a long twenty minutes.

Wozniak was a short man, heavy and balding, who had all the time in the world to give to Caldwell. It seemed to Caldwell that Wozniak didn't actually have much work to do, or else he'd had a good deal to drink with lunch and had written off the rest of the afternoon as a loss. They sat at Wozniak's desk and talked about the Detroit Lions for a while; they went over the recently completed season almost game by game. Wozniak had season tickets, and he assumed that Caldwell had tickets as well. After the football talk, Wozniak stood up. "Let's take a look around," he said.

"Fine," said Caldwell, "I'd like that." It was precisely what he hoped the man would say. It would relieve Caldwell of having to make technical small talk. He could just say "Uh huh" every time Wozniak pointed out some elementary marvel.

They walked around Wozniak's little kingdom. Caldwell noted the location of the room where the disks were stored. "I'd like to see that," said Caldwell.

Wozniak was surprised. "The library?" he asked. "That's nothing. That's just a room with racks and disks. It probably looks just like the one in your own department."

"Sure," said Caldwell, "but we're in the process of changing over to a whole new cataloguing system, and it's got everybody mad as wet hens. Nobody can find anything anymore, and it's slowing us down and costing us a lot of man-hours. That's one of the reasons I'm here. I'd like to see your system. It seems like filing should be such a simple thing; I mean, it's really just a matter of common sense. You know, assuming that people are going to put things back where they belong. But I've already lost one good systems analyst because she got fed up with our problems."

"Ah," said Wozniak. "In that case, come with me." Wozniak produced a passkey and opened the door to the library. The room inside was even larger than the libraries at General Motors and Chrysler. To Caldwell, who had never before been in such a room, it was bewildering. Finding what he needed would be like trying to identify a particular pebble on a gravel driveway.

"Your payroll data," said Caldwell, "is that kept separately? That's what I'm primarily interested in."

"Over here," said Wozniak, lazily waving a hand at a wall of racks. "Very complete records that go back as long as we've had the system on computers."

"How do you arrange them? Chronologically? Or . . ." Caldwell's voice trailed off. He couldn't think of any other way to arrange the disks, but a real computer expert might have had other ideas.

"Chronologically, of course," said Wozniak. "The most recent are—" A beeper on his belt began sounding. "Just a minute, Mr. Jahncke, I'll be right back." That would be the call from Van Eyck; Caldwell smiled. Everything was going along smoothly, for a change. Wozniak would leave him in the library— "I guess we're finished here, aren't we?" said Wozniak. "Come on, then. I have to answer this call."

Caldwell muttered a curse, but there was nothing else to do. He had to go out of the library with the man. "Do you mind if I look around a bit while you're on the phone?" he asked, a little hopelessly.

"Not at all," said Wozniak. "Just don't steal any industrial secrets." He smiled and hurried away toward his desk.

When he was sure he was alone, Caldwell went back to the disk library. He slipped the passkey Van Eyck had stolen into the slot. He waited; nothing happened. He remembered what Van Eyck had said, and he turned the passkey upside-down and tried again. Once more nothing happened. There were four ways the key could fit in the slot, and Caldwell tried each way at least twice. The door stayed locked. Caldwell put the key back in his pocket and promised himself that somehow Van Eyck was going to make it all up to him. The young man had been wrong; someone had noticed that the passkey was missing, and it had been invalidated. This business was causing everyone concerned more grief than had been advertised.

Wozniak came running back to the library. "That was your boss on the phone," he said.

"Mr. Salicki?" said Caldwell. Nominski had given him that name, in case he needed to demonstrate that he was, indeed, from General Motors. "My mother use to check up on me like that."

"No, no," said Wozniak, "he said there are some disks missing from your payroll department. All of the most recent disks and the quarterly master. He thinks they were stolen, and he thinks someone might have taken ours, too."

"No," said Caldwell, smiling, "it's exactly as I told you. They're probably just misfiled. He gets excited so easily."

"Well," said Wozniak, using his key to unlock the library door, "he told me some other things, too, so I thought I'd better check—" They went back into the room. Wozniak inspected the disks. "That's a relief," he said. "If they were gone, we'd know that somebody was planning some kind of crazy rip-off. I'd better get back to him. I left him hanging on the phone while I checked these disks. I'll tell him to forget the conspiracy idea. You're probably right; they're probably just stuck on the wrong rack somewhere." He walked away hurriedly, leaving Caldwell alone in the room. The library door closed and locked.

Caldwell was glad that Van Eyck's passkey hadn't worked; if things had gone as planned, Wozniak would have discovered that the disks had been tampered with. "Well," murmured Caldwell, "everything is fine now, unless I'm left to suffocate in here." He went to the payroll disks, identified the ones he needed, removed their labels, switched the disks with others around the room, and went out to find Wozniak. His prescription drugs had never made him feel as tranquil as he was now.

10.

Adrian van Eyck looked at Josie Frankel. The young woman was sitting on the floor in a corner, her knees drawn up under her chin, her slender arms hugging her legs. Van Eyck had prepared for certain eventualities, trying to foresee any possible hitch that might develop in the operation. A hostage situation had not been one of them. Nominski had been right when she said that they were all in terrible trouble now. If they were caught, the added charge of kidnapping would put them away for a long, long time. Van Eyck stared at the prisoner, trying to devise something reasonable to do with her.

"Why can't we just let her go when we've got the money?" asked Leyva.

"It's all right with me," said Van Eyck. "That's perfectly fine, as far as I'm concerned. I don't want to hurt her, either. But I'm not going to hang around Detroit. I'm taking my money and leaving. I have dozens of other people I can become. But you, Arthur, you wanted to stay here and keep on teaching. Miss Frankel will be able to identify you. Mr. Caldwell has a nice house and a family and a future here. Miss Frankel will present a definite problem to him, too. And I'm just as sure that if the police and the federal boys pressure *you* a little, neither Andi nor I will be safe for long. So you see, we're all in this together." Van Eyck rubbed his chin and thought. Frankel looked back at him, glum and frightened.

"Let me try," said Leyva. He sat down on the floor next to the girl. "Hello, Josie," he said.

"What are you going to do with me?" she said in a shaky voice.

"That's what we're trying to figure out. You've heard us talking. You know that we don't want to hurt you, but you can see that we think of you as a danger. We're worried that you'll lead to our getting caught by the police."

"Are you robbing Chrysler?" she asked.

"Well," said Leyva, glancing at Van Eyck, "yes, in a way."

"Look," said Frankel, "I don't care about that. You can let me go."

"How can we be sure, sweetheart?" asked Nominski.

The girl began to cry softly. "What do you want from me?"

Leyva looked at Nominski. "Why don't we bribe her?" he said. "Why don't we give her some money to keep quiet? That will make her an accomplice. She'll have to keep quiet about the rest of us then. She wouldn't be able to explain where she got the money."

"Good idea," said Nominski. She looked at Frankel. "If we gave you a hundred thousand dollars, would you pretend you never saw us?"

"Yes," said Frankel. "Yes, of course."

"A hundred thousand!" said Van Eyck.

Nominski lit a cigarette. "Sure," she said. "We give her the old man's share, then we get rid of him. It's his fault she's here. He brought her."

"Hell," said Leyva, standing, "this isn't getting us anywhere."

Josie Frankel began to sob loudly.

Not long after, Caldwell came in and announced that his visit to Ford had gone off without much of a problem. "Your damn passkey was worthless, though," he said, taking the card out of his pocket. and tossing it at Van Eyck's feet. The young man shrugged his shoulders but said nothing.

"What now?" asked Nominski.

Van Eyck was thoughtful. "For a while it seemed like everything was coming apart at the seams. Really, though, we're right where we're supposed to be. After all, the three sets of disks have been switched. No one knows anything odd is going on yet. They're just as in the dark and vulnerable as they're supposed to be, it's still early Wednesday, and all I have to do now is make a few phone calls. The only hassle is our guest here. Someone will have to stay here with her all the time, of course. But we'll work that out."

"In that case," said Nominski, "I'll leave. I have to get back to work. I'm on a long lunch hour as it is."

"Okay," said Van Eyck, "we'll see you later."

Nominski went out, and Van Eyck took his notebook and sat down by the telephone. "Here we go," he said. He dialed a number and asked for an executive vice president at General Motors. "Hello," he said to the man's secretary, "I'd like to speak to Mr. Bernside, please. No, I'm afraid you can't help me with this. No, I'm sure he'd want to speak to me personally. I'm afraid I can't tell you. Oh. Well, I'm sorry he isn't available. He'd damn well better be available, because this is in the nature of a criminal threat. I think he'd want to hear what I have to say. Thanks, that's a whole lot better." There was a short pause; Van Eyck looked intense. "Hello, Mr. Bernside? You don't know me, but I wanted to warn you that you will be unable to meet your next payroll. Yes, yes, I know that's impossible. Listen, I know what I'm talking about. I'm responsible. No, don't hang up. Let me explain, and then you can check for yourself. Thank you, you won't regret it. Very simply, all the computer information you need to process the paychecks, a job that begins this afternoon and runs all day tomorrow, is gone. We took it. You will have to explain to all your workers that they won't get paid. No, indefinitely. As long as it takes for you to meet our terms. I'm not going to tell you anything more now. Good-bye." Van Eyck hung up the phone and smiled.

"That was simple," said Leyva.

"I told you," said Van Eyck, "the hard part is over."

He dialed the phone again and spoke to an executive at Ford. Then he called Chrysler. He also gave the information to a high-ranking official of the United Auto Workers, who was part of the team negotiating the union's contracts with two of the three manufacturers. Afterward, Van Eyck leaned back in his chair. "I'm hungry," he said.

"Is that what you're doing?" said Josie Frankel. "Wow."

Caldwell looked at her. "It's a shame you weren't around from the beginning."

"That's what I've been thinking," said Van Eyck.

"You're holding up *all three* companies?" asked Frankel.

"Yes," said Caldwell.

"Wow," she said.

"She's impressed," said Caldwell to Van Eyck. "Maybe you can woo her a little and take her along with you."

"It's a thought," said Van Eyck.

"I already have a boyfriend," said Frankel. She sounded regretful.

Van Eyck didn't notice. "That's it for today, boys," he said. "Now let's talk about how we're going to get away with the money. That part is always a little ticklish." None of them said a word about Nominski, and their unspoken suspicion that she had committed the murder at General Motors. They wanted to pretend that everything was going to turn out all right.

Part Three

The Sticker Price

1.

It was like a game of tennis. With his telephone calls, Adrian Van Eyck had served the ball wickedly into the courts of the three major automobile manufacturers. His move was deceptive. He purposefully gave them little information. He wanted the executives to be deeply worried, but unable to do a single practical thing until the following day.

That didn't stop the executives from trying. At General Motors, the man who spoke to Van Eyck was Henry Bernside, a vice president with a great deal of experience in handling such disruptions as strikes and protests. When Van Eyck hung up, Bernside stared at the telephone for a moment. Then he paged through the plant's internal telephone directory and found the number for the Office of the Paymaster. He dialed the number. A woman's voice answered. "This is Henry Bernside," he said. "I'd like to speak to the person in charge of the hourly wage paychecks."

"I'm sorry, sir," said the woman in a strained voice, "but that would be Mr. Salicki, and—"

"Salicki?" said Bernside.

"Yes, sir. The man who was found shot to death this morning."

"Good Lord, this business is serious, then. Well, I've got to talk to someone there."

"I'm afraid I wouldn't know who else you'd want, sir. Mr. Salicki was the—"

"Never mind." He was sure that the murder of Salicki and the warning call from Van Eyck could not be mere coincidence. "I'll come down there myself and look around," he said.

Bernside's counterpart at Ford was Paul Koppe. He had responded to Van Eyck's words by calling in his secretary. "Bobbie," he said, "I've just had a call from a man who claims that he's going to stop our paychecks from going out."

"That would cause a lot of uproar on the line," said the woman.

"Uh huh. Well, there's probably no truth to the thing, but I'd like for you to check on it for me. Find out if everything is going along routinely in the Hourly Employee Record Division. I don't know who's in charge there these days. Look that up and give them a ring. Find out what's what. The guy on the phone said that he has the material necessary for making up the checks. He didn't say anything more. I don't know what he meant by 'material'; I don't know exactly what he has. Or says he has. Either he's telling the truth and we'll have a lot of trouble and headaches, or he's just a nut and we can forget about it. I'd like to know which as soon as possible."

"Yes, sir, Mr. Koppe," said the secretary.

"I don't foresee any problems, though," said Koppe. "Let me know as soon as you have an answer."

The supervisor of the Hourly Pay Office at the Chrysler Hamtramck Assembly Plant was explaining the situation to a company vice president by the name of Keith Bolander. Bolander was a young man who had not worked for Chrysler for very long. Only a few months ago he had been employed by *Rolling Stone* magazine. The payroll supervisor was losing patience with him, because for some reason Bolander couldn't follow what he was saying.

"I'll go through it one more time," said the supervisor. He allowed a little of his exasperation to show in his voice. "The employees come in every morning and punch the clock. They punch out again at night. That gives a record of how many hours and minutes they worked for the week. Once a week, each foreman collects the timecards of the employees under him. He takes the cards and puts the information on one of these sheets, see? There's a line for each employee. Next to the name we have the person's plant ID number, his Social Security number, his job classification code, his pay scale, his withholding tax rate, his other deductions, and all the rest. Understand?"

"I've got it now," said Bolander.

The supervisor nodded; he didn't like the kid at all. "When the hours are all entered on the sheet, the foreman hands it in to his supervisor. The supervisor puts all the sheets from all over his department together, and sends them to the Hourly Pay Office. It takes quite a while for us to transfer all of these figures onto the computer disks. Then the computers figure everything, including all bonuses, overtime, and deductions, and they print out the checks. That takes a while, too. Then the checks are distributed to the employees, and by that time the whole thing is ready to start all over again."

Bolander understood, or at least he thought he did. "So what this fellow did was steal all the timecards."

The supervisor was ready to hit him. "No, for Christ's sake! How the hell could he do that? The timecards are in the hands of a couple of hundred plant foremen all over the factory."

"He stole these sheets?"

"No, damn it, but you're getting warmer. He stole the computerized rosters of our employees, along with the information from the sheets that was on disks."

"So we can't make up checks for this pay period."

The supervisor nodded. "That's right."

Bolander looked puzzled. "Well," he said after a moment, "what can we do about it?"

"Nothing at all. We can't do a damn thing. My office doesn't keep the sheets after that information is transferred to computer disks. We'd have to dig up the old timecards and start from scratch. It would take at least another week."

"Well," said Bolander, "if we can't do anything about it, what the hell am I here worrying about it for? We'll just have to wait until that guy calls us and tells us what he wants."

The supervisor had nothing but contempt for Bolander. "You mean, just pay him what he asks? Give in to a blackmailer?"

"Not necessarily," said Bolander. "The police and the FBI will catch him with the disks. He has to show up somewhere to pick up the money."

"What if he doesn't call again?" asked the supervisor.

"That's not likely. Why would he go to all the trouble of stealing our disks, if he doesn't want us to pay to get them back?"

"He may just want to cause trouble. He may have a grievance with Chrysler, a former employee or an unhappy customer. Or he may be working for the union, trying to cause a disturbance among the workers."

Bolander had never considered these possibilities. At first he'd thought the problem was a minor computer foul-up, the kind of snag that happened all the time. Now it was shaping up to be much more than that, and he didn't like it. It looked like it was definitely going to interfere with his plans for the weekend. He didn't like it at all.

Jerome Spillman was a tall, thin, very intelligent man. He was a legal counsel for the United Auto Workers. Van Eyck had called him with the warning; Spillman seemed to be the one person who might see at once what a payroll default could mean during the delicate period of contract negotiations. Spillman was the right man, after all. He did understand the intricate problems and threats involved. He was deeply worried, though. Van Eyck probably didn't foresee how violent the workers' reaction could be. Spillman sat in his office, his head aching. He had a bad cold, but he couldn't afford the time to pay attention to it. He called in his assistant, a younger man named Clifford Schutt, and quickly outlined the situation.

"I don't understand," said Schutt. "If management wanted to pressure our members by withholding paychecks—"

"Which is an absolutely stupid thing to do," said Spillman.

"Of course. But they might claim something like a computer breakdown. That would sound plausible, at least. There'd be a lot of griping, sure, but no permanent damage. That might work for one employer; but how can all three companies expect us to believe that they all suffered the same kind of accident at the same time?"

"Arrogance," said Spillman. "Maybe they think they can act tough."

"The industry would shut down in half an hour. And the men and women on the line won't soon forget management's attitude."

Spillman massaged his forehead. "It doesn't sound right to me. They're not that foolish. We've got to think it through again from the beginning. The UAW contracts come up for renewal this year, and the target company is Ford. GM is mentioned, too, because of certain grievances."

"No monetary problems with GM," said Schutt. "They mostly concern working conditions."

"Uh huh. But Ford is the chief target for a strike. So they would be the logical place to search for whoever is originating this ugly scheme."

"Maybe it's retaliation," said Schutt.

"Retaliation? For what?"

"For the shooting. Didn't you hear about the murder?"

Spillman straightened in his chair. "No," he said, his face going pale.

"Some middle-management guy at General Motors was

killed today. Shot down, right at the plant. He worked in their payroll department."

"There has to be a connection," said Spillman, "but the idea of retaliation is ridiculous. That's not the way businesses operate. What are we dealing with now, terrorist groups among the employees?"

"I don't know," said Schutt.

"That's the whole trouble," said Spillman, "I don't either. And I don't know what to advise the membership."

2.

At seven o'clock Wednesday evening, Andi Nominski got out of her car and went into the apartment building on Woodward Avenue where Van Eyck had rented the room. She tried to move as quietly as possible. She took out her key, slipped it slowly into the lock, turned it, and opened the door. She surprised Van Eyck and Josie Frankel, who had taken off most of their clothing and were embracing uncomfortably on the cold, hard floor. "How about that," said Nominski, stepping into the room, "just as I expected. I thought I'd drop by early enough so that I wouldn't catch you too far gone. It looks like I made it just in time."

Van Eyck was not at all pleased to see her. "I was calming her, Andi. I was telling her that we wouldn't hurt her."

"Did you tell her that you'd still respect her in the morning, too?"

"What business is it of yours?" Van Eyck demanded.

"What are you doing?" asked Nominski, laughing harshly. "Playing Patty Hearst and the SLA?" She looked at Frankel. "They have a name for what you are," she said. "You're a gun moll. You're Adrian's gun moll. I think that's funny."

"They have words for what you are, too," said Frankel.

Nominski's face hardened, but she didn't reply. Instead, she turned back to Van Eyck. "Adrian," she said, "I'd like to talk to you about something that occurred to me this evening. How are we going to divide up the money?"

"You know that already, Andi. I take a hundred fifty, you and Caldwell and Leyva get a hundred each."

"So you say. But how are we going to collect the money?"

Van Eyck didn't get her point. "Me and Caldwell and Leyva will take care of that in the morning. Each of us takes care of one company."

Nominski was getting impatient. "Look, I guess I have to draw you a picture. What do *I* do tomorrow?"

"You go to work. You come back here afterward, and you get your money and go home."

Nominski sighed. "Let me make it a bit clearer, stupid. Tomorrow, your share will be a hundred and fifty thousand, right? How much are each of you taking in ransom?"

Van Eyck chewed his lip. "A hundred and fifty, if all goes well."

"Okay," said Nominski. "What's to prevent you from splitting right from the scene of the crime? Why would you need to come back here at all?"

"Because I have to," he said lamely.

"No, you don't. There isn't a reason in the world why you'd need to come back. What are Caldwell's and Leyva's shares?"

Van Eyck was beginning to understand. "A hundred each, of course," he said.

"And how much are they picking up tomorrow?"

"A hundred and fifty each. But you don't think—"

"Adrian," snarled Nominski, "why on earth would either of them come back here, just to give me my money? Why wouldn't they just run away with the extra fifty grand? They have new identities. There's no way at all that you can guarantee that I'll get my share tomorrow."

"Andi, be reasonable. Caldwell has a wife and kids, he's not going to run out on them. You know that. I can't say the same thing about Arthur, although he has a sister to take care of."

"You better give them the word, then," said Nominski. Her face was hard and vicious. "One way or another, I'm going to get my cut, if I have to hunt down all three of you bastards to get it."

"Good night, Andi," said Van Eyck. "Don't slam the door on your way out."

Nominski gave one short laugh and then turned and walked out of the room. Josie Frankel was crying on Van Eyck's shoulder. Van Eyck was lost in thought.

3.

Caldwell was reading in bed. He wasn't paying much attention to the book, because his thoughts were on what he'd have to do in the morning. Taking care of the disks at the Ford plant had been a challenge, an anxious nightmare. In the morning, though, he'd have another assignment. He had to waylay a Chrysler executive and persuade the man to give him one hundred and fifty thousand dollars. He would have no weapon, no other means of persuasion than his own limited talent for salesmanship. By morning, the targeted executive would know all about the missing computer disks. If for some reason he didn't, if the Chrysler management had clamped a tight lid on the situation, the whole scheme would collapse. Then Caldwell would have to beat a very fast and very empty-handed retreat. It would all have been for nothing.

The television was on in the bedroom, too, because Marianne wanted to listen to the news. Caldwell didn't pay attention to it until the news anchor came to the story of Salicki's murder. Caldwell listened closely.

The police said that they had no clues and no leads in the matter, but they speculated that the killing might somehow be connected with the on-going union contract talks. The anchorman mentioned that Salicki had been a supervisor in the Cadillac plant's payroll division. There was no longer any doubt in Caldwell's mind: He was certain that Nominski had murdered the man. Caldwell would face many uncertainties the next day; most of all, he would have to be on his guard against Andi Nominski. She was more dangerous than anything else.

4.

Thursday morning. Van Eyck and Leyva left the Woodward Avenue apartment in their rented cars. Andi Nominski telephoned to say that she would be there before five-thirty that evening, and that her share of the money had better be waiting for her. David Caldwell was left to guard Josie Frankel in the apartment until either Leyva or Van Eyck returned. Everyone was in motion. There was no more time for fear.

Thursday morning was dark and overcast, with the threat of a new snowstorm pushing in from Canada through Michigan's upper peninsula. The temperature when Arthur Leyva left the apartment was eighteen degrees Fahrenheit. With the windchill factor, Leyva thought he was going to die. In a rented Ford Escort he headed south and east, toward the luxurious homes of the affluent Grosse Pointe suburbs. He had a name and address on a slip of paper: Henry Bernside, 212 Harvard Circle, Grosse Pointe Woods. Mr. Bernside, a General Motors executive, lived well. Today, Leyva would see how well Bernside earned his salary.

It was eight o'clock when Leyva found Bernside's house. It was large. There were bigger houses, of course, more ostentatious estates, but then Bernside wasn't a top-level executive. His home was showy enough for Leyva's taste, though. Behind the house and to one side was a separate garage; its doors were raised, revealing a long, late-sixties model white Cadillac convertible in excellent condition. There were two other cars in the driveway, a Cadillac limousine and a black Corvette Stingray. Leyva wondered how many people lived in the house. Evidently, they didn't have to worry too much about getting around.

Leyva sat in his car across the street from Bernside's home, waiting. A box of Jordan almonds was on the front seat next to him. He had the engine running, the heater on, one window cracked a little for air. The radio was tuned to an FM station playing Smetana's *The Moldau*, one of Leyva's least favorite pieces of music. Still, it was better than what the other stations were offering. He tapped his fingers on the steering wheel and watched Bernside's house. A light was on in one of the upstairs windows. As he watched, the light went off. Leyva suspected that it wouldn't be long before Henry Bernside, all unaware, left his house to go to work.

An hour earlier, at seven o'clock, a light brown Toyota had pulled up to the curb a block from Arthur Leyva's house. The Toyota's parking lights were on, and its radio and heater. Behind the steering wheel was Andi Nominski. She had a few ideas of her own for the day, things she had decided not to discuss with Adrian van Eyck. She was feeling good, because she knew that by the day's end she would be at least a hundred thousand dollars richer. That would be the absolute minimum, in the event that everything she had planned failed. If all went according to schedule—she didn't realistically expect to win all down the line—if everything fell into place, she'd leave Detroit that evening with seven hundred and fifty thousand dollars. Three-quarters of a million in cash. With her false identification, she would begin a leisurely drive toward Chicago. From there she'd fly to Atlanta, where she would rent an apartment and apply for a passport. From there . . .

Nominski saw Arthur Leyva leaving his house, jumping down the bottom two steps, which were covered with snow and ice. She was waiting for him there because she wanted to make certain that he went to the apartment on Woodward and changed cars. He had screwed that up once, already. His car pulled away from the curb, and she followed. She let him get four or five cars ahead in traffic so that he wouldn't notice her. She saw that he was, indeed, driving toward Van Eyck's Highland Park headquarters, so she relaxed. She drove by the apartment building while Leyva was parking his car. She went around the block and stopped on the other side of the street, letting her engine run. He wouldn't waste much time here, just a moment to run inside and check with Van Eyck, then out again and into the rented car.

A few minutes later she saw him get into the second automobile. She pulled out of her space and headed up the street, thinking that she could take it easy and let Leyva pass her. Then she would follow him more closely. She was surprised when Leyva turned his car around and drove off in the opposite direction. Nominski wondered what he was doing. She made a left turn across two lanes of traffic, pulled into a driveway, backed out, and sped down Woodward after him. Maybe the old man was up to something crazy himself, but Nominski couldn't imagine what. He didn't have the money yet. It didn't make much sense to her. Nevertheless, with one hand she reached into her handbag and took out her .38 and put it on the seat next to her, covering it with her bag. She looked at herself in the mirror and smiled. "Calamity Jane" Nominski was ready for anything.

Henry Bernside was very tired; he hadn't gotten very much sleep. He'd met with other General Motors executives until nine o'clock the previous night. After that they had to deal with outraged union officials, who had been tipped off to the situation by some unknown informant. They learned from the UAW committee that the same thing had happened at Ford and Chrysler. The GM men were astonished by the news; the information changed the entire picture. Everything the General

Motors executives had decided during their long meeting went out the window. They had drawn up a list of possible explanations for the missing disks, with appropriate responses. Of the six scenarios, only two were now still plausible: one, that some lunatic individual or terrorist organization was responsible, for criminal or political reasons; and two, that the whole thing was a tactic of the union leadership, despite their protestations of innocence. Bernside had not gotten home until after one o'clock in the morning; even then nothing had been settled, no new facts had appeared, and no one had anything better to suggest than to call in the authorities and "wait and see." The union committee threatened that unless all paychecks were distributed on schedule, a full-scale strike would be called, not just against Ford, but against all three major car manufacturers. The implications of such a gigantic walkout were terrible to imagine. Bernside had spent most of the night tossing restlessly in bed and swallowing Valium on the hour.

He was about to get into his car when he noticed that there was someone standing in his driveway. He looked at the man for a moment. The stranger was moderately well-dressed, but clearly not a Grosse Pointe resident. He was waiting beside the pile of snow left by the last snowplow. It was too cold and too early for him to be idly strolling through well-to-do Grosse Pointe Woods. "Are you looking for something?" asked Bernside. Leyva seemed like a respectable older man; it never occurred to Bernside to connect him to the missing computer disks.

"Would you mind if I asked you a question?" said Leyva, moving closer to the executive.

"Not at all," said Bernside.

When they were only a few feet apart, Leyva took his hand out of his overcoat pocket. He held his pistol pointing toward Bernside's chest. "Please," he said, "I'd like for you to come with me. My car is parked just over there."

"What is this?" said Bernside angrily.

"Don't be foolish," said Leyva. "I'm standing here in your

driveway with a gun, and you have to ask me what this is. Didn't you get a phone call yesterday? Didn't someone tell you about your computer disks, and your paychecks?"

"My God," said Bernside, his voice barely above a whisper. "You're the maniac who killed that man Salicki."

Leyva's eyes widened. His hand faltered and the pistol's barrel dropped. "No," he said, "not me. It wasn't me. I didn't have anything to do with that. I've never hurt anybody."

Bernside smiled cynically. "But you're prepared to hurt me. Is that right?"

Leyva looked at the pistol in his hand. "Yes," he said.

"Then if you're not the man who murdered Salicki, you're just as bad. Do you plan to murder me when you're done?"

"No," said Leyva, "I promise you that."

"Your promises don't mean anything to me," said Bernside. "They might be true, but on the other hand you may have said the same thing yesterday to Salicki. I still think you might have killed him."

"Forget that," said Leyva angrily. "I have the gun, I'll do the talking. Now, open the door of my car and slide across the seat. Get behind the wheel."

"You want me to drive?"

"Yes," said Leyva impatiently. "One of us drives, the other holds the gun. And it's my choice."

"All right," said Bernside, acting braver than he felt. "Okay, so far." He got behind the wheel and started the car. "Where to?" he asked.

"Let's just go to your office," said Leyva.

Bernside looked at him sideways, his eyebrows raised. "You realize you'll be outnumbered there. We have lots of armed guards. And the police and the FBI have been called in, too."

"Yes, I know," said Leyva, "but I have you."

Bernside nodded and put the car into gear. They drove away from the snowdrift-covered curb. A moment later, Nominski's Toyota followed.

5.

In the suburb of Birmingham, in a rather nice neighborhood, one not so nice as Grosse Pointe but nicer by far than where the assembly-line workers lived, Adrian van Eyck was waiting for Paul Koppe, the Ford executive. Koppe's home was modest compared with Bernside's, because there was a rigid protocol built into the automobile industry. It governed even the spending of one's own money. Koppe was entitled by his position to have a house exactly like the one he owned; had he overextended himself and moved into a grander house, like those of his superiors, he might have jeopardized his future in the company. This wasn't an official policy, but it was a kind of unwritten law of jealousy and status among the lower executives. Koppe was not interested in hurting his future, and to tell the truth he was not interested in having a fancier house. That would come later, when he was promoted. It had taken Koppe ten years to unravel all the crazy knots of proper conduct in the industry, but he was fairly sure he understood it now.

The man in the driveway changed his mind about that. "Hello," said Koppe. "Cold, huh?"

"Cold as a well-digger's belt buckle," said Van Eyck.

"Ha," said Koppe. He stood in the drive, slowly breathing out clouds of white mist, waiting.

Van Eyck waited, too. He wanted Koppe to ask him what he wanted. Koppe didn't look like he was going to cooperate. At last, Van Eyck took the initiative. "I'm here to sell you something," he said.

"Oh," said Koppe, evidently disappointed. "You have a lot of ambition, getting out this early in the morning in weather like this."

"It's the only way to get ahead," said Van Eyck. "I'm sure you've learned that yourself. Now, what I have to sell you is something you'll really like to have back. I mean, they're yours to begin with, but you're going to have to pay to get them back."

"Ah," said Koppe, his face brightening, "the disks."

"That's right. I'm so glad you understand."

"Sure," said Koppe. "I'm not surprised you came here. The plant is swarming with cops and feds. Would you like to come inside to talk? It's a lot warmer in there."

"Thank you," said Van Eyck. "Is your family awake? I'd rather not have them involved."

Koppe frowned. "You didn't murder that man at the Cadillac plant yesterday, did you?"

"No, no way," said Van Eyck. "I don't even have a gun. I figured I wouldn't need one. You people really have to get those disks back."

"I'm glad to hear that. I thought from the beginning that the shooting was probably unrelated to the theft, but you know the police. They like to wrap things up all tidy. If you happen to get caught, you'll probably be charged with the murder somehow. I can't imagine how they'll tie it together. I'm just warning you to be careful. Come on inside."

"Thanks," said Van Eyck.

"By the way, who's behind all this? The union? Some political group?"

"Freelance," said Van Eyck. "Rob from the rich. That's all."

"That makes me feel better already," said Koppe. "I didn't want to get involved with some oddball cause."

"Don't worry," said Van Eyck, wiping his feet carefully before going into Koppe's house, "we don't believe in a goddamn thing."

Bernside drove the rented Escort while Leyva sat as far away from him as possible, pointing the gun at Bernside. The GM vice president glanced sideways and said, "You realize that when my wife notices that my car is still in the driveway, she'll wonder about it. She'll call my office."

"You're right," said Leyva. "When we get to your office, we'll have you call home with an explanation."

"What explanation?"

"You think of one."

Bernside looked again at Leyva. "You're from the union, aren't you? I'll bet you don't even belong to the union. They wouldn't be foolish enough to use their own members. They hired you, didn't they? To pull this job? And to kill Salicki, for some reason?"

"No," said Leyva.

"How did you get by our security? That's what I'm crazy to find out. We have the best in the country."

"I didn't get by your security," said Leyva. "I got by Chrysler's."

"Oh, you're working with others. And you took care of Chrysler. How did you get their disks out? Where are they now?"

Leyva grunted. "I can't tell you anything now. You know better than that. Besides, *I* have the gun. I do the talking, and you do the answering."

"I'm sorry," said Bernside with venom in his voice, "I keep forgetting."

"Never mind. Just drive."

"I hate you union bastards, you know that? You think—I

mean—your bosses think that all we do is sit around thinking up ways to screw our workers. Do you have any idea how much we've done to improve their lives? Do you have any notion of what it costs us? Yet every time the contracts expire, the union demands such an outrageous increase in wages that our whole profit picture goes right into the wastebasket, along with the economic index of the whole damn country."

"I don't represent the unions," said Leyva.

"Say, how *did* you get into Chrysler?"

Leyva gave a brief smile. "Charm," he said.

6.

"Well," said David Caldwell, "this is the first time we've been alone."

Josie Frankel looked at him suspiciously. "What do you mean by that?" she asked.

"Did that sound bad? I'm sorry, I didn't mean it that way. I was just trying to make conversation. Do you go to school?"

She shook her head. "I work. I work for the Chrysler Corporation, in public relations. You remember; that's why I'm here."

Caldwell was embarrassed. "Yes," he said, "but I thought you might, you know, go to school part-time or at night or something."

"No," said Frankel, "no, I don't."

There was an awkward silence. It went on longer than Caldwell could bear. "Did you have a good night with Adrian?" he said at last. He knew too late that it was a grotesque thing to say, under the circumstances.

She looked at him like he was a little light-headed. "Yes, thank you. He made me very . . . comfortable."

"Good, good."

There was another lapse.

"You don't seem like desperate criminals, most of you," said Frankel.

"We aren't, most of us," said Caldwell. "Look at me. I'm not desperate, and I don't think of myself as a criminal, really. I haven't done anything to hurt anyone, you know."

Frankel flushed. "That's just what you're telling yourself. You think this is a victimless crime. Adrian told me that unless your terms are met, hundreds of thousands of workers won't get paid next week. You might start a huge strike. You think that won't hurt those families?"

"The companies will agree to our terms. They'll get their disks back. Everyone will get his check."

"You're not desperate, and Adrian isn't desperate, and that older man isn't desperate. But *I'm* desperate. I don't want to be here, even though Adrian is kind of a nice boy. And that awful Andi woman, she's desperate."

Caldwell looked grave. "Yes," he said, "you sort of have to watch out for her."

"Will you let me go when you're done? When you get the money?"

"Yes," said Caldwell. "You can trust Adrian."

"Why are you doing this? Are you just after the money? You don't seem like the typical outlaw type."

"I teach college English," said Caldwell wistfully. "My first class of the spring term is this morning. I'm just not going to show up today. That will get me in a lot of trouble. What I really want is to leave you here all alone, go downstairs to my car and get in it and drive to the campus. I want to get my notes in order and face a classroom of sleepy sophomores. I don't want anything more to do with this business. I wish I hadn't drifted along into it. I want to get out, but it's too late. As nice as Adrian is, he can be very hard about some things. I don't think he or Andi or even Arthur would stand for me running out on them now. There's nothing left but to go through with it. It started so easily, and I let myself get caught up in it. Now there's no way out. However it ends, I have to see it through all the way."

"You'll go to jail, you know," said Frankel. "I'm sorry, but that's what's going to happen."

Caldwell felt an intense sadness. He covered his eyes with one hand. "I know," he whispered. He wondered if it was too late to make a deal with the authorities. He could call up the police and say—what? What could he say? He had two choices: He could say that he knew the identities of the thieves, and the location of the disks, and that he'd spill it all in exchange for immunity. Then he would warn Adrian, so they could escape under their alternate identities. That wouldn't work, though; Nominski would throttle him. Well, he could avoid mentioning the others. He'd just promise the police that he wouldn't go through with his ransom collection, that if they forgave what he did at the Ford plant he'd be a good boy from now on. And Nominski would still chop him up.

He needed protection. He saw himself making a deal, something that would protect both himself and his family. He would meet a crusading D.A. (Humphrey Bogart again, a good guy this time in *The Enforcer*) on a fog-shrouded pier, late at night. The District Attorney wouldn't want to make a deal, of course, because the good guys held all the cards. Turning himself in was Caldwell's only hope, if he wanted to avoid the vengeance of his gang. It wouldn't end happily. The D.A. always won, the poor worried stoolie always ended up in the Jersey marshes. There was no way out, whether he followed his conscience or Van Eyck's plan.

"What are you thinking?" asked Frankel.

"I was having a daydream," said Caldwell. Suddenly he looked a little more cheerful. "I wish I were Jimmy Cagney. It would make me feel really good to push half of a grapefruit in Andi Nominski's face."

"She'd cut your heart out," said the girl.

Caldwell knew she was right.

7.

Leyva stared out at the bleak city. It was a landscape arranged in black, white, and dirty gray, with dashes and slashes of color in the most unexpected places: bright orange flame burning like pennants atop crackling towers; pulsing red lights on the wings of landing aircraft; distant, unreadable neon signs blinking green, flashing blue. Leyva watched it all go by, unaware that his hand had grown tired and the pistol was now resting on the seat between the two men. After a while, Leyva realized something. "You're not heading toward the Cadillac plant," he said accusingly.

"That's right," said Henry Bernside. He didn't seem very concerned.

"Why not?"

"I'm trying to think of a way to get that gun away from you."

Leyva remembered the weapon and raised it once more. Bernside laughed. "Stop screwing around," said Leyva. "Let's just get there already. You're asking for trouble."

"Am I?" said Bernside.

"If I say so," said Leyva. "I mean, I have the gun."

"You have the gun; but I have this automobile traveling at fifty-five miles an hour. While we're on the freeway, it's a standoff. You can't do anything to me, and I can't get the gun away from you. At least, I don't think I can."

"That's right," said Leyva, "you can't."

"Well," said Bernside, "before I die, I'd like to know a few things. What does the union think it's going to get out of this? Public support? It won't be long before the papers find out that this whole thing was a union-instigated plot. It will hurt the union worse than anything in its history. You don't know about that, you're just a paid goon. But this is going to be some scandal."

"I'm not connected with the union. I've told you that before. We're just a gang of get-rich-quick fortune hunters."

"Sure you are. You couldn't have gotten into the protected data libraries of the Big Three without a lot of help from the inside. There are going to be a lot of people losing their jobs over this. You don't know what you're starting. You could damage the economy of the whole United States. I'm talking about something so bad that it'll make an ordinary recession look like burnt toast."

Leyva decided to stop arguing with Bernside. He just put the gun against the man's temple. "Shut up," he said. "Just get us to the factory. Right now."

"Why don't you just tell me where the disks are?"

"I will. For one hundred and fifty thousand dollars."

"Ha! A hundred and fifty thousand! I'm supposed to pull that out of my desk drawer?"

"I don't care where it comes from," said Leyva. "It's the only way you'll ever get those paychecks made up."

"Do you know how little I care about those goddamn checks? If we have to, we'll tell everybody that they'll get double wages on the next check."

"An awful lot of workers are going to be upset. They'll end up cheated, and they'll know it."

Bernside turned to look at Leyva. His expression was placid. "They and you," he said, "can go fuck off." He made a lunge for Leyva's wrist. The gun went off, deafening both men in the close quarters of the front seat. The car swerved hard to the right, into a black stone wall that bordered the freeway. There was a hideous scream of bending steel.

"Watch it!" shouted Arthur Leyva.

Bernside pulled the wheel to the left, and the car skewed back across the lane and into the next lane, where the driver's side was struck by another car. Another car ran into the back of the Escort, and both automobiles spun perpendicular to the flow of traffic. Bernside tried to turn their car around. There was another tremendous jolting crash, and the gun in Leyva's hand went off. Bernside slumped forward. The car lurched ahead, back across the right lane toward the wall. "My God," was all Leyva could whisper before the car crashed into the barrier. Leyva's head smacked onto the edge of the dashboard only an instant before the car was struck one final time by a green pickup truck. The Escort careened back toward the center lane; it rocked over and came to rest on its side, wheels spinning, one door thrown open. Leyva had been flung clear of the wreck and sprawled broken and lifeless on the highway, amid a sparkling litter of shattered glass.

Some distance behind the collisions, Andi Nominski watched with little emotion. She felt only disappointment. The total take would be a hundred and fifty thousand short, now. One of the wrecked cars had begun to burn; she watched as flames and smoke obscured the road ahead. She waited calmly, knowing that it would take a while before the police could clear the freeway. She lit a cigarette and listened to the radio. As she heard the first sirens approaching, she thought to hide her own pistol under the front seat.

8.

Less than an hour later, about half past nine, Nominski was in a small luncheonette on Woodward Avenue not far from Van Eyck's hideout. She swallowed the last of her coffee, picked up her check and paid it, then went to the pay phone in the back of the diner. She looked in the telephone book for the number she needed, dropped the coins, and punched the buttons. The phone rang eight times before it was answered.

"Hello?" said a woman's voice.

"Hello. Is this Marianne Caldwell? Mrs. David Caldwell?"

"Yes, it is. Who's calling, please?"

Nominski smiled. "My name isn't important, Mrs. Caldwell. I'm just a friend, a concerned friend. Your husband is in trouble, Mrs. Caldwell."

Marianne's voice got louder and higher in pitch. "Who *is* this? What are you talking about?"

Nominski was enjoying the conversation. She wanted to draw it out a little longer, to make Caldwell's wife stew a little more. "Oh, don't worry, dear," she said. "He isn't hurt. At least, not yet."

"Will you please tell me what's going on?"

"It's always difficult to break this kind of news. Your husband is right now in a shabby apartment on Woodward Avenue, alone with a nineteen-year-old girl named Josie Frankel."

"I don't believe it. My husband has class today. He'd never miss his class."

"Why would I lie to you, Mrs. Caldwell? But relax, he isn't—well, he *hasn't* been having an affair with this Josie person. Of course, they've been alone there for some time this morning, and who knows what might have happened between them? You can never tell about men. That isn't what you ought to be concerned about, though. The plain truth of the matter is that your poor husband has been shanghaied into some insane, crooked scheme. Three people have been killed already. Your husband hasn't had anything to do with that, but he's already done enough to be sent to prison."

Marianne's voice was steady. "I don't believe any of this."

"His student, Adrian van Eyck, is the leader. They're blackmailing the three automobile manufacturers. They've stolen valuable computer disks so that none of the auto workers in Detroit will receive their next paychecks. That will touch off a vicious strike and cause violence and bloodshed all across the country."

"You're crazy."

"I expected you to say that. Do you know Arthur Leyva?"

"Of course. He's in David's department."

"He's dead. He killed an executive of one of the corporations less than an hour ago. Your husband is going to meet with some other executive himself in a little while."

Marianne laughed. "Arthur? *Killed* someone? Now I'm sure you're crazy. I'm going to report this call to the police."

"I wouldn't do that, honey. It would put a noose right around your dear David's neck. Think for a moment: Doesn't this explain where he's been, this last couple of weeks? You never really believed his excuses, did you? You see, I know more about you and your David than you could ever imagine." Nominski laughed.

"Where is he now?"

"Not yet, sweetheart. I want to make a deal."

"What kind of a deal?"

Nominski tried to make her voice sound reasonable and persuasive. "You want your husband to be safe. I'm only interested in money. You don't care about the money, do you?"

"No! For God's sake, no!"

"Fine. Here's my idea; it will work out nicely for both of us, I think. Your husband is supposed to visit Chrysler this afternoon. Now if you show up at the apartment on Woodward and tell him you know everything, he won't go. Just tell him I'll go in his place. He'll accept that. He'll welcome it, as a matter of fact; he doesn't really want to do it. He's looking for an excuse to get out of it. He's a good man, your David. So you and he can go home, Adrian can keep the money from Ford, and I can keep the money from Chrysler. We'll all get away happy."

Marianne thought for a minute. "Are you sure everything will be that simple?"

"Yes," said Nominski, "we can't be traced. Trust me."

There was another moment of silence. "All right. Who are you, and where is David?"

Nominski gave her the address of the apartment. "Just say that Andi called you and offered to trade."

"I still don't believe any of this, but if it's true, thank you for getting my husband out of trouble."

"Thank *you*, honey. I'll send you a postcard from St. Tropez." Nominski hung up the telephone and shook her head. It never ceased to astonish her how easily most people can be manipulated.

9.

Representatives of the Big Three had agreed to keep the news of the missing disks secret until they could find out who had taken them, and what it would cost to get them back. But the union leaders knew, and rumors began to spread among the workers. The personnel in the three payroll offices were aware that their routines had been suspended. When it came time to print out the paychecks, computer technicians learned the disks were gone. The corporation executives had to say something soon, but there was nothing they could say that wouldn't make them look very, very bad. It was unlikely that their employees and the public would believe that the disks had vanished without a trace, from the midst of the three payroll-department staffs, and under the watchful gaze of the strictest industrial security system in the country.

At General Motors a meeting had been scheduled for nine A.M. It had been put off indefinitely pending the arrival of Henry Bernside, the man with the ultimate responsibility in the matter. The other executives waited nervously in the meeting room.

At the Ford plant, Paul Koppe had not come to work yet, either. His secretary had been answering frantic calls from other department chiefs, telling them that as soon as Koppe arrived he would brief them all. She assured everyone that the problem was not desperate, that if the worst came to the worst, Mr. Koppe said the payroll staff would work through the night to make up for the lost time.

At Chrysler, Keith Bolander didn't have the faintest idea of what to do. He was terrified. He was still new at his job, and he hadn't been prepared to handle a crisis more severe than petty pilferage of company property. As soon as he got to the assembly plant, he went straight to the office of the General Services Supervisor, a man by the name of Norman Sutton. Sutton's title didn't have any real definition, which meant that he often got stuck with all the worst foul-ups that occurred in the plant. When he saw Bolander's face, he knew he was going to inherit another.

"Mr. Sutton?" said Bolander. "I have a problem."

Sutton only nodded wearily.

Bolander's knees felt weak. He sat down gratefully by Sutton's desk and explained the situation. Sutton was stunned. He wondered what Bolander expected of him. He knew as little as Bolander, and he had never faced anything of this complexity, either. "Sorry," he said.

Bolander looked like he might break down. "But you *have* to help me," he pleaded.

"Where does it say that?" said Sutton angrily.

Bolander couldn't reply.

"Do you think the union is behind this? Or some sneaky gang of geniuses? What are they going to want? Money? It makes a difference. If all they want is money, it will be a cinch. We catch them at the point of transfer. There's no way they can avoid it. Sooner or later they have to pick up the money, and then the cops will collar them. If it's the union, brother, I don't want any part of it."

"Listen," said Bolander, "if it's just a matter of, like you say, money, some thieves holding us up, I'd be grateful if you handled it. If I screwed the thing up, I'd lose my job and I'd never get another one. You could manage it, though. But if it's the union, then it's over my head and yours, too, and we'll have to pass it on upstairs."

Sutton thought for a moment. "This is a tremendous thing you're asking of me."

"I'll pay you back, somehow."

"How?" asked Sutton.

Bolander was taken aback. "I . . . I don't know."

"We'll think of something," said Sutton.

"Then you're going to help me?"

Sutton nodded. Bolander silently gave thanks for getting out from under the problem.

Of course, by this time the Detroit police and the FBI were swarming around the data-processing departments of all three corporations, doing their investigative things, dusting and questioning and photographing, but they were coming up with nothing. After several hours of inspection on Wednesday night, they settled down in the offices they had commandeered. They drank coffee, installed telephone lines, established command centers, talked about the Detroit Pistons, waited for the perpetrators to contact their victims, napped on tables, got in the way of the regular employees, and tried to analyze the situation.

The union leadership was taking more positive steps. In a meeting room in one of the union halls, Jerome Spillman was nervously chewing on a pencil. He looked at his watch; it was a little after ten A.M. He picked up his telephone and dialed the number of Henry Bernside at General Motors. He was told that Bernside had not yet arrived. That was difficult to understand; Spillman wondered idly if Bernside were somehow involved with the theft of the disks. That idea was sheer nonsense. Spillman called Paul Koppe at Ford. Koppe's secretary said that he, too, hadn't yet gotten to work. There was no sensible explanation, to Spillman's way of thinking. He called Keith Bolander at Chrysler. At least he was there, but he told Spillman that the matter was now being handled by Norman

Sutton. Bolander had the call transferred to Sutton's number.

"Sutton? This is Jerome Spillman. I don't think we've ever met. I'm a legal advisor to the UAW, and I'm deeply concerned about this paycheck situation. Have you heard anything more about it? What's going on over there?"

Sutton was displeased that Bolander hadn't told him that the union already knew all the details. It would make his job a great deal more difficult. He had made tentative plans to stifle any reaction from the workers; he had notions of blaming it all on "human error" or something like that. Bolander had misled him, had left out certain important points. Now Sutton was beginning to see just what a dangerous trap he had walked into. "I don't know what's going on," he said. "That's the truth. There are so many cops and detectives that I can't get to my own desk without showing my identification twelve times."

"Good," said Spillman. "I want to tell you one thing: I don't trust you as far as I can throw you. There is one almighty big fishy smell emanating from your factory. If anything at all out of the ordinary happens—and that includes the failure to distribute paychecks on schedule, even with a damn good reason—we're going to nail your hide to the barn door. Why aren't Koppe and Bernside in their offices this morning?"

"Koppe and Bernside?" asked Sutton, genuinely puzzled. "Who are they?"

"You really keep on top of things, don't you, Sutton? You're really keeping the lines of communication open."

"Right. Talk to you later." Sutton angrily slammed the phone down. He'd take this all up with Bolander later. When he was finished with Bolander, the kid wouldn't be able to get a job selling ices from a pushcart.

10.

At ten o'clock, Paul Koppe and Adrian van Eyck were having breakfast in a quiet restaurant near the River Rouge plant. It wasn't a first-class restaurant because it wasn't a first-class neighborhood, but it was clean and the food was good. The two men were talking over various areas of mutual interest, and they found that they got along rather well together. Van Eyck did not seem at all homicidal; Koppe knew that might be an illusion, that Van Eyck might actually be the man who shot the General Motors employee. Koppe preferred not to believe that, at least partly because Koppe was Van Eyck's prisoner until their business transaction was completed.

That was what they were negotiating in the restaurant: a simple business transaction that would see the computer disks returned to the Ford Motor Company, and a certain, as yet unagreed-on, sum to be paid to Van Eyck.

"What do you think is a fair price?" asked Koppe.

"I'll tell you," said Van Eyck, "I didn't expect to get into haggling over this. I expected to present a figure and have it accepted or rejected. Take it or leave it. Then I would get the money, or you would get a lot of grief. I have a clear idea of what will happen when those paychecks don't go out. We let the union in on it for just that reason. You won't be able to duck the issue, and you won't be able to come up with a satisfactory cover story. It might take you two weeks of labor to figure up new paychecks from scratch, and it would cost you hundreds of thousands of dollars. Not to mention the fact that your assembly lines would be shut down."

"That's enough," said Koppe. "All right, I don't deny any of that. We stand to lose millions. How much do you want?"

"A quarter of a million dollars," said Van Eyck quietly.

"Ha!" Koppe cried. "From all of us together, or just from Ford?"

"From each of you."

"You'll never get it."

"I know," said Van Eyck. "That's why I'm only going to ask for a hundred fifty thousand. Look, Paul, we're not a gigantic crusher of a heist. We're a small sting. A hundred fifty grand. Your insurance will cover that. You can earn that much back in a few hours. But it would almost be corporate suicide to turn me down."

Koppe laughed. "You never had any intention of sticking me for two-fifty, did you? Well, anyway, one-fifty sounds like it's getting into the right ballpark. Could I whittle you down to an even hundred thousand?"

"No," said Van Eyck. "We're on a tight budget."

"I see," said Koppe. He swallowed some of the warm coffee in his cup. "All right, then. We'll see what we can do. How soon after we pay up do you return the disks?"

"Half an hour, at the most."

Koppe raised an eyebrow. "And you don't think you'll be in danger?"

"None at all," said Van Eyck.

"It's your funeral," said Koppe.

Andi Nominski had another phone call to make before she went to the apartment on Woodward. It was a call she had to make in private. She dropped more coins into the pay phone and dialed the number of the General Motors Cadillac plant. "Hello," she said when a switchboard operator answered, "I'd like to speak to whoever is in charge of the payroll department."

"Just a moment," said the operator.

"Yes?" said a man's voice. Nominski was surprised. This was her own department, and she expected that the phone would be answered by Dottie, the regular secretary. The man was probably a cop, she thought. If he only knew who she was. She smiled to herself.

"I'd like to speak to Mr. Henry Bernside," she said.

"Mr. Bernside isn't in today," said the man.

"Is Mr. Salicki there?"

"No, I'm afraid he isn't available, either."

"May I speak to whoever is filling in for him, then? This is very important. I'm an employee, and I have to be excused today."

"I'll give him your message. What did you say your name was?"

"No, you don't understand. I have to speak to a supervisor directly."

"What was your name?" asked the cop.

Nominski took a deep breath and let it out slowly. "Carla Guzzo," she said, naming another woman in the department.

"Just a minute." Nominski waited.

Finally, another man's voice came on the phone. "Hello?" he said. "This is Duncan Prasky."

"Mr. Prasky," said Nominski, "I want you to listen closely. Mr. Bernside won't be coming in today. He was killed in an automobile accident on the freeway this morning. He was with a member of the gang that stole your computer disks. I'm the only person alive who knows where those disks are. If you want them back, you'll have to make it worth my while. You'll have to pay me two hundred and fifty thousand dollars, or suffer the consequences. I'm sure you've been filled in on what those consequences might be. Do you understand?"

"Just a second." Nominski could tell that he had covered the mouthpiece of his telephone with one hand. He was evidently directing the police and the FBI to listen in. "Two hundred fifty thousand," he said in an obvious attempt to stall. "That sounds fair. I suppose we'd be glad to agree. How do you want to make the exchange?"

"Do you have the cops listening in, you goddamn son of a bitch?" asked Nominski.

"Well, look, there isn't any other way. They're all over here, and we can't do a thing without bumping into them. They're monitoring all the calls anyway. It isn't my fault. We can still work out some kind of deal. I'm sure we wouldn't press charges against you—"

"You moron! Three people are dead already, and you say you're not going to press charges." Nominski hung up. Her stomach felt sour. She had to take it out on somebody. She wondered who it would be.

David Caldwell had exhausted all the polite conversation he had in him. Josie Frankel was sitting on the floor, her back propped up against a wall. They were very studiously looking away from each other, to avoid the necessity of exchanging further pleasantries. Caldwell wished that Van Eyck had thought to supply them with a deck of cards or a Monopoly game or something. The only thing he saw that they could do was to turn on the radio again and dance. It seemed moderately indecorous under the circumstances.

About ten-thirty, Caldwell was relieved to hear a key turn in the door. He was less relieved to see that it was Andi Nominski, and not Van Eyck or Leyva. "What are you doing here?" he asked. "You're supposed to be at work today."

She waved her hand airily. "I decided I could use a day off," she said.

"You're endangering all of us. They must know that someone on the inside helped. By not going to work, you're practically signing a confession."

"A lot I care. I wasn't planning on ever going back anyway."

"But Adrian said—"

Nominski gave her short, humorless bark of a laugh. "Adrian! What does he know? None of you has figured out that I'm pulling the rug out from under you. Listen, have you heard? Leyva and that General Motors executive he went to see are both dead. Smashed up on the freeway. It ought to be on the news at noon. It's a shame we don't have a television in here. It was spectacular."

Caldwell was too horrified to ask how she knew the details. "Arthur?" he said.

"Poor old Arthur. Wouldn't hurt a fly."

"Oh, my God, why?"

Nominski shook her head. "It's a dangerous game we're playing, David, my boy. We have to be prepared for these things."

"But Adrian said—"

"Will you stop *saying* that already?" Nominski screamed. "Adrian doesn't know his ass from his elbow."

Caldwell didn't say anything more. His expression showed his anguish. Josie Frankel sat down next to him, a consoling gesture.

"That's sweet," murmured Nominski. She waited a few minutes, a decent interval, enough so that Caldwell would be getting over one shock before she presented him with another. "By the way," she said, "your wife knows everything and she's coming over here right now."

Caldwell felt a rage and a murderous fury unlike anything he had ever experienced in his entire life. Suddenly he understood why Nominski was the source of all this information. The implications of what she had told him were clear. He stood up and walked slowly toward her. She did not move. He grabbed her shoulder with his left hand, holding her still, and raised his right hand to strike her. She smiled contemptuously, and she did not flinch. He couldn't hit her. He dropped his hand and pushed her back against the wall. She shook her head pityingly. "Caldwell, I did it for your own good. This is your chance to get out of it. You and your wife can go home and be clear of the whole deal. Listen. I'll take your place, I'll go to Chrysler and get the money. Adrian can bring you your share tonight. Understand?"

"You can go to hell!" cried Caldwell. "You tried to turn my wife against me. I can't believe you did that. You can't scare me off now, Andi. You can stay here and watch our hostage, if you feel like it, or you can leave. I'm going to do my job. I owe it to Adrian, and I owe it to Arthur. Hell, I owe it to myself and to Marianne. But Adrian is going to hear about this, and you know what that means. He's going to kick your ass, and you know it." Caldwell put on his coat and gloves. He looked at Josie Frankel. "I have to go now," he said.

She was frightened. "Please," she said, "I don't want you to leave me alone with her."

"I have to. She won't do anything crazy; Adrian would kill her. He'll be back soon. I ought to be back within an hour or two. Then it will be all over."

"Lots of luck, you bastard," said Nominski. Caldwell went to the door without even glancing at her.

After the telephone call from Nominski, Marianne Caldwell sat down on the bed and thought. The story she had heard was fantastic, but that didn't mean that it, or parts of it, weren't true. She was positive that her husband had been involved in something for the last couple of weeks. She had been unable to imagine what it might be. She acknowledged that his excuse—that he had been concerned about his health and his family's well-being—was true as far as it went. She still ruled out the possibility that Caldwell was having an affair with another woman. That kind of thing wasn't like him. The idea of his being involved in a large criminal venture was wild; but Marianne found that she could believe it, if she were given enough evidence.

She dressed herself and the children quickly. She put the scrap of paper with the address in her coat pocket, checked to make sure she had her keys, took the children and went out to her car. First she drove to her mother-in-law's house, where she left little Davey and Risa. Then she headed across the city toward Woodward Avenue.

She was thankful to the woman—"Andi"—for offering to bail Caldwell out of the situation. He would be angry to see her, of course. She knew that he was risking everything to provide for his family. He would resent her interference; his pride would be hurt, as well. She would have to make him see that it was for the best. They could sell one of the cars or something to get some cash, and she still had her job. They'd get along, somehow. Anything was better than the danger he was in. She pushed the speed limit a little recklessly.

When she turned onto Woodward, she began looking at house numbers. She was unhappy to see that she still had a long way to drive. The traffic on Woodward was moving slowly. She was impatient, and she hit her fists against the steering wheel at every traffic light, at every halt in the traffic flow. When she got to the right block, she pulled over. While she was parking the car, she didn't see her husband run out of the building and get into an AMC Concord. Marianne slammed her car's door and hurried along the sidewalk. She spotted her husband's own Vega parked across the street. Caldwell was already two blocks away, making a right turn. Marianne went up the steps of the apartment building.

11.

"Hello, is this the Ford Motor Company?"
"River Rouge Assembly Plant."
"I'd like to speak to the payroll department, please."
"Just a moment." (Pause.) "Hourly Employee Record Division. May I help you?"
"Yes. May I speak to whoever is handling the problem you're having with the paychecks?"
"Oh, my. Yes, just a second." (Pause.) "Mr. Koppe's office."
"Hello. I'd like to help you get your computer disks back."
"Ah. I'm sorry, but Mr. Koppe isn't in at the moment. May I have him call you back?"
"Don't be an idiot. I'm not giving you my phone number."
"I see. Would you care to speak to anyone else."
"A cop? An FBI man? Are you crazy?"
"Would you care to leave a message for Mr. Koppe, then?"
"Yes, I think I will. Tell him that a man by the name of Adrian van Eyck will offer the disks to him for one hundred and fifty thousand dollars. Tell him to refuse. I'll give him the disks and the names of everyone involved for an even hundred grand."
"What was that man's name again, please?"

"Van Eyck. Adrian."

"And how will Mr. Koppe be able to identify you?"

"Carla Guzzo will call him later."

"Thank you. We'll be waiting for your call. Mr. Koppe ought to be in at any moment."

"Right. Talk to you later." Nominski hung up the phone and was looking for another telephone number when she was interrupted by Josie Frankel.

"Are you really turning Adrian in?" asked the girl.

Nominski nodded. "It sure sounds like it."

"Why? Whatever for? What did he ever do to you?"

"Nothing," said Nominski. "I'm in this for the money. I never needed those three fools for anything. They're lucky I let them into the deal."

"They're real lucky to know you," said Frankel.

Nominski laughed. She walked over to Frankel and knelt down beside her. She reached out her hand and began to stroke Frankel's hair. She touched the girl's cheek, and she cringed away. "Aw, hey, don't be like that," said Nominski. She took the .38 from her handbag and put it on the floor. "Be nice," whispered Nominski.

There was a loud knock on the door. Nominski was startled; no one should be knocking. Van Eyck and Caldwell both had their own keys. Nominski frowned in thought. The knock came again. "Be quiet," she warned Frankel. She picked up her pistol and went to the door. "Yes?" she called.

"It's Marianne Caldwell. Let me in."

Nominski smiled. "Yes, certainly, just a second." She gave Frankel a warning glance and put her pistol back in the bag. She unlocked the door and opened it. "Hello, Marianne. My, you're pretty. I had no idea you were such a pretty woman. Come in. We've spoken on the telephone."

Marianne came into the apartment, wrinkling her nose a little at its shabbiness. "You're, uh, you're Andi, then?"

"Yes. This is Josie Frankel. She's a friend of Adrian's. I'm sorry we don't have any furniture. Try to make yourself comfortable. Lord, I wish David had told me how pretty you are."

"Where is David?" asked Marianne.

"He just left, not ten minutes ago. You just missed him. Didn't she, Josie?" Frankel was weeping, and did not answer.

"Did he leave to do what you mentioned? Is he really part of—"

"He's on his way to the Chrysler plant right now. The best thing to do, I guess, is sit here and wait for him and for Adrian to come back. I don't know what else we can do. Besides, I'm waiting to make a telephone call."

Marianne turned toward the door. "I guess I'd better leave," she said.

Nominski hurried across the room to get between Marianne and the door. "Where are you going? Home?"

"No," said Marianne. "I don't know who you are, or who this girl is; but if David is in some kind of trouble and I can't help him, I'm going to talk to someone who can."

"You're going to the police?" said Nominski.

"Yes," said Marianne.

"You're a fool, too." Nominski pulled her pistol from the bag and pointed it at her. Marianne gasped. "Sit down over there, next to the girl. We'll all sit here and wait for the boys to come back with my money. I can't think of a lovelier way to spend the afternoon, can you?"

12.

David Caldwell, unaware of Andi Nominski's intrigues, parked the Concord in the Chrysler visitors' lot. He clipped on his William Jahncke identification badge, and once more slipped into the persona of a computer expert from General Motors. He looked at the name of the man he was to see at Chrysler: Keith Bolander. Caldwell steadied himself, then got out of the car and walked toward the entrance.

A receptionist looked up politely. "Hello," she said. "May I help you?"

"Yes," said Caldwell, "my name is William Jahncke. I'm a computer analyst in the payroll department of the Cadillac Division of General Motors. I would like to see Mr. Keith Bolander. I don't have an appointment, but this is a serious emergency. I'm sure he will want to talk to me. It's something I couldn't discuss over the telephone. Tell him it's about the disks."

"Thank you, sir. Just one moment. Please have a seat." The receptionist dialed Bolander's extension. She relayed the information. "He'll send someone to get you," said the woman.

"Thank you." Caldwell sat on a couch and read a magazine for about ten minutes.

"Mr. Jahncke? My name is Norman Sutton. I've taken over the handling of this problem from Keith Bolander." They shook hands. Sutton seemed a little suspicious. "I hope you don't mind, but would you show me some identification? You understand. In this situation we have to be careful. We've been penetrated once already."

"Certainly," said Caldwell. He handed Sutton his GM picture ID. He was grateful now for Van Eyck's attention to detail.

"Thank you. Now, what's the trouble? Or do you have some information?"

Caldwell rubbed his chin. "I have some information, I think; but I've come to discuss it with you, to see how meaningful it might be. You can understand that I didn't want to speak with you by phone. Not with all the police hanging on every word. I think we have to keep a little apart from them, if you know what I mean."

"They don't really appreciate our problems. They aren't looking out for our best interests," said Sutton.

"Exactly."

"Let's go up to my office. I'd rather not discuss it any further here in the lobby."

Caldwell froze for a second. "No," he said at last, "your office would be just as bad as mine. Come with me. We'll go out to my car."

Sutton gave Caldwell a thoughtful look, but said nothing. They walked quickly across the parking lot. "I wish you'd warned me," said Sutton. "It's pretty damn cold out here."

"Sorry."

When they got to the car, Sutton looked at it skeptically. It was obvious that he thought it odd that a General Motors executive would drive an AMC Concord. "It's my wife's car," said Caldwell. "The Eldorado is in the shop. I'm having the leather upholstery mink-oiled."

"What?" said Sutton, startled.

"That's a joke. One of my wife's. Her jokes are as bad as her driving. Get in, and we'll talk. I have something to show you, too."

Sutton got in the car, still looking dubious. Caldwell started the engine and backed out of the parking place. That told Sutton that something was up. "Who are you?" he asked. Caldwell drove out of the lot, heading away from the plant with no destination in mind.

"Call me William Jahncke, but it isn't my real name. I'm not an employee at General Motors. I didn't steal your disks, but I know where they are. I'm your contact. You deal with me to get them back. You pay me; half an hour after I get away, I'll call you and tell you where to find them."

Sutton was silent. He was surprised that the thieves would contact him this way. He hadn't been prepared for it. He wasn't sure how to respond. "First off, how can I be sure you're who you say you are? How do I know you know where the disks are? After I pay you, how do I know you'll call?"

It was Caldwell's turn to be surprised. "You haven't told many other people about this, have you? So no one else knows. You have to trust me, or you'll never get the disks back. If that happens, you'll have to sweep the pieces of Chrysler away with a broom and start from scratch."

"That's good as far as it goes," said Sutton, "except for the fact that only about ten or twenty thousand people know what happened by now. I'm surprised the news people aren't covering it already. So that kills your main argument. But anyway, let's hear what you want. How much?"

"A hundred fifty thousand dollars."

"Is that all? No political prisoners you want released? No appearance on nationwide television? No getaway jet?"

"Be serious," said Caldwell. "We just figured you'd be ready to pay a token hundred fifty thousand. Were we right?"

"Yes," said Sutton. "I can get an okay on a sum like that, if I go through the right channels. I can't give you the money myself. I have to get a check signed by at least a vice president. They're waiting to hear a ransom figure, so it won't take long to get it."

"A check?" said Caldwell. He didn't like that.

"Sure," said Sutton, "what do you think we are? Do you think we keep that kind of money around the plant in petty cash?"

"You're bluffing. You said you expected a ransom demand, so you have established access to a large quantity of cash. You had all last evening and this morning to anticipate this moment."

Sutton nodded. "Well, as a matter of fact, you're right."

"Good," said Caldwell.

"It will probably be marked," said Sutton.

"My boss said not to worry about that. He said he could launder it easily enough."

"You must have some boss," said Sutton. "In that case, let's go back and get down to business."

"You're willing, then? You'll cooperate?"

"I'll see a vice president and ask for the check. You'll have to wait in the lobby while I go upstairs. Then we'll go over to the bank and get your cash."

Caldwell didn't like the sound of that, either. "No way," he said. "You have the police and the FBI up there."

"I'm trusting you. Now you trust *me* a little."

"No. I hold all the cards."

"But you can't cash them in," said Sutton.

"If I don't, you'll be standing in line for unemployment with all your Chrysler coworkers on Monday morning."

They looked at each other. There was a long silence. Finally, Sutton broke it. "All right," he said. "Drive me to my house. I live in Royal Oak."

"Why?"

Sutton sighed. "Come on, do it. You'll get your money."

Caldwell wasn't happy about it. It was another instance of the plan failing, of events moving out of his control. But despite a twinge of doubt, he made a turn onto an expressway and followed Sutton's directions. At least he was heading away from the growing horde of people trying to capture him.

As they rode up in the elevator, Paul Koppe and Adrian van Eyck discussed the effects of a full-scale strike against the automobile industry. "We don't want to think about it," said Koppe. "The UAW doesn't, either. They're shrewd people, they know what might happen. I've spoken with Jerome Spillman, one of their legal hotshots. Have you met him? He seems like an intelligent man. Anyway, he says they're every bit as scared over there as we are."

"I was counting on that, to tell you the truth," said Van Eyck.

"You seem very young to have devised such an elaborate job," said Koppe. The elevator came to a stop and they got out. Koppe indicated that they were heading to the left. "I expected a gang of hulking safecracker-types with black masks and guns."

"I'm sorry."

"No, really, the main reason I'm recommending that we pay you the money is because you've never threatened me. Of course, once we hand over the money, you realize that the gloves come off. It's our duty to get that money back. You'll be followed when you leave here. We'll try to trace the call when you notify us about where to find the disks. We'll give this nationwide media exposure. We'll spend ten times what you're taking from us, if we have to, to hunt you down. It's a shame in a way, and I'm sorry, but we have to. The industry can't afford to be vulnerable to every crackpot gang that needs money."

"But you *are* vulnerable," said Van Eyck. "I've proved that."

Koppe smiled as he opened a door. "No, you haven't proved that yet," he said. Both men went into the office. "Mr. Grossberg, this young man can help us retrieve the disks."

Grossberg, a senior vice president, a man of considerable authority and imposing appearance, studied Van Eyck in silence for several seconds. Then he grimaced. "This kid? This kid is responsible for holding up three of the biggest corporations in the world?"

"Yes, sir," said Van Eyck.

"It's my opinion, sir, that we ought to play along with him for now," said Koppe. "Once we get the disks back, it won't be difficult to track him down. The FBI and the police are just champing at the bit. Right now, though, the important thing is preventing a strike. We have to have those paychecks ready—"

"I know, I know," said Grossberg, waving a hand. "I hate the idea of this kid coming in here and holding a gun to my head."

"No gun, sir," said Koppe.

Grossberg's eyebrows went up. "Oh? That's a pleasant surprise. A smart move, son. If you played it tough with me, I would have had those disks out of you the hard way, believe me. You'd have begged me to take them off your hands. And then you'd have gone to prison. Which you're still going to do, by the way. But this way you'll be able to walk in there under your own power."

"We'll need you to sign the check, sir," said Koppe. "Just a formality."

"Hold on," said Grossberg. "How much?"

"A hundred and fifty thousand," said Van Eyck.

"Is that all, son? You surprise me again. That's less than we predicted. I tell you, it isn't worth it. I make more than that going to the bathroom."

Van Eyck just stood there smiling. Paul Koppe moved alongside Grossberg's desk. They prepared a check for one hundred fifty thousand dollars. "Here you go," said Koppe.

"Thank you," said Van Eyck. "Now we have to cash this sucker. I'd appreciate it if you'd give me a hand down at the bank. Both of you. If you'll come with me now, we'll have the disks back here within the hour. You won't have any trouble catching up on the payroll then."

"I'm sorry, I just can't—" said Grossberg.

"I think, sir," said Koppe, "that under the circumstances it would be better if we continued to cooperate."

Grossberg looked angry. "Why the hell should I? He has his check, doesn't he? I didn't like giving it to him, but I went ahead with it because at the moment he seems to be calling the shots. You don't need me at the bank. They'll honor the check. What he's asking is adding insult to injury. It will be a public embarrassment for me. He's acting like he's got a gun, after all."

Koppe smiled placatingly. "He has better than that. He still has the disks."

Grossberg grumbled. "Yeah. Okay, kid, but *this* I resent."

The three men left the office and headed toward the elevator, greeting on the way a uniformed police lieutenant.

Marianne Caldwell looked at Andi Nominski. Nominski was watching Josie Frankel. Frankel was reduced to a quiet, tearful hysteria. Marianne knew that something was very wrong. She knew that whatever plans Van Eyck had made, they had gone horribly sour. Arthur Leyva had been killed. The smooth-running machine they had bet their lives and liberty on had broken down. It wasn't difficult for Marianne to guess that the cause of the trouble was in the room with her. David would never permit himself to be involved in anything that concerned guns; he had an aversion to them. Marianne didn't know what kind of person Adrian van Eyck was, but she didn't imagine that he could be cruel or violent. Not if he had had the cooperation of David and Arthur.

Yet something evil had worked its influence here. Marianne wondered what that evil had yet to accomplish, and who would follow Arthur Leyva to destruction. She was frightened by that thought and its implications: that Andi Nominski's pistol had a practical purpose as well as a decorative one, and that she might not allow the others to get away alive.

"Will you two be all right if I leave you for a moment?" said

Nominski. "I have to run out to the car for something. I won't be long. Can you two be trusted to stay put?"

"Yes, of course," said Marianne.

"If either of you two makes a move while I'm gone, you're both dead little girls, understand? I'm just going out to the curb, and I'm coming right back. Just sit tight."

"Okay," said Marianne.

Nominski started to the door, then cursed softly. "God, am I a fool!" she said. "I forgot about the telephone. That presents a problem. I guess I'll just have to take you with me. You're going to sit on the steps while I go to my car. I want you both to act nice out there, or I'll blow you away before you can open your mouths. I killed a man yesterday, so it doesn't make any difference to me if I have to kill anyone else today. Got that?"

This time Marianne didn't answer.

"Come on, then. Frankel, get on your feet. Come *on*, damn it! You—Caldwell's wife—you help her. I don't have all day. Come on." They left the apartment and went out the front of the building. Marianne steadied Frankel. On the front steps they sat close together. They didn't have their coats with them, and they suffered in the cold, wet wind. Nominski went straight to her car, opened the trunk, and took out a ball of clothesline, a knife, and some old rags. She came back to the two women, and they all returned to the apartment. "That was fine," said Nominski. "I'm proud of both of you." She indicated that Frankel was to sit down on the floor where she had been. Nominski wadded up a rag and stuffed it into Frankel's mouth. Frankel made protesting, gagging noises, but Nominski didn't seem to notice; she proceeded to tie Frankel up, hand and foot. "I like this," said Nominski, winking at Marianne. "I've read about it, but I never thought it would be this much fun."

"Are you going to do that to me?" asked Marianne.

"Only if you insist," said Nominski. "I like talking to you.

Josie, here, hasn't been much company. I'm hoping you'll be more stimulating."

"Probably not."

Nominski's face clouded. "Watch it, bitch," she said.

"I'm sorry," said Marianne, frightened. "Listen, I know you're not going to let me leave—"

"That's for damn sure."

"My two children are with David's mother. I was hoping you'd at least let me call her. I was supposed to pick them up tonight. Now David will have to—"

"What makes you think he'll be able to go get them?"

Marianne was afraid, but she had reached the point where the fear of Nominski and her pistol was nothing compared with her fear for her husband and her concern for her children. "All right, that's enough," she said. "I'm going to call my mother-in-law right now. You go ahead and shoot me if it gives you a thrill." She picked up the telephone and dialed the number.

Nominski was amused. She moved close to Marianne and began stroking her cheek. "You can call. I'll listen to make sure you don't say anything you shouldn't. Don't get upset with me, sugar; I want to be your friend. I don't want to shoot you. I have no reason to hurt you or your husband."

Marianne put her hand over the phone. "And get your goddamn hands off me," she said.

Nominski backed off. "I didn't know you used language like that, sweetheart. I thought you were a nice girl."

"Hello, Mother? Listen, there's been a kind of emergency. No, I'm all right. So is David. But we won't be able to pick the kids up for a while. No, I'm not sure. No, there's nothing for you to be worried about. I'll tell you all about it later. I was hoping that you— Yes, that would be wonderful. I'd be so grateful. Thanks, Mother. We'll be home in a little while. Thanks again."

"Marianne," said Nominski, "why don't we sit down and try to get to know each other?"

"What the hell are you talking about? You don't have anything I want and I don't have anything you want. I'm not preventing you from doing anything. When David gets here, your little power trip will come to a screeching halt. So just forget it, forget I'm even here. The sooner somebody slaps you down, the better. Until then, the hell with you."

Nominski was livid. "Slaps me down?" she cried. She struck Marianne a heavy blow across the face. Marianne stumbled and fell, holding her reddened cheek. "I'll take care of you just the way I took care of the other one." Nominski forced a rag into Marianne's mouth and bound her with the clothesline.

Nominski was alone again, for all practical purposes. She walked back and forth, trying to decide what was the best thing for her to do now. She couldn't think of anything positive to do. She could only wait. The one thing she might try, admittedly a long shot, was to call Paul Koppe at Ford one more time. She went to the phone. When the switchboard operator answered, she asked for Koppe's extension.

"Mr. Koppe's office," said his secretary.

"Hello," said Nominski, "this is Carla Guzzo again. I spoke with you a little while ago."

"Yes, I recall. I'm sorry, but Mr. Koppe still isn't in. Would you care to speak to a supervisor? He'd be able to take care of you as well as Mr. Koppe."

"I'll bet he could," said Nominski suspiciously. "Put him on."

"Just a moment, I'll transfer the call." There was a click and then silence on the line.

Someone picked up a phone on the other end, and a man's voice answered. "Hello, this is Larry Olejnik. Can I help you?"

"This is Carla Guzzo. Do you know why I'm calling?"

"Yes," said Olejnik, "you're asking for a hundred thousand dollars to tell us where our disks are."

"Word travels fast, doesn't it?"

"What did you expect, Miss Guzzo? It was the secretary's duty to keep me informed."

"I guess so. Tell me, Larry, what exactly is the job description of your position with the Ford Motor Company?"

"Huh? What? I'm, uh, the, uh—"

"You're a goddamn cop, that's what you are." She slammed the phone down, angry. These companies were out of their minds. They could have had the information cheap, but they insisted on trying to trap her, as if she were dumb enough to fall for it. Stupid and cheap. There was nothing for her to do now but wait for Van Eyck and Caldwell to come home, and get her money that way. She lit a cigarette and sat cross-legged on the floor, idly tapping the barrel of her pistol against her thigh.

13.

Van Eyck, Koppe, and Grossberg drove in Van Eyck's rented car to the main branch of a bank in Detroit's downtown area, almost in the shadow of the Renaissance Center. "We made arrangements with this bank early this morning, anticipating this very situation," said Koppe. "They contacted the Federal Reserve people, so by now they ought to have plenty of cash in here, all in nice small bills, all marked and recorded."

"Doesn't concern me," said Van Eyck. "I can pass marked bills."

"They'll be ready for you," said Grossberg. "They're going to be photographing you. The FBI won't let you just fade away."

Van Eyck pulled into a parking lot. "That doesn't bother me, either. I think I've got the FBI licked."

Koppe whistled and Grossberg made a disgusted sound. "Look, kid," said Grossberg, "don't get the wrong idea. I don't give a tinker's dam if you get caught and salted away for the rest of your life. You're not Robin Hood, you know, whatever you think of yourself. But I still want to give you a piece of advice: *Nobody* licks the FBI. Dillinger couldn't lick the FBI, and you're not even in his league."

"Please, don't worry about me," said Van Eyck. They got

out of the car. They walked toward the bank, their shoulders hunched against the cold.

"Fine," said Grossberg, "that's the last word I'll utter on the subject."

"I want to keep an eye on what you do in there," said Van Eyck. "I could have gone to another bank. Any of the larger banks would have enough cash handy. But if I'm going to avoid delay, I'm going to have to use your bank. I want to make sure, though, that nobody tries any last-minute tricks."

"Okay," said Koppe, shrugging.

They went into the bank, and Grossberg and Koppe spoke with one of the bank officers, a short, heavy, worried-looking woman. Van Eyck saw her staring across the lobby at him; he smiled and waved. The woman took the check, examined it, and carried it away. Van Eyck, Koppe, and Grossberg waited. Nothing out of the ordinary appeared to be happening in the bank. They were apparently not attracting any attention.

Ten minutes later, the officer returned, carrying a brown paper bag from a supermarket. She handed it to Grossberg, who gave it to Van Eyck. No one said a word. The bank officer watched nervously. Van Eyck took all the packages out of the bag; there were fifteen packs of hundred dollar bills, with one hundred bills to a pack. The money was crisp and new. "Okay by me," said Van Eyck. "Thank you, ma'am." He shook hands with the bank officer. "Let's go."

They left the bank. No one seemed to be following them, but that didn't mean that no one was, however.

"You don't mind the hundreds?" asked Grossberg. "It was supposed to be small bills."

"It's all right," said Van Eyck imperturbably.

"What now?" asked Paul Koppe.

"Now, I think, we'll go to lunch," said Van Eyck.

"What?" said Grossberg. "What about the disks?"

"I promise you, half an hour after I leave you, I'll call Mr. Koppe's office and tell his secretary exactly where you can pick up your disks. Where would you like to eat?"

"The Pontchartrain," said Koppe. Grossberg gave him a warning look.

"Don't worry," said Van Eyck, "the lunch is on me."

"All right, then," grumbled Grossberg.

When Caldwell and Sutton arrived at the Chrysler executive's house, Caldwell parked the Concord in the driveway. "Now, what's this all about?" he asked.

"Come inside with me," said Sutton. "Meet my family."

"Ordinarily I'd love to," said Caldwell in a tired voice, "but I'm in the middle of a brilliant crime, and I'm in kind of a rush. Another day, perhaps. My wife and I will have you folks over for dinner sometime. Right now I don't have the time."

Sutton got out of his car and was walking toward the house. Caldwell didn't have a choice; he followed. He didn't want to let Sutton out of his sight. Sutton unlocked his front door and let Caldwell in. The house was moderately expensive, decorated in a manner a trifle too vigorous for Caldwell's taste. There were two four-foot-high ceramic leopards guarding the entrance to the parlor. On either end of a long, white sofa there was a gaunt brass stork, taller than the leopards, staring down a sharp, evil beak; the storks looked like they were ready to peck the eyes out of anyone foolish enough to smudge some dirt on that sofa. On a wall overlooking the conversation pit hung the kind of overwrought green seascape that is sold by the square foot. "Very charming," said Caldwell.

"Thank you," said Sutton. "My wife decorated it all herself. Let me find her. Have a seat. Would you care for anything?"

"No, nothing. We ought to be going."

"Just a few seconds." Sutton went off to get his wife. Caldwell felt afraid, trapped in the man's house. He knew that Sutton might be calling the police, but Caldwell's conventional sense of propriety prevented him from walking uninvited about the man's house.

"Hello," said Sutton's wife. She was very puzzled. She didn't know what her husband was doing home so early; she didn't know who the strange man in her living room was; and she didn't know why Sutton was acting so excited. Mrs. Sutton had on a large cardigan sweater over a housedress. Her brown hair was disheveled and she wasn't wearing any makeup.

"Hello," said Caldwell, standing. They looked at each other.

"And this is my daughter, Jeannie, and my other daughter, Marcy," said Sutton, ushering in two teenage girls still in pajamas and robes. "I let them stay home from school today."

"Pleased to meet you all," said Caldwell. He was embarrassed.

"Now, go put on your coats and boots, because we're all going with Mr. Jahncke here," said Sutton.

"What?" said Caldwell.

"What?" said Mrs. Sutton.

"Aw, Daddy," said the two girls.

"Mr. Jahncke, you do have a gun, don't you?" said Sutton.

"No, sir, I'm afraid I don't."

"Just a second." Sutton disappeared again.

"What's going on?" cried Sutton's wife.

"I'm trying to finish a robbery," said Caldwell. "I'm holding up your husband's company. I don't know exactly why he brought me here."

"He brought you here?" said Mrs. Sutton.

"Yes, ma'am."

"Here you go, Bill." Sutton came back with a .45 caliber automatic. "From my army days. It's got a full clip in it." Sutton slid out the magazine to show Caldwell.

"Thanks, but—"

"Here, take it. This has to look right."

"Look right for what, Daddy?" asked Jeannie or Marcy.

"Let's go out to the car now. I'll drive, Mr. Jahncke. You can sit in the back with the kids."

"Norman," cried his wife, "what the hell is going on here?"

"Don't you see?" said Sutton happily. "We're all hostages. Everything is going to work out fine."

"Daddy, you're crazy."

Caldwell's throat was very dry. He felt a heavy throbbing pain in his lower abdomen. The automatic in his hand felt heavy and obscene. He watched Sutton bundle his family up and head them toward the door. He wished he knew what was happening.

"We'll go to the First Peninsula," said Sutton. "I'll get you some of your money."

"We have to go back to the plant and get your boss to sign the check first," said Caldwell.

"No, we'll do it my way."

"Wait a minute," said Caldwell, getting just a little irritated. "Who's running this?"

"I'm glad you asked that," said Sutton as he settled himself behind the wheel of Caldwell's car. "*I* am. If you hope to get your money and get away, you'll do what I say."

Caldwell said nothing. He was uncomfortable in the backseat, jammed between the unhappy daughters. In the front, Mrs. Sutton was alternately glaring at her husband and giving Caldwell sick glances. "Please don't point that gun at my daughter," she said.

"Sorry," said Caldwell.

"That's better," said Mrs. Sutton. "Maybe you should let me hold that until we get to the bank."

"Sure," said Caldwell, passing the pistol forward.

"Sheila," cried Sutton, "just shut up! Give him back his gun!"

"Yes, dear." She passed the pistol back to Caldwell.

They drove in strained silence. Sutton parked the car. He looked back at Caldwell. "I'll be in there just a minute. Don't worry. I won't try anything foolish while you have that gun."

"We'll all go in," said Caldwell.

Sutton frowned. "If you say so."

"Daddy," objected Marcy or Jeannie, "we can't go in there looking like this!"

"She's right," complained Sheila Sutton.

"Get out of the car," said Sutton. "And hurry it up, it's cold."

The Sutton family and Caldwell went into the bank. Caldwell put the pistol in his overcoat pocket, hoping that it wouldn't fall out while they were in the bank. He was having visions that were almost tangible, all of them horrible nightmares of what might happen. Nothing did go wrong, though. He and Mrs. Sutton and the two girls waited by the deposit slips while Sutton talked to one of the bank officers. Sutton produced a checkbook and two savings passbooks. The officer asked to see some identification. Sutton complied, and the officer went into the vault for a few minutes. When he came back, he was carrying a cloth bag. He gave it to Sutton. Sutton brought it to Caldwell. "Here," said Sutton, "count it."

Caldwell opened the bag and counted the money. There was twenty-five thousand dollars. "What's this?" he asked.

"I've cleaned out my bank accounts. You hold that and my family as insurance. Now we'll go get the check from the company."

"Mr. Sutton," said Caldwell, totally bewildered, "I don't know why in hell you're doing all this. We could have saved a lot of time by just going to get that check in the first place."

Sutton shook his head. "Trust me," he said.

"God, Norman," said his wife, "you'd damn well better know what you're doing."

"I know what I'm doing," said Sutton. "Now, let's go get the rest of the money."

They left the bank, unaware of the stares they were attracting from employees and depositors. They took the same seats in the car, and Sutton drove to the Chrysler plant. He pulled the car into the executives' parking lot, then guided his family and

Caldwell to the entrance. A security guard there stopped them. "Hello, Mr. Sutton," said the uniformed man, looking questioningly at the pajama-clad girls.

"Say, Tommy," said Sutton, "would you let my wife and kids and Mr. Jahncke here wait for me inside the building? Just inside the door would be fine. I'll be right back. I have to go upstairs and get something; it won't take long."

"Sure, I guess so, Mr. Sutton, if you'd be willing to take the rap if somebody gets on my back about it."

"Okay, Tommy. I'll be down in a minute." Before he left them, Sutton pulled Caldwell away to speak privately. "You still have the gun with you?"

"Yes," said Caldwell. He sincerely wished that he knew what was going on.

"Well, if you see anything out of the ordinary, if you see cops coming after you, you use that gun. Start with my wife. Don't shoot the kids until you're sure you have to."

Sheila Sutton overheard his words. "Norman!" she screamed.

"Don't worry," he said, "everything will be fine. I just want Mr. Jahncke to realize that he can trust me while I'm upstairs. I want everybody to stay calm and quiet. I'll be back in a little while, and this afternoon we'll all go somewhere special."

"But, Daddy," said one of the girls, "I have to use the—"

"Shut up," Sutton snapped. He nodded to Caldwell, then hurried down the hall. He turned a corner and was out of sight.

"What now?" asked Mrs. Sutton.

"We wait," said Caldwell, sighing.

"What are you up to?" asked one of the girls. "Are we kidnapped?"

"I don't think so," said her mother. "Daddy made us come along."

"What are you up to?" asked the other girl

"I don't want to say, really," said Caldwell. "Sort of robbing the place. In a way."

"That's neat," said the girl.

241

There was a long, tense silence as everyone waited for Sutton to return. A clock on the wall moved slowly. Five minutes passed, then ten, then fifteen. Caldwell was sure that he was going crazy. He had a strong urge to run out of the plant and speed away in his car, to forget the whole thing. He clamped a lid on his panic and waited.

Sutton reappeared. "Got it!" he called. He practically ran toward them.

"Good," said Caldwell.

"Now, listen," said Sutton, pulling Caldwell away to speak privately once more. "I'll trade you this check for my twenty-five thousand."

"Sure, but I still don't—"

"Let's go cash it and get this over with."

"Fine," said Caldwell, "that's okay with me. But this check is for two hundred thousand. That's fifty thousand more than what—"

Sutton looked disappointed that Caldwell didn't immediately understand. "Well, I just thought that my time, inconvenience, and help were worth *something*."

"They were, they definitely were," said Caldwell, catching on to what Sutton was up to.

"So why not let me take care of cashing the check? That way there won't be any pictures taken of you. Keep my twenty-five thousand in cash, and I'll give you a hundred and twenty-five more at the bank. Then I can deposit my twenty-five thousand back in my accounts, and keep an extra fifty that the IRS doesn't have to hear about."

"Terrific," said Caldwell with some amazement. "You've made my whole day."

"I'm glad," said Sutton. "Just don't tell Sheila about it."

Part Four

The Trade-In

1.

Van Eyck got out of the cab with his brown grocery bag. He paid the driver, then turned and walked up the steps of the apartment building. He was very happy. He was hoping that he was the last of the three to get back to the apartment; that was why he had delayed his return by going to lunch with Koppe and Grossberg. He was very good at planning and just as good at execution, but the one talent he didn't have was the ability to wait and worry. He looked up and down the block, but neither of the other two rented cars was parked nearby. Perhaps, like Van Eyck, they had chosen to come back by taxi, to shake an FBI tail. Van Eyck didn't expect that was the case, however. He supposed that he would, after all, have to wait.

He opened the door to the apartment. "Hey, Josie, look—" he began to call, but he didn't finish. There was an unusual tableau waiting for him. Andi Nominski was in the apartment, when she ought to have been at work. On the floor, bound and gagged, were two women. One of them was Josie Frankel, but the other was someone Van Eyck had never seen before. He was worried. This was an unpleasant development, something he would have to deal with before they could make a clean getaway. It seemed that they were acquiring hostages; he hoped Leyva and Caldwell would bring no more with them when they returned. Van Eyck knew he would get into an argument with Nominski about it, too.

"I got the money all right," he said, tossing the bag of hundred dollar bills at Nominski's feet. "No problem at all. Actually, it went much smoother than I even hoped. Open the bag. Isn't that a pretty sight?"

She looked into the brown sack. She took out a package of bills, tossing it lightly on one hand. "It has a nice feel to it. Are they all hundreds?"

"Yes," said Van Eyck.

"They'll be a problem to spend, won't they? Hundred-dollar bills attract attention."

"Not if you're careful. You can always take a few into a small bank or savings and loan and have a bank check or cashier's check made up, or buy traveler's checks. That doesn't look suspicious. Then cash the check somewhere else."

"How did you get away?"

Van Eyck dropped his overcoat in a corner of the room. He lay down on the floor and massaged his scalp. "I took these two Ford execs out to lunch after we got the money. I knew we'd be followed. There was probably someone outside watching my car and someone inside the restaurant, too. After we ordered our meal, I got up to go to the men's room. I left the bag of money at the table, so Koppe and Grossberg would know I was coming back. While I was away, I told the headwaiter to call me a cab, and to signal me silently when it arrived. Then I just sat back, enjoyed a nice shrimp cocktail and a glass of wine, and waited. When I got the signal, I jumped up, hurried out—I left a hundred bucks with the headwaiter, just to take care of things—and got in the cab. If there was someone watching me in the restaurant, I left him in the snow on the sidewalk. We drove around town for a while, then I had the cabbie let me out by the Plaza Hotel in the Renaissance Center. I went up to the twentieth floor and got off. I was all alone. I walked downstairs to the fifteenth floor, got on an elevator the rest of the way down, left the hotel, and climbed into another cab. I was certain I wasn't being followed then. And that was it."

"Very nice, Adrian. A little showy, perhaps, but effective. I guess that's what counts."

"Why are these people tied up, Andi?"

She looked at him, deciding how to answer. "Adrian, what are you planning to do now?" she said, avoiding the subject.

"Wait," he said. "What else can I do?"

"Well," said Nominski, "you have your one-fifty in this bag. I half-expected you to run out immediately. I'm surprised you even came back."

"Well, I had to see to Josie."

"Yes, there's Josie. We have to decide about her."

Van Eyck grew wary. "What's to decide? After Arthur and David get back, we'll split the money and let Josie go. She won't be able to hurt us. Then we all go our separate ways."

"She knows Caldwell. Caldwell isn't planning to leave town, like you are. I think she's a danger to me, too. She knows my real name. My picture will be in every paper in the country and on television, too, if she identifies me. I don't like leaving here knowing that."

Van Eyck rubbed his eyes. "What a mistake Arthur made, bringing her here. I guess it's my fault; I thought the best way to go was with amateur help. Someone more experienced would have known better than to take a prisoner."

"I knew better, Adrian," said Nominski. "I didn't take a prisoner."

"Yes, I know; but murder isn't what I had in mind, either. You both could have done your jobs without the flourishes. With a murder attached, our little project isn't going to be forgotten so easily."

"I know. That's another reason we have to come to a quick decision about her."

Van Eyck looked at Josie Frankel, helpless on the floor. Her face was red and puffy from crying. She was making unintelligible small sounds. "I think we can trust her. We could follow your suggestion and give her some money, just to be certain."

"None of my share," said Nominski. "I'm getting everything that's coming to me, and not a penny less."

"You'll get what's coming to you, Andi," said Van Eyck. "But you played a minor role in this. As I recall, you were only supposed to make a few phone calls. You didn't risk your neck, except when you started playing Dragon Lady and waving your gun around at General Motors and bumped off that poor guy. You could get us all put away for good. You ought to be penalized instead of rewarded."

"I'd like to see you try," said Nominski, giving him a cold smile.

"I think you'd be surprised."

"It would give me a lot of pleasure to kick you around," she said. "It would help relieve some of my tension."

"It's me, Leyva, and Caldwell who handled the hard parts. You were supposed to be at work this morning. I don't like you being here at all. People are going to think of you as a likely suspect, and that's just what you're afraid Josie will start. You're bringing it on yourself."

"Let me worry about that. As long as I get my hundred thousand."

"There shouldn't be any trouble. The split will go just as we planned."

"No, it won't," said Nominski, relishing the bad news she was about to deliver. "Arthur Leyva won't be coming back. He and his man from General Motors were killed on the freeway this morning. He never got the money from them."

"Killed?" said Van Eyck. He was appalled. He had planned the job to go off without harm to anyone.

"He had his gun on the man's head. Either he shot and the car went out of control, or the other way around. The car crashed into a wall, got hit by a truck, then flipped over. It tied up traffic for a long time."

Van Eyck closed his eyes. He felt genuine grief. Arthur Leyva had trusted him, and Van Eyck hadn't been worthy. Van Eyck felt responsible for Leyva's death. It was no good telling himself that Leyva had been at fault, because of the damn gun. It seemed to Van Eyck that he'd never shake the sense of guilt he felt now.

"Just a second," he said, looking up quickly, "how the hell do you know all about it?"

Nominski's eyes widened. "Well," she said, "I was on my way to work. By a remote coincidence, I just happened to be behind him on the freeway."

"Andi, from your house, you should have been traveling in the other direction."

Nominski smiled. "I was only looking out for my interests."

Van Eyck was furious. He wanted to crush every trace of her crazy smugness. He looked at her with disgust.

"The way I see it, Adrian," she said, "they'll pin it all on Leyva. This executive with him was from GM, so they'll link Leyva to Salicki. They'll be more than happy to blame Leyva. It will make their job easier—"

"Leyva had your .32. You killed Salicki with a .38."

"That doesn't mean anything. Look, Adrian, I'm sorry he died, too; but that doesn't change the situation. He's dead, and we have to make the best of it. We might as well use it to our advantage, if we can. We'll be one hundred and fifty thousand short, now. When Caldwell comes back, the total pot will be only three hundred thousand. But there's three of us now, instead of four. So let's forget about—"

The door opened; Caldwell had returned. He carried a cardboard box with Chrysler's ransom money in it. "Here we are," he said cheerfully. "I can't tell you how glad I am to get back here. I've been scared out of my skin all the way."

"Were you followed?" asked Nominski.

"No," said Caldwell. "The guy I dealt with at Chrysler, this Sutton fellow—"

"Sutton?" said Van Eyck. "You were supposed to call Keith Bolander."

"Bolander chickened out and passed it to Sutton. Anyway, Sutton took the opportunity to cheat his own company out of an extra fifty thousand for himself. I let him get away with it so that he'd protect me through the whole business. He covered for me at the plant. We went to get the cash before he reported anything to the cops."

"You should have beat him out of the extra fifty grand," said Nominski. "We could use every penny, since Leyva isn't coming back."

Caldwell took off his coat. He looked more closely at the two prisoners tied up on the floor. "Adrian," he said in a calm voice, "would you mind telling me why you have my wife trussed up like a Thanksgiving turkey?"

"Your wife? Marianne?"

"Didn't I tell you who she was?" said Nominski.

"Andi," said Van Eyck, "you're going to pay for this. I don't care where you go or what name you use, I'm going to find you. And you'll pay for this."

"Ha," said Nominski. "We'll talk about all that later. Now I want to count the money."

"Will you please untie my wife?" cried Caldwell.

Nominski knelt beside Marianne and cut the clothesline that bound her hands and feet. She was careful not to remove Marianne's gag until last. "David!" gasped Marianne when she was finally able to talk. She rubbed her wrists.

Caldwell helped her to her feet. "Are you all right?" he asked.

She clung to him, not able to say anything more for a moment. "David, are *you* all right?"

"I'm fine," he said. "Everything's over now."

"My wrists and ankles hurt," said Marianne. "I'll be okay. David, why did you do this?"

Caldwell winced. "Please, Mari, don't ask me that. I don't want to talk about it yet. I'll explain everything to you, but, please, let it rest for a few days. I've been through too much."

"All right, for now," said Marianne. She looked at Nominski, who smiled. "She's a monster, David."

"I know," said Caldwell. "She must be, to have called you today."

Van Eyck frowned. "Do I understand you right, Mr. Caldwell? Did you say that Andi called your wife and told her what was going on? Where you were and what you were doing?"

"This morning, yes," said Marianne.

"Ah," said Van Eyck, "thank you." His expression was placid; that ominous calmness of Van Eyck's frightened Caldwell.

"Why did she tie you up?" asked Caldwell. Nominski answered. "Both of them, they were trying to escape. Mrs. Caldwell told me that she was going to the police. I had to do it. This Frankel girl, too."

"David," said Marianne, "while both you and Mr. van Eyck were gone, she telephoned somebody and tried to make a deal for herself. She was trying to get money by turning the rest of you in."

"That's a lie!" shouted Nominski.

"Ask the girl," said Marianne.

"Her word won't mean anything," said Nominski. "Of course she'll say the same thing."

Van Eyck still seemed serene on the outside. His voice was low and apparently without emotion. "Why would they make up a story like that?" he asked. "I don't see their reasons."

"Then I'll tell you," said Nominski. "They want to cut me out of the money, but it won't work. They think they can split my share. The Caldwells would get half of my hundred thousand, and Frankel thinks she can get the other half. But they're forgetting who they're dealing with. They think you'll believe them instead of me, but remember, Adrian, that I was in this from the very beginning. You couldn't have managed without me."

"Andi, my love," said Van Eyck, "it has reached the point where I don't know what to believe anymore. If I had to choose between you on the one hand, and Mrs. Caldwell or Josie on the other, it seems likely that you'd come out on the short side."

"Adrian," said Nominski, beginning to worry, "I wasn't really turning you in. It's only that after you left this morning, I came up with a clever way to double our take. I thought that if I spoke with a different set of executives and sold them the same information you were selling to your contacts, they'd pay twice. Giving them your name wouldn't help them at all. I knew that you'd be using another as soon as this was over."

"Why did you come here, instead of going to work?" asked Caldwell.

"It's a good thing I did," said Nominski. "If I hadn't, you'd have waited forever for Leyva to get back. You'd just now be leaving to go to Chrysler."

"What did you plan to do here?" asked Van Eyck.

"I told you. But they wouldn't go for it."

"Lucky thing for you," said Van Eyck. He knelt and cut Josie Frankel loose.

"I heard what she did before Mrs. Caldwell got here," said Frankel. "She was trying to set up a trap for you to walk into. She gave all the details to some secretary, but they didn't act on it. Adrian, watch out for her. I'm afraid of her. She kept touching me."

"That figures," said Van Eyck. "Don't worry, though; we'll take care of her."

"What does that mean?" asked Nominski.

"There's three hundred thousand, just like you said. I plan to divide it evenly."

"Good," said Nominski, relaxing a little.

"First, I have to make a few phone calls. Then we'll take care of the money, and then we can get out of here and go far away."

Nominski looked suspicious. "Who are you going to call?"

"The companies, of course," said Van Eyck. "You remember. I promised I'd tell them how to get their disks back."

"Oh, forget that," said Nominski. "Let's just split the money and leave."

"Hold on," said Van Eyck, waving a hand. "The money's not going anywhere, and we're safe here. Let me make the calls."

Nominski grumbled, but Van Eyck took the list of telephone numbers from his pocket. He dialed the phone. "Mr. Paul Koppe's extension, please," he said, when the Ford receptionist answered.

"Hello, who is this?" said Koppe.

"Hi, Paul," said Van Eyck. "I'm sorry for leaving you in the restaurant like that. It was very ill-mannered, but I hope you understand my reasons. Thanks for all your help."

"My pleasure," said Koppe, a slight edge on his voice. "And now?"

"Now I hold up my end of the bargain. Your disks never left your plant. As a matter of fact, they never left the Hourly Employee Record Division. They're still in the data library. We removed their identification and shuffled them in among the other disks. You'll have to search for them, but they shouldn't be too difficult to find. It won't take you more than an hour to recover all of them and put them to work."

"Anyway, it's all up to the police now. They'll be hot on your trail as soon as you hang up."

"Confidentially, I don't plan to have a trail," said Van Eyck.

"Lots of luck, then," said Koppe. "We're grateful that you kept a low profile."

"It didn't completely succeed," said Van Eyck. "There were hitches I hadn't planned for."

"There always are," said Koppe.

"I learned that. Next time, I'll do better."

"Next time?" Koppe gave a startled laugh.

"Yes, next time. Don't worry, though; I think I'm through with your industry."

"Thank goodness. Well, I hope I never see you again except on the post-office walls."

"You won't even see me there," said Van Eyck. "You wait and see. I don't think I left any useful traces at all."

"I've got to go. We have to get those paychecks printed up. Thanks for lunch."

"Anytime," said Van Eyck. He hung up. Then he telephoned Chrysler and told them where to find their disks, and he telephoned Jerome Spillman, the union's attorney. Spillman was relieved to hear the news. When Van Eyck finished, he hung up the phone with a sigh. "It's sort of like the end of the World Series," he said. "It was beautiful while it was happening, but now all we have are the memories."

"And the money," said Caldwell.

"But it was doing it that was the exciting part," said Van Eyck, "and that's all over."

"Until next time, Adrian," said Caldwell. Van Eyck smiled.

"You won't be in it next time, will you, David?" asked Marianne.

Caldwell shook his head emphatically. "Nothing could make me go through all that again."

"You didn't believe that you could do it this time," said Van Eyck. "You're just natural-born degenerate scum like the rest of us."

"I did it for Marianne and the kids," said Caldwell. "Now I can go into the hospital without worrying about them. It was worth it, I guess."

"Except for Arthur," said Van Eyck.

"Yes," said Caldwell, "except for Arthur."

"The kids!" said Marianne. "I have to call your mother and tell her we'll be there soon."

"Wait just a minute," said Andi Nominski. "There's something I think we'd better get cleared up before we continue with this bittersweet celebration. You people can do all the laughing and crying you want, later this evening; but I don't particularly enjoy that kind of thing, and I'd just as soon get out of here."

"Maybe she's right," said Caldwell.

"Okay," said Van Eyck. "I have a couple of ideas, though, about how we ought to divide it."

"What ideas?" said Nominski. "A hundred grand each."

"Well," said Van Eyck, "you remember that at first you were going to get a hundred thousand, and I was to take an extra fifty. Now, though, I think we all ought to donate a little to Arthur's sister. And I don't think he should be buried by the city. We ought to see that he's laid to rest."

"I think so, too," said Marianne.

"You don't have anything to say about it," said Nominski angrily.

"And I think we ought to give something to Josie," said Van Eyck, "to compensate her for the trouble we've caused her."

Nominski slammed her fist against the wall. "Didn't you compensate her enough last night?" she said. "Give her some money, if you want, but don't give her any of mine."

"Take whatever you want, Adrian," said Caldwell. "You're right about all that, and we wouldn't have any of the money without you."

"If you've come this far just for money," said Marianne, "and you don't stop to remember Arthur, then you've been corrupted by it. You have your money, and there aren't any more risks to take. What difference does it make whether you have a hundred thousand dollars or ninety?"

"The difference," said Nominski, "is ten thousand dollars. And you can't tell me that ten thousand dollars doesn't mean anything. We all know how much ten thousand dollars is worth."

"But isn't your conscience worth more?" asked Josie Frankel.

Nominski stared at her in disbelief. "Did she really say that?" she said. "Can't you shut her up?"

"I'll tell you this," said Frankel. "I don't want any of the money. Does that make you feel better? But if you don't go along with Adrian, if you don't give something for Mr. Leyva, I'll go straight to the police and tell them everything I know."

"I'll tell you what," Nominski said. "I'll make everything very simple." She opened her bag and took out the pistol. "This will make all the decisions from now on."

"Put that away," said Marianne.

"That won't get you anywhere," said Van Eyck.

"We'll see," said Nominski. "It helped persuade Salicki to do what I wanted. I found it very useful. And you have to admit that with Salicki dead, everybody else took us very seriously. They might not have been so helpful otherwise."

"What do you want?" said Caldwell.

Nominski pointed at the money. "All of it," she said. "I'll take the whole three hundred thousand. Then you people can sit here and decide what to do about Leyva's burnt-up body. I'm the only one here with the foresight to bring a gun. Bullets always cast the deciding vote in case of a disagreement, you know."

"This doesn't surprise me, Andi," said Van Eyck. "I expected you to do something like this."

"Oh, really? And did you plan something to stop me?"

"Yes," said Van Eyck.

"What?" said Nominski, pointing her pistol at his chest.

"I'm going to bash your skull in."

She laughed. "I'll make a note of that, Adrian, darling. Will you track me to the ends of the earth?"

"Andi," said Van Eyck in that rare, chilling voice, "you won't live to spend a dime of that money. You're going to live and die in Detroit, and I'll keep that promise. I said that you'd get everything that was coming to you."

"I don't have the time to listen to you, sweetie. Caldwell, grab that box of money. Let your wife carry Adrian's grocery bag. I know you two won't try anything. Adrian, put your hands on your head and don't move unless I tell you."

Caldwell looked helplessly at Van Eyck, hoping the young man did, in fact, have some plan. Nothing seemed forthcoming from Van Eyck, however, so Caldwell gave the bag of hundred-dollar bills to Marianne and took the box himself. Van Eyck clasped his hands on his head and waited quietly.

"What about me?" asked Josie Frankel.

"Ah, yes," said Nominski, "I haven't forgotten about you. We'll have to settle this before I leave here. Adrian, tell me the truth. Are you planning to take Miss Frankel with you into your life of exile?"

"No, Andi, I'm not. She wants to stay in Detroit. Anyway, I don't want to take anybody with me. I'm going alone."

"Into that dark night," said Nominski. "Well, Josie, dear, you don't want any of the money—you wouldn't get it, anyhow—and you don't have Adrian's protection. What do you think I ought to do with you? Try to put yourself in my position."

"What do you mean?"

"Well, how do you feel about coming with me? Maybe you should think it over."

"Why don't you just let me go, please?" begged Frankel. "I won't do anything. I just want to go home."

Nominski laughed. "You know what they say about going home again. For some people it's more true than for others. Josie, you've made some very bad choices. You've lined yourself up on the wrong side in this little drama. I'm really sorry."

"Stop it, Andi," said Van Eyck. "You're talking like some kind of television tough guy."

"Go to hell, Adrian," shouted Nominski. "I don't want you talking unless I ask you a question. All of you people, you're going to do exactly what I say from now on. Caldwell, you and your wife and Adrian here, I want you all lined up against the wall. No, turn around. Face the wall."

"What is this, Andi, the St. Valentine's Day Massacre?" said Van Eyck. He still didn't seem very worried.

"What's she going to do to us?" asked Marianne in a shaky voice.

"I don't know," said Caldwell. "I'm sorry I got you—"

"Shut up! Just stand there and be quiet. I'm not going to do anything to you. Now you, Frankel. Over there by the window. That's good."

There was silence for a short while. Caldwell, with his face to the wall, wondered what Nominski was doing behind him. He guessed that she would try to club them unconscious, the way they do it in the movies: a quick smack to the base of the skull. His shoulders hunched involuntarily. Caldwell knew how tricky that maneuver was. It rarely does knock the victim cleanly unconscious; most often, it just hurts a hell of a lot and makes a bloody wound on the head. Sometimes, if the blow is too heavy, there are the dangers of concussion and skull fracture. Caldwell waited, wishing that he could do something to protect his wife. She was sobbing quietly beside him. Van Eyck stood facing the wall, his hands still clasped on his head.

"Stop," said Frankel. "Please."

Caldwell wondered what Nominski was doing to the poor girl.

"Don't," said Frankel.

There was a single, stunningly loud gunshot. In the small apartment the noise seemed like the thunder of the earth exploding. It seemed to roll and echo for minutes. Then there was only the sound of Caldwell's murmured cursing and Marianne, fallen to her knees, crying.

"She did it," muttered Van Eyck, amazed.

Caldwell couldn't help himself; he turned around. The sight was much worse than he had imagined. Andi Nominski stood over Josie Frankel's body, the gun forgotten in her hand. She seemed fascinated by the sight of the corpse. Frankel's face was an unrecognizable mass of ruined flesh. Her blood had splattered against the wall and the window, and was now pooling on the floor. Nominski took a couple of deep breaths. "No more witnesses, Adrian," she said. "You don't have to worry anymore."

"I wasn't worried, Andi," said Van Eyck calmly. "But I have this feeling that you aren't planning to let me walk out of here. You know that without my money I'll be very unhappy, so for your own peace of mind you're probably thinking of sending me after Josie. Am I right?"

"I have been toying with the idea," said Nominski, "but your usefulness isn't over yet."

"I'm glad to hear that. What about the Caldwells? They don't pose a threat to you."

"Except that I ought to make things neat, Adrian. You should understand that. I really shouldn't leave any loose ends."

"Oh, my God, my God," said Marianne softly.

"Adrian, for Christ's sake, do something!" pleaded Caldwell.

"Andi," said Van Eyck, "I'll make a deal with you. Let the Caldwells go, and I'll face you unarmed. You can keep the gun if you think it will help you, but let them go first."

"No deals, Adrian," said Nominski. "But if you keep annoying me like that, I just might forget my plans and take care of all three of you right now."

Caldwell felt a surge of desperate fury in him. He turned and lunged at Nominski almost without conscious thought, uttering a brutal growl that was not entirely sane. Nominski stared, unbelieving. Caldwell's eyes were lit with a crazy gleam, and his lips were drawn back in a grimace of murderous hate. Nominski backed away a step, her face showing fear for the first time. The pistol still hung unremembered in her hand.

"David!" cried Marianne.

"Caldwell, don't!" shouted Van Eyck.

He didn't hear them. Nominski waited until Caldwell was close upon her; then she kicked at him, catching him in the pit of the stomach with the toe of her heavy boot. Caldwell made a small grunting sound and sank to the floor in a sitting position. He looked around the room with blank eyes, holding his belly. Then he gave a choked cry and collapsed on his side.

"Damn nice try," said Nominski scornfully. She stepped over him. "Adrian, grab the box. Get the woman on her feet. Come on, lady, you're going to have to pull yourself together if you want to live through this. Hand me that bag of money. Now, listen: We're leaving here right now. I don't want any funny business when we get out on the street. Mrs. Caldwell, you'll come with me. Adrian—"

"Wait one minute, Andi," said Van Eyck. "Once we leave this apartment, whatever happens between us is for keeps. I want you to know that I'm prepared to die if that's what it takes to stop you. When we get out on the street, I'll do everything I can to keep you from getting away. This whole thing is my responsibility. It's my fault that Arthur and Josie are dead. The only way I can make up for that, just a little, is to make sure that you never hurt anyone else ever again."

"How romantic you've turned out to be, Adrian," said Nominski. "You thought you were a dashing, gallant pirate. It turns out you've got something no good crook can afford. You've got a conscience, Adrian, and it's going to cost you your life. You're talking awful big right now, but, honestly, you don't scare me. You're just trying to kid yourself into believing you're going to live to see dinnertime."

"As soon as we get outside, you know you've had it," said Van Eyck. "You say you're not scared. Think of the number of ways I can get that gun away from you. That's the only thing that's standing between you and the grave, Andi, the fact that you're holding the gun. But outside, it's all different. There are other people out there. I could start running. I could throw a handful of snow in your eyes. You could slip on the ice. In here you're safe, but outside is where the real contest starts."

"Adrian, if you got the gun away from me, what would you do with it? You wouldn't shoot me. You don't do things like that."

Van Eyck grinned. "How do you know?"

Nominski suddenly looked uncomfortable. She didn't know much about him after all, she thought. She knew only the face he had chosen to display; she had already seen some evidence that day that there was something more beneath his mild surface. Her fear passed quickly; she was in control, and she couldn't let him distract her. "Mrs. Caldwell," she said calmly, "you'll come with me. You'll be my insurance that Adrian and your husband will behave themselves. Take the box of money from Adrian. I'm sorry, you'll have to carry it and the bag, too. Mrs. Caldwell and I will drive in my car. Adrian, love, you will help Mr. Caldwell into his rented car and you'll follow me. Understand?"

"You've injured my husband," said Marianne. "Can't we take him to the hospital?"

"Not yet," said Nominski. "I come first. Now remember, no tricks."

Van Eyck helped Caldwell to his feet. Caldwell was dazed, but a little more conscious than just after Nominski kicked him. He had a great deal of trouble standing. The pain in his abdomen was intense, as bad as anything he had ever felt. He had a cold rush of fear; he was suddenly certain that Nominski's boot had ruptured one of the tumors. If that was true, he had to get to a hospital and into surgery very soon. He panted in pain, leaning against Van Eyck for support. His face was shiny with sweat. "I can't," he said in a hoarse voice.

"Get him moving, Adrian," said Nominski, "or I'll leave him here in a condition where he'll never feel pain again."

"Come on, Mr. Caldwell," urged Van Eyck, "you have to make the effort. For your wife's sake. Please."

Marianne, carrying the whole three hundred thousand dollars, went to her husband. "David, try to hold on a little while. We'll get you in the car, and as soon as she gets away we'll call the doctor and take you to the hospital."

"Right, right," said Nominski impatiently. "Adrian, drag him outside. Mrs. Caldwell, you go next. All of you remember that my gun still has more than enough bullets in it, and I won't mind using it outside."

"Are we just going to leave Josie here?" asked Adrian.

"What do you want me to do with her?" asked Nominski. "Tonight you can all come back and do whatever you want. I don't care. For now she can rest in peace."

Outside, on Woodward Avenue, it had begun to snow. All the old, dirty ice and gray slush was being covered by clean, virgin white. The air was sharp and the street was hushed and peaceful. Adrian van Eyck came out of the building first. He paused on the stoop and looked up and down the street. A few cars passed; he watched them, thinking of futile things he might do to attract attention. For all his talk, he had no idea of what he could do to thwart Andi Nominski. He realized perfectly well that when she drove away, he would not be alive to worry about the Caldwells. At the moment, he was thinking only of saving himself; he didn't actually believe that Nominski intended to murder David and Marianne, although she had proven to be more psychotic than he had supposed.

He helped David Caldwell down the icy steps. Caldwell was doubled over, holding his arms tight across his abdomen. His face was an unhealthy gray, and he was loudly sucking air in irregular gasps. He was in a lot of danger.

"Get the keys to that car out of Caldwell's pocket," said Nominski. "Be careful. I have my gun on Mrs. Caldwell. Don't make me use it."

Van Eyck opened the passenger door and helped Caldwell in. He closed the door and went around to the street side. He got behind the wheel and started the engine. He waited for Nominski.

The two women followed. "Come with me," said Nominski. She indicated the rented car, the Concord Caldwell had used that day, where Van Eyck was smoothly revving the engine. "Let me have the keys for a moment, Adrian." She took the keys and opened the trunk. She stowed the box and the bag of money, then gave the keys back. "You can't get away with the loot," she said. "Maybe you will try something, because you don't think I'd shoot Mrs. Caldwell; but I will. I know what you're thinking, Adrian: You're thinking that once I shoot Mrs. Caldwell, I won't have any more protection, and then you can take off with the money. But—"

"Andi," said Van Eyck, "it sickens me to think that you put me in the same class as yourself."

"Never mind, Adrian," she said lightly, "just drive carefully." She went to her brown Toyota. "Here we go, Marianne. You don't mind if I call you Marianne, do you?"

Marianne didn't answer; she was almost in shock. The terror of the last few hours had been too intense. The uncertainty of the next hour seemed even worse. Marianne could only picture herself and her husband lying dead, robbed of life by a homicidal woman. There was something more upsetting than death in store for them, also. The way Josie Frankel had died cheated her of her humanity and her God-given dignity. She had been violated in an ultimate sense. That disturbed Marianne more than the bare fact of death.

Van Eyck trailed Nominski in the Concord. The driving became more difficult as a new dusting of snow covered the streets. The visibility was poor. The two cars followed Woodward Avenue downtown, moving slowly in the sluggish traffic.

"What do you think she could do here, in the middle of town?" asked Van Eyck.

"Adrian," muttered Caldwell, his eyes tightly closed. His voice was low and hollow. He seemed only vaguely conscious.

"Mr. Caldwell, I know you're in pain, I know you're suffering; but please try to hang on for a little longer. Try to stand it, because I may need you when we get to wherever Andi's taking us. I don't know what's going to happen, but you have to be ready."

"I'm . . . okay, Adrian," whispered Caldwell. He tried to sit up straighter, but groaned and slumped again. "I'll be all right."

Van Eyck gave him a worried glance, then turned his attention back to the road. "You know, I've learned the hardest thing about a life of crime is the getaway. You can have the most brilliant plan in the world, but the hitch is getting away with it. Pulling off a perfect theft or a perfect con is easy enough; that's just cleverness. Sooner or later, though, you have to deal with separating yourself from your victims and your gang. I never realized it before, but both groups have a lot of power over you. I thought it would be easy. I thought everything would be finished once we got the cash, but I was wrong. That's where the problems really start. From now on, I'll have to give the most thought to the end of the game. The getaway. That's the whole secret."

"Adrian," said Caldwell, "I could have told you that."

Caldwell tried to take a deep breath and found that the pain had eased. He still felt a sharp stab every time the car dipped into a pothole, but he was able to talk and sit without feeling that every moment was his last. He relaxed in the seat. He forgot what he had witnessed in the apartment. He forgot that he had entrusted the young man beside him with saving all their lives, for all intents and purposes surrendering his fate to Van Eyck's skill and judgment.

With a start, Caldwell realized that he felt gutshot. He remembered ruefully his daydream, the day he had gotten the bad news from his doctor. He had met some children on the sidewalk. The children had been the key to his fate, he had believed; but somehow things had gone wrong. He had not been brutal with them. He had smiled and been charming, yet here he was with the fires of hell devouring his belly. It wasn't fair. If he was going to be punished for the worst, he wished now that he had lived the worst. He had never had a blonde chorine for a mistress. He had never been fingered by his best friend, a nightclub owner with gangland ties. He had no henchmen. He had no crooked judge in his control. There were no crusading newsmen out to get him. He was little; in the language of the mob, he was nickel-and-dime small-time. He was very small-time. He was so small-time, the best thing to do was die and save everyone else a lot of trouble.

He didn't have a natty suit. That distressed Caldwell. Jimmy Cagney had died in a natty suit in *The Roaring Twenties*. Caldwell was going to die in a sixty-dollar suit off the rack in a department store in the Fairlane Shopping Mall. It would be worse than embarrassing: It would be damning. It was all Caldwell could think of in his partial delirium. "Not like this," he muttered.

"What?" said Van Eyck. Hie brows were furrowed as he concentrated on a way to get out of the trap.

"I don't want to die like this," said Caldwell.

"Me, neither," said Van Eyck.

"No diamond stickpin," said Caldwell.

"No," said Van Eyck, wondering what Caldwell was talking about.

"I want my Velma."

"She's in the other car, with Andi."

Caldwell blinked. His fantasy faded. He recalled where he was, what was happening. With a guilty shock he realized that he had totally forgotten the danger to Marianne.

His wife, at that moment, was peering through the rear window of Nominski's car. The window was fogged, and there was little visibility through the falling snow. She couldn't make out her husband, although the Concord nosed through the bad weather at a cautious distance. "Are you going to kill him?" she asked.

"Kill who?" said Nominski. "There are two of them back

there." She smiled, pleased with herself. Her best hope to get away with the money and her murders was to keep everyone guessing at her real plans.

"Adrian," said Marianne. "The way you were talking, you sounded as if you intend to murder him next, when we get where we're going."

"Why should I tell you?"

"Why should you be worried? What can I do?"

"I'm not worried," said Nominski, "and you can't do anything. I still don't see any point in telling you what's going to happen to Adrian. It's for your own good, sweets."

"Then what about David? I have a right to know."

"There is no such thing as rights, Marianne. You should have learned that by now. Josie Frankel had a right to live, didn't she? You'd say that. But I had a right to kill her, because she was a threat to me and I had the gun. As long as I have the gun, I decide who has rights and who doesn't. At this particular point in time, I have all the rights. I don't see that changing any."

Marianne stared through the windshield. Ahead of her was a city snowplow, heading to some part of town to remove the new accumulation of snow. It was moving very slowly. Behind her was the car with Van Eyck and her husband. Together they made a capsule of fear in an uninterested landscape. Marianne's pulse speeded up when a Detroit police cruiser passed them going in the other direction. What could she do? Was there some clever trick she could try that would disarm Nominski and save her husband's life, without causing a fatal traffic accident? She knew that a movie heroine would have a whole variety of brilliant things to do in the same situation. Marianne considered grabbing the steering wheel away from Nominski. That wouldn't solve anything; Nominski would grab it back, take out her pistol, and use it. Marianne could jam on the brakes. Nominski would respond in the same way, with a bullet. Nominski was right about one thing: Whatever ploy

Marianne might devise, the pistol overruled her at every turn.

Neither Marianne nor the two men in the rented car did anything heroic. Nominski turned off Woodward in the downtown shopping area. She headed west for a few blocks, until she stopped outside a parking garage. She left the motor running. "Come with me," she said. She got out of the car and Marianne followed her. They walked back to Van Eyck's car, and Nominski signaled for him to roll down his window. "I'm taking my car into the garage," she said. "You wait here. I want to park my car and leave town in this Concord. I'm going to leave you here with the money, but I'm taking Mrs. Caldwell with me. You know, of course, that if I come back and find you talking to the police, she'll get it right on the sidewalk."

"I've got that all firmly in mind, Andi," said Van Eyck. "Go do what you have to do. We'll be here. If a cop comes by, it's only because we'll be stopping traffic. So hurry up."

"Okay," said Nominski. She went back to her car and pulled into the parking garage.

Van Eyck watched her. "This is it," said the young man. "How are you feeling?"

"All right. Why?" said Caldwell.

"Because we have to move now."

"What are we going to do?"

Van Eyck smiled sadly. "I still don't have the faintest idea, but this is Andi's weak point, I know it. Just like I left myself vulnerable at the apartment, she hasn't thought this part through well enough. Sometime, for one tiny instant, all four of us are going to be outside the car here, and the money is going to be inside. That's the time to move, I think."

"No," said Caldwell, "you're wrong. You'd be sacrificing at least one of us."

Van Eyck looked at him curiously. "Well, what do you suggest?"

"Run after her. She'll be leaving her car in there and coming back on foot, with Marianne. She probably won't have her gun in her hand. She won't be expecting you. If you get her by surprise in there, before she gets down to the street—"

Van Eyck chewed his lip. "Mr. Caldwell, you're thinking better than I am. Maybe I'm not so good under pressure. Do you think you can walk? I'm going to need you. If I go after Andi, I need you to get Marianne to safety, and to come back down here and call the police. I'll need help, David, or I'm done for."

Caldwell swallowed. He hurt, but he didn't feel crippled any longer. "I'll be there," he said. "I'll do my best to keep up."

"Okay," said Van Eyck, "then let's do it."

He got out of the car. Caldwell opened his door and eased himself to a standing position. Van Eyck gave him a worried look, but Caldwell raised a hand, indicating that he was all right. Van Eyck went into the parking garage. He studied the ground floor warily because he didn't know how far up Nominski had driven her car to find a parking place.

Caldwell's adventures had begun in just such a daytime home for cars, and it looked to him that they would end in a daytime home for cars. He couldn't move as fast as Van Eyck. He hurried through the growing blizzard to the drive-in entrance of the garage. Caldwell tried to keep up with Van Eyck, fearing that if he didn't, his wife would suffer the consequences.

Van Eyck had only a hazy idea of what he would do. He knew that Nominski had not parked on the ground level, that she had driven up to one of the four upper levels. There was no elevator here, only a narrow spiral stairway. Van Eyck ran up the steps three at a time, and stopped at the second level. He ran out halfway into the level and climbed on the trunk of a grimy blue Volvo. He looked, but he couldn't see Nominski or her Toyota. He hoped that he hadn't missed her; she might still be sitting in her car, talking to Marianne. Van Eyck made another quick survey and decided to go up another level. He went back to the stairs. He felt the crushing burden of guilt, the need to redeem himself, the overriding imperative of finding Nominski before she came upon Caldwell.

On the fourth level, Nominski finally found a slot for her car. "Here's where we dump it," she said to herself. "Come on, Marianne. It's time to go to our reward."

"David and Adrian won't be waiting for us in the car," said Marianne. "They won't be led like sheep. If I know them, you're going to be in big trouble when you leave here."

"If you're right, honey, *I* won't be in big trouble. *You're* the one who's going to take it in the teeth if they're planning to surprise me. You walk ahead of me. On the parking level I can see in all directions. They can't jump out at me without giving me enough time to get off at least one clean shot. That one is for you. On the steps, with you walking ahead of me, I'll have all the protection I need."

"They'll think of something. They'll sabotage the car. Maybe they're hiding the money."

"I'll check everything downstairs," said Nominski. "They're smarter than that. They know if anything's funny, you'll pay for it. They'll be there, don't worry."

"Then what?"

"Here's what I've decided. You and your husband are going to get out of this, through the goodness of my heart and the fact that I don't have the time or the inclination to put bullets through your heads in the middle of downtown Detroit on a Thursday afternoon."

"And Adrian?"

Nominski laughed. "Adrian is another story. He threatened me, so he's made it a matter of pride."

"Please, can't I say anything that will—"

"No, nothing," said Nominski. They started down the stairs.

Caldwell made slow progress. He took one step with his right leg; then he had to swing his left leg around slowly. If he moved too quickly, a hot streak of pain ignited agony in his side. He made his way through the parking garage, holding his lower abdomen. His face was twisted with pain, and he felt faint. He forced himself to keep moving because so much depended on what he and Van Eyck could do in the next few minutes. He cursed himself viciously to make himself go on, but he had a black fear that he was going to fail in the vital moment. All the dreams and hopes he had about the money disappeared. His idle fantasies turned sinister. The old gangster movies he loved always dealt with the rise and fall of some desperate character. Caldwell thought it extremely unfair that he should have his fall without at least a few minutes of exultation and glory.

He toppled forward when he reached the stairs, grabbing a metal railing with both hands. He steadied himself. He listened for a moment, trying to make out footsteps above him—Adrian's, perhaps—or voices, but he heard nothing. He stepped up on the first stair with his right foot. The effort to raise his left leg was too much for him. He grunted and felt hot tears come to his eyes. He clenched his jaws and forced his left foot onto the stair. His body blazed with a rending pain. He fell to his knees on the stair, gasping for breath. He couldn't believe what was happening to him: He was dying there in the garage.

He waited a moment for the knife edge of pain to recede, then he slowly stood up again. He climbed to the next stair with an effort of will. The pain did not lessen, but he was able to ignore it by concentrating on one thought—it was a choice between the agony and Marianne's murder. He would buy her life with his torment. He had never loved her so much.

After a timeless stretch of torturous labor, he reached the landing halfway to the second level. He permitted himself a short rest. He could still hear nothing from above. From below came automobile sounds: car horns, wheels squealing around turns, a radio playing loud music. He wondered what Van Eyck was doing. He took a few deep breaths and continued upward. Sometimes he felt as if he were in an impenetrable fog, isolated from all sensory impressions; at other times every sight and sound and smell was supernaturally vivid. The piercing anguish did not lessen.

On the second flight of stairs he reached his limit. His intent was still as firm, but his strength had run out. He tried to lift his leg, but it would not move. He tried to crawl up the stairs, but his body could only twitch. He was stranded halfway up the stairs, unable to go up or down, unable to cry out, unable to save himself if some violent climax swept over him. He held his belly and wept. He had failed Marianne, he had given up, and he was glad he was dying. He hoped that when he met them all in eternity, they would pity him; he could not hope for their forgiveness. He would need no further punishment, because his memories would always be the greatest source of his torment.

He felt his life ending. He could barely move. He felt as Edward G. Robinson must have felt, after being gunned down in one or another of his pictures. Before losing consciousness, Caldwell's last thoughts were of his early fantasies, and how they had all led to this. "Mother of mercy," he said in a croaking voice, "is this the end of Caldwell?"

Not far above him, Adrian van Eyck was racing up to the third level. He paused, almost panic-stricken, and searched the parking area with his eyes. Once again there was no sign of Nominski and Marianne. He was almost convinced that he had passed them on the way up, that they had been in a car hidden among the hundreds of others below, that he was sealing his fate and Caldwell's by going higher. The temptation to give up and run back downstairs grew almost irresistible, but he forced himself to continue. He had to make at least a cursory search of the fourth and fifth levels. Then he would go back down and deal with Nominski on the street.

He leaped to the landing between the third and fourth levels and turned the corner, jumping up the stairs. He almost bumped head-on into Marianne Caldwell, who was coming down the stairs ahead of Andi Nominski. Marianne shrieked and flattened herself against the wall. Van Eyck threw himself down, trying to avoid the bullet he was sure was aimed at him. Nominski laughed. "Adrian!" she said. "How lovely to meet you here." She rather relished coming upon him. It would make things much easier for her.

"Adrian," said Marianne fearfully, "where's David?"

"Andi," he said, getting up. He stared up at Nominski, looking right down the barrel of her pistol. "I don't know," he said absently. "I think he's down there behind me."

Marianne started down the stairs. Nominski stopped her. "Stay where you are, Mrs. Caldwell," she said. "I'm still running things."

"But David—"

"I'll worry about him later. He won't do anything foolish, not while you're with me. Right now I have to consider how I'm going to take care of our boy Adrian."

"You don't understand," pleaded Marianne. "David needs to get to a hospital."

"Just wait a minute," said Nominski, "and you can take Adrian with you."

Van Eyck climbed a step closer to Nominski. "I'm going to make it hard for you, Andi," he said.

She shook her head. "Stay where you are. It won't be hard at all. You'd be surprised."

He climbed another step. "I'm not Josie Frankel. I'm not a terrified young girl. I'm not completely helpless."

"You're wrong, Adrian. You *are* completely helpless."

He climbed to the step just below hers. "Don't kid yourself, Andi, I still have an ace in my sleeve."

"Won't do you much good there, boy," she said. She held the gun out a little, and it pressed into his chest. She had the uncomfortable feeling that Van Eyck wouldn't be acting so boldly if he didn't know something that she didn't. He had bluffed her before; but now, with his life and the Caldwells' hanging in the balance, she didn't expect to see him so confident. "What are you talking about?"

"It's something I saw when I was eleven or twelve years old," said Van Eyck. "In a movie, I don't remember the name of it. One of those serials made in the forties. It was playing one Saturday afternoon at my neighborhood theater. The hero said that if you feel a gun in your back, you can spin away from it before the other person can shoot. Now you and I are going to find out if it works this way, too." He pivoted on the end of the pistol, at the same time slapping Nominski's gun hand away from him and Marianne. Nominski fired, and the roar of the gun sounded impossibly loud in the garage. Van Eyck raised his right fist and clubbed Nominski's temple, stunning her. Her hand opened and she dropped the pistol. It rattled down the stairs. Marianne grabbed it, holding it in horror. She retreated down a few steps.

Nominski's knees buckled. Van Eyck caught her and put his hands around her throat. He began to tighten his grip.

"Adrian!" cried Marianne. "Adrian, what are you doing?"

Van Eyck didn't answer. His face was flushed and he breathed heavily from his exertion. Nominski's face turned red, then pale as he strangled her. She began to turn the blue cyanotic color of death. She struggled wildly, but her attempts to get free did no good. She tried to talk, to beg for her life, but her thick blue lips and swollen tongue choked off her words. Van Eyck was madly determined.

"Adrian, stop!" said Marianne, still shrinking against the wall several steps below. "You're killing her!"

"No," he said, panting, dropping the body to the stairs, "I've *already* killed her." He stood up straight, his hands at his sides, and stared blankly over Marianne's head. She crossed herself in a childhood reflex.

"What now?" she asked.

"Now it really *is* over, or almost over. We have to think for a minute. Your husband is in desperate shape. We have to get him to a hospital. We have to do something with Andi. Our car is still out at the curb with its motor running and the money in the trunk." He was silent for a few seconds. "Okay, I've got it, I think. You go down and sit in the car. If a cop comes to tell you to move—"

"Hey," shouted a man's voice from below, "what the hell is going on up there?"

"Nothing," called Van Eyck.

"I thought I heard a gunshot or something."

Van Eyck pointed at Marianne. She closed her eyes and gritted her teeth. "Just the goddamn kid," she answered. "It was a cherry bomb he got in Canada."

"They're illegal here, lady. You better watch him."

"Don't worry," said Marianne, "he'll be sorry."

"All right. I don't need the police hanging around here. My job is hard enough."

Van Eyck grinned at her, but Marianne just shuddered. "You better go down and get in the car," he said. "I'll be there in a minute with your husband."

"Okay, Adrian. Hurry."

Adrian Van Eyck stood alone in the stairwell, looking down at the grotesque corpse of Andi Nominski. There had been enough death, he thought, and he was to blame for it all. He might be able to pass off Salicki's murder—Van Eyck hadn't been aware yet of the extent of Nominski's paranoia. He might be able to dismiss the deaths of Arthur Leyva and Henry Bernside, because it was Leyva's foolishness that had been responsible. He might be able to console himself for Josie Frankel's death, because at that point they had all been in the power of a lunatic. But Nominski had died at his own hands, and no matter how much she deserved it, he would never, ever, forget how it had felt to throttle the life slowly from her body.

He bent and hooked his arms under her armpits. He lifted her a little and dragged her up the stairs. He was surprised at how difficult it was to move the dead weight. He sweated and labored and got her to the next level. He stopped for a moment to decide if it was better to leave her there or take her up to the top. He figured that, as much as he wanted to leave her on the fifth level, he stood the chance of meeting someone coming down the stairs. Rather than risk that, he dragged her a few feet into the fourth level. He looked around. There was a car pulling out of a parking place not twenty yards away. It came toward him. Van Eyck felt his heart race and his throat tighten.

The car stopped beside him. The driver rolled down the window. "What's wrong?" he called.

"My girl fainted. She's going to have a baby and she faints a lot. It's all right. My sister went down to call a doctor. We have our car, and if we have to take her to the hospital or something, we'll be okay."

"You sure you don't need anything?"

"Thank you very much. We'll be all right."

The driver nodded, relieved that he didn't have to do anything for these strangers. He rolled the window up again and drove away. In a moment, Van Eyck was alone. He looked around for a place to hide Nominski's body; there were no hiding places. He looked for a utility closet or a restroom, but there was none. He shrugged. The only thing to do was leave her as far from the stairwell and the automobile ramps as he could. He chose a spot, and began dragging Nominski's corpse across the concrete. He was vulnerable now to anyone who might come along, but his only thought was to finish the business for good.

At the same moment, Marianne was kneeling beside her husband, dismayed by his delirium and pallor. She roused herself with an effort, hating to leave him in this condition, but she knew that the best thing was to do exactly what Van Eyck had said. She went out of the garage and was glad to see that the Concord was where they had left it. It seemed to her that they had been in the garage for hours, but it had only been a few minutes at the most. She opened the driver's door and got behind the wheel. The snow fell, and she listened to the lulling sound of the windshield wipers. She waited.

Van Eyck hurried down the stairs. He grunted when he saw Caldwell. The man was in much worse shape than he had anticipated. He wasn't going to be able to help Caldwell to the car. Van Eyck knelt beside him. "Mr. Caldwell?" he said, having little hope that he would be understood. "I'll be right back. I'm just going down to get the car. We'll take care of you now. You'll be all right." Van Eyck ran down the stairs and out to the car. He got in and slammed the door.

Marianne put the car in gear and turned into the garage. She stopped at an automatic barrier and took a ticket; then she sped heedlessly through the ground level. She stopped the car beside the stairwell on the second level. "You'll have to help me get him into the car," said Van Eyck. "I can't carry him, and I don't think he can make it on his own."

"Let's go," said Marianne. Together they supported Caldwell and led him to the car. Van Eyck got into the backseat so that Caldwell could have room in the front.

"His doctor—" said Van Eyck.

"Dr. Loetz," said Marianne.

"What hospital is he connected with?"

Caldwell had had surgery in two different hospitals where Dr. Loetz had operating-room privileges. Marianne chose one. "It's the nearer of the two," she said.

"No," said Van Eyck, "we can't take him to the nearest. We're going to save your husband's life and his name, too. This will give him the perfect alibi. At the time of the crime, your husband will have been on the operating table."

"But the other hospital is all the way across town," said Marianne. "He needs help now. It will take half an hour to get him there."

"Not if you ignore all the traffic lights and stop signs. Just lay on the horn and keep your eyes open."

"In this weather?"

Van Eyck slammed his hand on the seat. "Listen, Marianne, he's gone through all of this, taken big risks. There's one more risk to take, just one, but I think he'll make it all right. If he's in a hospital miles away from everything that happened today, he'll never have to worry about someone collaring him. Do you want the two of you worrying about that for the rest of your lives?"

Marianne shook her head. "All right, Adrian," she said. "How do I get to the Lodge Freeway?"

They drove in silence, each wrapped in his own thoughts. They had a lot to remember and a lot to forget. Caldwell's ragged breathing was the only sound in the car. Marianne drove recklessly, praying that some divine guidance would protect them all from other reckless drivers who wouldn't see them coming. After a few minutes, they heard a siren coming up from behind. "That's what I was hoping for," murmured Adrian.

"Aren't you afraid?" asked Marianne.

"Traffic patrol, that's all," said Adrian.

"Should I pull over?"

"I guess so."

Marianne changed lanes, then slowed and came to a stop on the freeway's shoulder. The police car stopped behind her. The cop looked past Marianne and saw how bad Caldwell looked. "We have to get him to the hospital," said Van Eyck. "He has terrible internal injuries, and he needs to get to surgery immediately. His doctor's waiting for us."

"Right," said the police officer, "follow me." He hurried back to his patrol car and sped away with his siren screaming, clearing the way for Marianne.

"A police escort for my getaway," said Van Eyck. "Well, everything will be just fine now."

"If we get David to the hospital in time," said Marianne.

"We will," said Van Eyck, with a certainty that would allow no question.

Caldwell came out of a hazy, disturbing dream to find himself lying on a gurney in a hospital corridor. He was aware of the familiar antiseptic odor at once. He had been given a shot of Demerol, and that was very pleasant. There was no pain. He had been shaved from armpit to groin and prepped for surgery, and he was dressed in a pale green hospital gown. He was experienced enough to know what had happened. His only real anxiety was that he didn't know how serious his condition was. The last thing he recalled was struggling to get up the stairs in the garage. Perhaps he had been shot and didn't remember. He panicked; he wanted to find out what had happened to Marianne and Adrian after he passed out, but he was alone in the hallway. There was nothing to do but lay back and wait.

"How are you feeling, Mr. Caldwell?" asked a young woman, masked and wearing a green outfit and cap.

"All right," he said dreamily. "My wife—"

"She's waiting for you. You'll see her when you come out of the recovery room."

Evidently Marianne was safe. "My friend, Adrian, is he with her?"

"There's no one with her," said the young woman. Caldwell wondered what had happened to Van Eyck. There were only a few possibilities: Adrian had seen Caldwell safely to the hospital and then made his escape; he had gone out for a while but would be there, smiling, when Caldwell awoke; or—and Caldwell hated to think of it—he had died in the parking garage, shot by Andi Nominski. Caldwell wasn't going to learn the answer before his surgery.

"Dr. Loetz?" asked Caldwell weakly.

"Your wife called him, and he's here now. We've been waiting for him, and everything's about ready for you. Now, that's enough talking. Take it easy, and we'll wheel you into the operating room in a minute." She left Caldwell alone. He closed his eyes and drifted.

A short while later a tall young man, dressed in the same surgical green, pushed Caldwell's gurney into the operating room. Caldwell felt a chill, the same timorous feeling he always got when he saw the gleaming chrome of the instruments and equipment waiting for him.

They lifted him from the gurney to the operating table. They removed his gown. They spread his arms out to the sides, in a cruciform position. Men and women moved about the room, murmuring incomprehensibly to each other. Caldwell closed his eyes so that he wouldn't see any more.

"How are we doing?" said Dr. Loetz. Caldwell opened his eyes; his surgeon was almost anonymous in his mask, cap, and scrub suit.

"All right," said Caldwell fearfully.

"We'll take care of you now, David," said Dr. Loetz. "Just try to relax. You'll be asleep soon. When you wake up, it will be all over."

"I know," said Caldwell.

"I'm going to give you the pentathol now," said a man's voice behind him, out of sight.

A woman held a black rubber mask. "Just take a few deep breaths for me, okay?"

"No," murmured Caldwell. The woman placed the mask over Caldwell's nose and mouth.

"Breathe," said the woman.

Caldwell felt as if he were dissolving. "Top of the world, ma," he whispered. He filled his lungs.

Caldwell awoke in a private room. The drugs he had been given made it difficult for him to remember where he was or what had happened. Marianne was sitting beside his bed. She held his hand and listened patiently to his slurred speech. He fell asleep again.

An hour later he woke again, and this time he was more coherent. "Am I all right?" he asked.

"Yes, Davey," said Marianne. "Dr. Loetz said the operation was completely successful. You shouldn't have any more trouble."

"That's good," he said. "The kids—"

"Don't worry, your mother has been with them all day. They're staying over at our house."

"What time is it?"

"About three. In the morning."

"You must be exhausted, Mari."

"It doesn't matter. Do you hurt? Do you want something for the pain?"

"No, not yet," he said, not wanting to lose consciousness again until he learned what he needed to know. "What happened?"

Marianne frowned. She sat on the edge of his bed and stroked his hair. "You mean back in the parking garage?" she asked. He nodded. "Adrian came up the stairs. He surprised Andi. She shot once, but missed us." Marianne looked away for a moment; the memory distressed her. "He killed her. Strangled her."

"It must have been awful for you, honey," he said softly.

She nodded. A tear glistened on her cheek. "Adrian and I brought you here. He stayed for a while, but he had to leave. Do you remember when he made the phone calls, before Josie Frankel died? He didn't call General Motors then. He thought he could still collect from them, if he got to them before they heard anything from the other companies. He was going to talk to whoever was filling in for their executive who was killed with Arthur."

"Did he collect?" asked Caldwell. "Or did they catch him?"

"He came back just about fifteen minutes ago," said Marianne with a little smile. "He left this for you." She handed him a box of candy.

"No, not now, I couldn't eat—"

"Open it, Davey."

He lifted the lid. Inside, there were twenty packages of hundred dollar bills, a hundred bills to a pack. "There's two hundred thousand dollars here," said Caldwell. "He gave me an extra hundred thousand."

"I know," said Marianne.

There was also a little paper cup with three pastel-colored Jordan almonds, in memory of Arthur Leyva. There was a card. Caldwell took it out and read it: *GM came through. Kept*

50G, gave you 50G, gave 50G to Arthur's sister. A boy has never wept nor dashed a thousand Kim. It was signed *The Napoleon of Crime.*

"I read it, but I don't know what that last part means," said Marianne.

"Those were the last words of Dutch Schultz," said Caldwell. "I think it's Adrian's good-bye to us."

"Then it makes me sad," said Marianne.

"Me, too."

"Do you think we'll ever see him again?"

"I hope not," said Caldwell. "He's going on to other projects and other intrigues. If we ever hear of him again, it will be because he got caught."

"Then I hope we never do," said Marianne.

"You take care of this," he said, handing the box to her. "I'm tired. I'm very tired." He closed his eyes. He felt Marianne kiss his lips, and then he slipped into a warm and peaceful oblivion.